DIMITRI

Roxie Rivera

Night Works Books
College Station, Texas

Roxie Rivera/Night Works Books
3515-B Longmire Dr. #103
College Station, Texas 77845
www.roxierivera.com

Publisher's Note: This is a work of fiction. Names, characters, places, and incidents are a product of the author's imagination. Locales and public names are sometimes used for atmospheric purposes. Any resemblance to actual people, living or dead, or to businesses, companies, events, institutions, or locales is completely coincidental.

Cover Photograph © 2013 ArtemFurman/Fotolia.com

DIMITRI (Her Russian Protector #2)/Roxie Rivera. – 1st ed.
ISBN-10: 1630420069
ISBN-13: 978-1-63042-006-2

DEDICATION

For Patricia, little sister extraordinaire.

CHAPTER ONE

With a loud grunt, I tried to drag the heavy sack of flour from the unloading dock to the storeroom. I'd already moved six of them and felt what little energy that remained with me start to drain. My four o'clock alarm and a full day of running from the kitchen to the bakery counter had done a number on me.

An irritating heat prickled my eyes as the stress of it all started to beat me down. I stretched my neck, hoping to ease my tense muscles, and closed my eyes while I drew a slow, steady breath into my lungs. Giving in to the panic of my craptastic situation wasn't going to help me.

My ears perked to the sound of someone coming in the side employee entrance. *Finally!*

"Johnny? Is that you?"

There was a long pause before my younger brother finally shouted back at me. "Yeah."

I frowned and let the sack of flour slump against my leg. "You're three hours late. I needed you to help me close today. Where have you been?"

"Hey, I got here when I could." He appeared in the doorway of the stockroom looking every bit the hooligan and scowled at me. "Get off my case, Benny"

I bit my tongue at the sight of his baggy jeans and that god-awful tank top. His sneakers were immaculately clean and bright white, of course. The gang tattoo on his neck still infuriated me. When he'd come home a few days before his high school graduation with that ugly thing emblazoned on his skin, I'd almost had a stroke.

"Look, I need your help. The supply truck was late today and I've got to get everything into the storeroom."

He didn't move. "Why didn't you have Marco or Adam do it?"

"I can't afford the overtime, Johnny. We're barely making ends meet." I wasn't telling him anything he didn't already know. We'd discussed our financial difficulties numerous times over the last few months but I don't think he gave it much thought. Apparently he assumed I would fix the problems—just as I always did.

"Maybe you should think about selling to that real estate guy," Johnny suggested and finally started to help me. He tossed the bag of flour onto his shoulder and carted it into the storeroom.

The thought of the slick real estate developer who had been pushing a sale contract at me for the last few weeks made my jaw tighten. Gentrification my ass! "We aren't selling, Johnny."

"Why not? It's good money, Benny."

"Money isn't everything, Johnny. This bakery isn't just part of the neighborhood's history. It's our history. Three generations of our family have worked here. Our grandparents built this *panaderia* with their blood and sweat and tears." I shook my head. "We're in a rough patch and we'll get through it. We are *not* selling."

"That's what the yarn shop lady and the furniture guy down the street said before they got smart." Johnny brushed by me to grab another sack of flour. "That's your problem, *nena*. You don't think big. You know what we could do with that kind of money?"

I rolled my eyes. Lately, Johnny had all these big plans. What he lacked was follow-through and drive. It was so easy to make concoct schemes but even harder to put in the work required to make them a success.

"First of all—stop calling me *nena*. And secondly? There wouldn't be that much money left over after the sale."

He frowned as he carted the heavy sack into the storeroom. "What do you mean? I saw what the guy offered us. That's a shitload of money, Benny."

"Yeah, it is but how do you think we paid for Abuelita's chemo and all the hospital bills? Before that, she'd taken out lines of credit on the building to pay for grandpa's diabetes problems. There are lines of credit and second mortgages." I rubbed the back of my neck as the stress of it all made me tense. "It's complicated, Johnny."

His eyes narrowed accusingly. "Why did you let her get all those loans?"

"I didn't, Johnny. I didn't find out until she opened the books to me. By the time she told us she was sick, she'd already gotten in way over her head."

"But the bakery makes good money."

"It's not that simple. The costs of supplies have increased. We had to replace all the ovens and the proofing boxes. We lost a quarter of our breakfast and lunch income when the layoffs at the gas plants hit." I couldn't even bring myself to mention what kind of a nosedive our business would take if the rumors of a Starbucks going in down the street were true. "Our health insurance premiums are way up."

"So cut them off," he coldly suggested. "Let them pay for their own doctor visits."

I glared at him. "Do you ever listen to the crap that comes out of your mouth? Some of our employees have been with the bakery since the day our grandparents opened, Johnny!"

He shrugged. "Yeah. So? People should pay their own way."

Frustration welled up inside of me. "I guess I should have made you pay all the lawyer fees for your last arrest, huh? I mean, you want to pay your own way, right?"

Johnny's eyes narrowed. "How many times are you going to throw that in my face?"

"Oh, I don't know, Johnny. As many times as it takes for you to realize what a dumb ass you are with all this gang bullshit."

"It's not bullshit, Benny. My crew is my family."

"Your family?" Anger surged through me. "I'm your family, Johnny. I'm the one that loves you just the way you are. I'm the one who has been there for you since we were little."

"You don't get it, Benny. You never will."

I couldn't even look at him. Glancing away, I said through gritted teeth, "Just finish moving the heavy stuff, okay? I can get everything else."

He started to argue with me but slammed his mouth shut and got back to work. We didn't say a word as we carried the stacks of baking supplies from one room to another. I'd learned that arguing with him only pushed him farther away from me. There was nothing I could say that hadn't already been said.

For some reason I couldn't fathom, he liked playing homeboy with the Hermanos. Some days I got the feeling it was all a big game to him. Only it wasn't a game. Not even close. The Hermanos were a brutally violent street gang that ruled over a huge section of Houston. I worried that Johnny would soon find himself in over his head—and then what? There was no walking away from the life he'd stupidly chosen.

His cell phone chirped and he dropped the buckets of shortening he carried to answer it. A second later, a car horn started blaring in the back alley. He shoved his phone back into his pocket. "I gotta go, Benny."

"What? No! You've got to help me finish this."

As if bolstered by the close proximity of his crew, he snapped, "I don't have to do shit for you, Benny."

Before I could even respond, a harsh male voice growled, "Don't talk to your sister that way!"

Both of our gazes jumped to the open doorway leading to the loading dock and alley. Dimitri Stepanov, our family's longtime tenant, loomed there. Tall, blond and rugged, he narrowed those icy blue eyes at Johnny. "You apologize to your sister."

"Fuck you, Dimitri." Johnny shot him the finger.

"Fuck me?" Dimitri took a step into the room and never let his unwavering glare leave Johnny. "Those are tough words, Johnny. You want to step out into the alley and see if you can back them up?"

"No." I moved between the two men and tried to put a lid on the simmering tension. "We're not going to have a street brawl behind my bakery."

Dimitri's harsh gaze softened as he glanced down at me. "He should not speak to you like that."

"Tell your boyfriend he better back up out of my business," Johnny warned.

My face went hot at the mention of Dimitri being my boyfriend. As if a man like Dimitri would give a short, thick-hipped girl like me a second look!

"When you disrespect Benny like that, you make it my business."

"I'm about to make whipping your ass my business, Dimitri."

"Johnny!" I gawked at him. "What is wrong with you?"

"What's wrong with me?" He stepped closer and poked his finger down into my face. "What's wrong with you? Why do you always take his side over mine?"

"What? Johnny, that's not—"

He threw up his hands. "I don't need this shit. I'm outta here."

"Johnny!" I chased after him but he darted out the back door and disappeared. Moments later, I heard the squeal of tires. Shoulders rounded with defeat, I stared at the empty doorway.

"I'm sorry, Benny. I shouldn't have gotten involved." Dimitri spoke gently, his words colored by his light Russian accent. "I didn't mean to make things worse."

I pivoted to face him and shrugged. "Johnny was in the mood to fight. You simply gave him a target."

Dimitri closed the distance between us. His familiar scent wrapped around me and left me yearning for his touch. Towering over me, he dared to touch my cheek. The feeling of his rough fingers moving over my skin made my belly do wild somersaults. "I'm sorry that I upset you."

I smiled and grasped his wrist. "You didn't upset me. I'm fine."

His hand fell from my face. Instantly, I missed the warmth of his touch. "Let me help you get all of this moved."

I shook my head. "No, Dimitri, this isn't your job. You're not my employee."

"No, I'm your friend—and I don't mind."

After five years of friendship, I recognized that arguing wasn't going to work. "Thank you."

He waved it off and grabbed the nearest sacks of sugar. As if their combined hundred pounds of weight were nothing, he hefted them onto his shoulders. "You should have told me you had a delivery coming today. I would have come home early to help you."

"I already asked you to help me with the plumbing when the sinks were leaking last week." I followed him into the storeroom with two boxes of sprinkles and colored sugar. "I feel like I'm taking advantage of you."

Dimitri snorted with amusement and dropped the sugar sacks into place. "You can take advantage of me anytime you want, Benny."

I was glad my back was turned. His double entendre made me blush with embarrassment. I could tell he was only joking with me but I couldn't help but wonder if my crush on him was that obvious. Clearly, Johnny had picked up on it. He'd made that cutting remark earlier because he knew it would hurt me. So much for brotherly love...

With a nervous laugh, I turned around—and slammed right into Dimitri's chest. He grabbed my shoulders to steady me. The scent of him punched the air right out of my lungs. All that soothing body heat radiated from him in waves, washing over me and filling me with such a longing need. Years of denying my attraction to the dead sexy Russian were finally starting to take their toll.

"Careful, Benny," he murmured.

"Sorry."

When his hands dropped from my shoulders, they skimmed my arms. The sensation of his fingertips gliding over my skin left me momentarily dizzy. I tried not to let my mind go to the dirty place it wanted to visit.

He stepped away from me and glanced around the overstocked storeroom. "This is a bigger order than usual."

Finally getting a grip, I said, "It's for that Tasting Houston thing Lena convinced me to do."

A few weeks earlier, an old college friend, Lena Cruz, had traipsed back into my life. By the strangest coincidence, one of her friends was dating one of Dimitri's friends. She currently worked at one of Houston's mega PR firms and offered to do me a huge favor by helping me drum up business.

"On Saturday, right?"

I nodded. "She thinks it will be a good way to build our brand. I'm not so sure about all that marketing and branding talk but she seems to really know her stuff."

I didn't add that I was desperate for her marketing plan to work. We needed to increase our customer base and grow our revenue stream if the bakery had any hope of surviving this tight spot.

Deep down inside, I feared that nothing would work. Jonah Krause, the real estate developer who wanted my building wasn't the kind of man who liked the word *no*. I'd managed to fend him off for a few months but I was starting to worry that he would ratchet up the pressure on me. I'd heard some eyebrow-raising tales from my neighbors about the tactics he'd used to strong-arm them into selling.

Glancing around for my clipboard and checklist, I realized I'd left it in my office. "Be right back. I need to grab my list. Marco supervised the delivery but his eyes aren't what they used to be. Sometimes he miscounts."

He nodded and I scooted by him, careful not to bump into his arms or chest. Every time we made accidental contact, it made it harder and harder for me to ignore the throbbing heat in my lower belly.

It was stupid, really, my infatuation with Dimitri. Over the years, I'd had the misfortune of seeing some of the bombshells he'd dated. Nothing made this petite Latina with a slightly too-curvy figure more self-conscious than a mental comparison of myself with the leggy, willowy beauties I'd seen on Dimitri's arm.

All thoughts of my wicked crush on Dimitri fled the moment I stepped into my office. The bank bag on my desk was upside down and the papers under it had been disturbed. One of my desk drawers, the one where I kept important contracts and papers, was slightly ajar. Even before I grabbed the bag and unzipped it, I knew what I would find.

My stomach dropped like an out of control elevator as I counted and recounted the day's takings. Three hundred dollars were now missing—and I knew exactly who had taken it. At the time, I hadn't given a second thought to Johnny coming in the side entrance instead of the alley door. Now, of course, I understood why he'd come into the bakery that way.

Awash in ugly feelings, I crashed down into my squeaky office chair. His betrayal left me shaking with anger and such profound sadness. What the hell was wrong with him? The knowledge that I didn't know my brother anymore hit me hard.

But it was the realization that I'd failed him and broken my promise to my grandmother on her death bed that made my stomach churn so painfully.

Like a dam bursting, a flood of stress exploded inside me. With my head buried in my hands, I started to cry. Big, ugly loud sobs tore through me until I was choking on them.

"Benny?"

*

Finding Benny sobbing into her hands caused such a painful tightness in Dimitri's chest. He crossed the distance between them in a few quick strides and crouched down in front of her. Tears ran down her face and dripped onto her shirt.

"I'm sorry." Her cheeks were flushed with embarrassment. "I'm being stupid."

"Don't," he whispered softly. There were tissues on the corner of her desk and he plucked a handful of them free. "You're not being stupid." Ever so gently, he dabbed at her face. "What's wrong?"

Lower lip wobbling, she gestured to the bank deposit bag and the stacks of cash on her desk. He took one look and figured it out. Swearing roughly, he vowed to kick that little bastard's ass the next time they crossed paths.

"How much?" Dimitri demanded.

"Three hundred," she said and sniffled loudly. "I can't believe he would steal from me."

Dimitri could. Even though Benny knew Johnny was getting into trouble, she had no idea the extent of his criminal behavior. She didn't know because Dimitri had been shielding the ugliness from her. She'd been through so much in the last few years. He couldn't bear to see her heart broken anymore by her worthless little shit of a brother.

"Dimitri?"

"Yes?" He fought the urge to cup her beautiful face and kiss the sadness out of her.

"Why do you think he needs money?" She nervously licked her lips, drawing his gaze to her pink pout. "Drugs?

Worse?"

"I don't know," he lied. "It could be anything. Maybe it's something stupid like buying alcohol or gambling."

She held his gaze. "I don't think so. I think it's something much more serious."

He couldn't bring himself to confirm her suspicions. Three hundred dollars would be enough to buy an unmarked piece and a box of ammunition from one of the backstreet dealers who worked the area. If Johnny thought he needed a gun to defend himself, it meant Benny wasn't safe. His gut twisted at the idea of Benny being hurt by her brother's stupid choices.

"Listen," he said and rubbed his hands over the denim covering her thighs. "Why don't you come up to my apartment? Let me cook you dinner."

And keep an eye on you...

"Oh, Dimitri, you don't have to offer to make me dinner. I'll be okay."

"I want to make you dinner." He didn't add that he wanted so much more than that with her.

For more than a year, he'd been secretly in love with Benny. The change from friendship to infatuation had come upon him so slowly; he hadn't even fully realized how he felt toward her until the day her grandmother had passed.

Overcome with grief, Benny had rushed into his arms and he'd cradled her on his lap as she wept. Holding her felt like the most natural thing in the world—and he'd never wanted to let her go. He'd been overwhelmed with the realization that he loved her.

But he hadn't been brave enough to say it then. Nor had he found the courage to do it any day since. The few times he'd come close to asking Benny out for dinner or a drink, he'd lost his nerve. He was keenly aware of the huge burdens she shouldered and he liked that she felt comfortable coming to him for help. The idea that making his move might upset the balance of their friendship and push her away from him stopped Dimitri from taking a chance.

Moving his hands to her jean-clad knees, he said, "We'll open a bottle of wine and you can relax while I cook you something delicious. And we'll talk. We'll figure out a way to deal with Johnny and his mess. Okay?"

Something flashed in her dark eyes. Interest, perhaps? He didn't dare hope for anything more.

With a smile, she acquiesced. "Okay."

"Wonderful." He stood and gestured to the desk. "You recount the money. I'll go check the list and lock up the back."

She handed him the keys and clipboard. Their fingers briefly touched and the searing heat of it made his gut clench. He couldn't help but wonder what it would feel like to have her soft, small hands touching other parts of him.

Taking a step back, he said, "Come find me when you're ready."

"I will."

He quickly retreated from the office and returned to the storeroom. List in hand, he checked and rechecked the delivered supplies before locking up and shutting off the lights. He heard her come into the back room of the bakery and waited for her to find him. The sweet smell of her, the bare hints of vanilla beans and cinnamon, curled around him and heightened his awareness of her. It took every ounce of his control not to reach for her hand and pull her toward him in the darkness.

Her gentle voice rolled over him. "I'm ready."

God, how he wished that was true.

CHAPTER TWO

An hour and a half later, I sank into the comfy corner of Dimitri's couch and curled my bare feet up onto the cushion. He'd insisted I kick off my shoes the second I came in the door. After being on my aching feet all day, it was a request I was happy to meet.

I'd only been in his apartment a handful of times since he'd signed his first lease five years ago but each time I noticed something different. Tonight it was the display of photos he'd placed on the far wall. Some of them were from his time in the Russian military and one of their Special Forces units. A maroon beret in a shadow box caught my eye. I'd never really asked him about his time working in the elite unit but a little Google-fu had shown me what kind of dangers he'd faced and survived during the various engagements with terrorists and the wars that had taken place during his service.

I spotted familiar faces in the photos from his time here in Houston. Ivan, Yuri and Nikolai, his childhood friends from Russia, were in most of them. The men all shared the same commanding dispositions. They were the types of men you met only once but never forgot.

My gaze lingered on a framed news clipping. Two years ago, the paper had run a series of spotlights on successful businesses headed by immigrants. My grandmother had been interviewed one week. Dimitri's private security firm had been showcased the next week. Using his background in the military and a windfall from a shrewd investment in timeshares, Dimitri had founded a small firm that selected and trained bouncers for the city's hottest nightspots. Some of them also worked security at places like Ivan's elite mixed-martial arts gym.

With all the money he had, I often wondered why the heck he stayed here in this apartment. Even with the improvements he'd made to the space—the hardwood floors and gorgeous tiling—it was still an apartment with no backyard and very little privacy.

Dimitri finished loading his dishwasher and joined me in the living room. He tried to pour more wine into my glass but I put my hand over the cup. "I shouldn't."

"You should." He gently pushed my fingers aside and splashed more of the dark, rich wine into my glass. "It's your second glass. Enjoy it. *Relax.*"

It was the relaxing part that worried me most. Being in his home, sitting at his table and eating the delicious dinner he'd cooked for me had been more wonderful than I'd ever imagined. His friendly offer had given me a glimpse of what I'd craved for so long. I tried to ignore the pang of longing growing heavier and heavier in my chest. *Why can't you see me?*

Dimitri settled onto the other end of the couch and turned so he could look at me. With one foot resting on his knee, he looked so at ease. "Let's talk about the business."

I sipped my wine and grimaced at the very idea of

opening that Pandora's Box of fiscal nightmares. "Let's not."

"No," he said firmly. "You need to talk about it. I can see that it's eating you up. I'm terrified you're going to have a heart attack or stroke from the stress of it all." He nudged my bare foot with the toe of his boot. "Talk."

How could I deny him anything?

With a sigh, I said, "I'm struggling to make ends meet." Because that wasn't quite the truth and I hated to hide anything from him, I clarified my statement. "Actually, I'm basically holding it all together with chewing gum and duct tape. It's...bad." My gut soured as I admitted, "I haven't drawn a salary in ten months and I withdrew from classes last week because I can't afford to keep going right now. I wanted to finish my degree but it's not feasible at the moment."

Dimitri let out a shocked sound. "Ten months, Benny? How the hell are you surviving?"

"I had some money left over from Mom and Dad's life insurance payout. It's running low so I've got to make some drastic cuts to my home budget."

"Why didn't you tell me? I would have loaned you money!"

I squirmed uncomfortably. "I don't want your money, Dimitri. That would make things weird. No money between friends, right?"

His pale blue eyes seemed to darken. I could tell he wanted to say something but he bit his tongue. Instead, he asked, "Can you recover?"

I nodded. "It will be painful, but yes."

"How?"

I ran my finger over the rim of the wine glass. "I'm going to sell the house."

He went rigid. "Your home? But where will you live?"

"I'm not sure. I'll probably try to get an apartment closer to here." Trying to make myself feel better about losing the house I'd grown up in, I said, "Johnny and I don't need that much space. We're never there so we don't get to enjoy the big yard or the pool. The market is really hot in our neighborhood. We own the house outright so I hope we can get enough from the sale to clear the business debts."

Dimitri downed the rest of his wine and set aside his glass. "You should move in here."

At first I didn't understand him. The wine made my thoughts a little fuzzy. Then it hit me. "You're moving out? When?" My voice climbed higher and higher as I spoke but I had to know. "Why?"

He peered at me so intently the fine hairs on my arms and the back of my neck stood on edge. "It's time. This place was always supposed to be a transition for me but I got comfortable here."

"Isn't that a good thing?" I couldn't believe how pathetic I sounded.

"Sure," Dimitri replied gently, "but that mess downstairs proved to me that it's time for me to go."

"I don't understand."

"I shouldn't have gotten involved with you and Johnny this evening. Every time I do, he gets nasty with you. I try to help you but I'm only making things worse."

"That's not true. I know you've gotten Johnny out of some bad scrapes." He started to protest but I shook my head. "I hear things, Dimitri. I know you've put your ass on the line for him once or twice. I don't...I don't know what I'd do if I didn't have you here."

"Even if I'm not living here, I'll always be there for you and Johnny."

It was a small comfort but it didn't ease the painful

ache surrounding my heart. "I worry Johnny is going to get into real trouble one of these days."

Dimitri exhaled slowly. "Becoming a man isn't an easy thing, Benny. Some men find it easier than others. If Johnny wants to play grown-up, let him deal with the consequences."

The idea of Johnny getting hurt made my belly ache. "I don't know if I can."

"You have to cut the apron strings." He made a scissor-like gesture. "You have enough on your plate without worrying about Johnny too. God, Benny, you deserve to have a life of your own."

I snorted softly. "A life? I can't even remember what that was like." Loose-lipped from the wine, I confessed, "I haven't had a date in nearly two years. Hell, I can't even remember the last time I was kissed or had sex."

The second my embarrassing confession escaped my lips, I wanted to die. I dropped my gaze to my lap and wished a hole would open up and swallow me.

I held my breath as Dimitri moved. I prayed he wouldn't say something trite or make an awkward joke to ease my uncomfortable gaffe. When his fingers closed around my wine glass, I let him take it away. The message was pretty clear. He was cutting me off.

But then he did the most shocking thing. He slid so close our thighs touched. Those big, strong hands cupped my face and forced me to meet his gaze. I felt the air rush out of my lungs as we stared at one another.

"We just broke your streak."

I blinked. "What?"

His thumb made lazy circles on my skin. "We just had a date."

Feeling a bit dizzy, I asked, "Did we?"

His lips twitched with amusement. "We did."

And then he kissed me.

I held my breath as his lips moved against mine, the kiss so tender and sweet it stunned me. Imaginary fireworks burst around me as Dimitri deepened the kiss, daring to swipe his tongue against my lips and coaxing me to let him inside. I clutched at his arms as he plundered my mouth, kissing me like no other man ever had. I melted into his warm embrace and prayed the moment would never end.

When it did, I experienced a quiver of embarrassment as the reality of what he'd done hit me. I couldn't meet his gaze. "You didn't have to do that."

"Do what?" he asked softly and brushed his fingers through the ends of my ponytail.

Face aflame, I said, "I don't need your pity kisses, Dimitri."

He grasped my chin and lifted my gaze. I was surprised by the frustration written so clearly on his handsome face. "Is that what you think? That I pity you?"

I gaped at him. "I don't know. I mean—look at you. You're, like, so far out of my league."

"League?" He growled with disgust. "Jesus Christ, Benny, is that what you think? That I don't find you attractive?"

"I—"

He cut me off with another kiss, this one punishing and demanding. I gasped as he grabbed me by the waist and dragged me onto his lap. The way he so easily manhandled me made my belly clench. His hands rode the curve of my back to settle on my bottom.

I inhaled a shuddery breath as he clasped my backside. Suddenly my jeans felt incredibly thin. "Dimitri…"

"Hush," he whispered and kissed me again. "Do you know what I see when I look at you?"

Feeling totally out of my depth and completely off-kilter, I simply shook my head.

"I see the prettiest brown eyes and the most tempting lips." He nuzzled our noses together. "If you only knew how many nights I've dreamed about having your soft, swollen lips wrapped around my cock."

My eyes widened at his frank admission. Lightheaded with surprise and desire, I couldn't believe this was happening. *Am I dreaming?*

Dimitri's hand left my bottom and slid around to my front. He palmed my breast through the thin cotton of my bakery t-shirt. "I fantasize about seeing you naked. I imagine what it would be like to lick and kiss your breasts while you're pinned beneath me in my bed." His other hand gave my backside a little swat. "Some nights I stroke my dick and imagine that it's your tight, wet pussy squeezing me. That it's your ass bouncing on my lap while you ride me and come on my cock."

Breathless now, I began to tremble. White-hot currents raced through me. Was this really happening? My inner cynic shouted this was all some kind of colossal prank but the hungry look in Dimitri's pale blue eyes assured me he was dead serious. *He* wanted *me*!

Dimitri's hand moved to the back of my head and he tugged me down for another one of his wildly sensual kisses. My toes curled against the couch as his tongue darted into my mouth. He nibbled my lower lip. "You're staying with me tonight."

I gulped. "Am I?"

He shot me a devilishly sexy grin. "Yes."

Suddenly, I became self-conscious to the extreme. Working dough, icing trays of pastries, rushing from the hot kitchen to the crowded front room—it was all hard, sweaty work. Feeling less than sexy, I asked nervously,

"Could I maybe, um, get a shower first?"

He chuckled and kissed me again. "Only if I get to join you."

"Oh!" I chewed my lower lip. The idea of Dimitri seeing me stark naked under the bright lights of his bathroom made me more nervous. "Well..."

"That wasn't a request." He shifted me off his lap but gripped my hand in his as he stood. I got the feeling he feared I would dash for the door if he let go. He was probably right. Even though I'd fantasized about spending a night with Dimitri, I found my courage fleeing at the reality of it happening.

Wordlessly, he tugged me along behind him. He dragged me to the front door and flipped the deadbolt before pulling me across the living room to the bedroom in the back of the apartment. I still couldn't quite believe what was happening. I felt sure that any moment I would jerk awake and find myself slumped over my desk, passed out from the sheer exhaustion of working twenty-hour days for months on end.

But it was real. This was really happening.

I was shaking by the time we reached his bathroom. I hadn't seen the inside of the space since he'd moved into the apartment. I knew he'd done work to the place—Abuelita let him have a break on the rent any time he made improvements—but I had no idea it looked this nice. The soft blue glass tile in the shower made the small space look so much bigger. He'd switched out the faucet and cabinets for something sleeker and more modern.

After he turned on and adjusted the water temp, Dimitri faced me. For a long moment, we simply stared at one another. He toed off his boots and jerked off his socks. When his fingers started to flick through the buttons lining the front of his steel grey shirt, a thrill of excitement coursed through me. My eyes widened with appreciation as he shucked the piece of clothing.

Incredibly toned, his lean muscles rippled as he moved. I raked my gaze over him, taking in every delicious inch of that ridiculously sexy chest. Old war wounds and scars dotted his skin. I understood then why he never spoke of his time in the Russian army. I doubted the memories were very good.

When he turned to drop his shirt into the hamper against the wall, I caught sight of the tattoo covering most of his back. It was beautiful with bold bursts of color and heavy dark lines. Unlike the obvious prison pieces I'd seen on Ivan's hands, the tattoo on Dimitri's back showed real skill and artistry.

"A phoenix?" I asked, surprised by the mythical beast he'd chosen.

He quirked an amused smile. "Why does that surprise you?"

"I don't know. I suppose I expected that if you had tattoos they'd be more..." I searched for the right word. "Primitive. Primal."

"I had this done when I left the service and came here." He gestured to his back. "It seemed like a good representation of the change I was making. Here? In this country? I could be anything I wanted. I was starting over from the ashes of my old life."

His reasoning resonated with me. As the granddaughter of immigrants, I understood his story and related to it. From birth, my grandparents had drilled into my head how lucky I was to be born here, in a place where anything was possible with enough hard work and dedication.

"I get it, Dimitri."

"I knew you would." He started to unbuckle his belt

and my heart began to race. The *whomp-whomp-whomp* of blood rushing by my eardrums accompanied my discovery that Dimitri preferred boxers. I thought for sure he would keep them on but he slipped out of them without a moment's hesitation.

It was all I could do to stop my jaw from dropping to the floor. His magnificent cock jutted forth from neatly trimmed curls—and pointed right at me. Whatever doubts I'd harbored about his attraction to me fled in that instant. There was no faking that response.

Dimitri took a step toward me and I took one back. His grin turned a bit playful and he continued to advance upon me. With one hand, he shut the door and backed me up against it. Caught between Dimitri's hard body and the stiff wood at my back, I had no choice but to surrender to his seeking mouth and roaming hands. The ruddy head of his thick cock rubbed against my belly and caused my mind to race with filthy thoughts.

My brain began to misfire as his rough palms slipped under my t-shirt to stroke my bare skin. Heat flooded my core. I squeezed my thighs together to ease the throbbing there. Years of running myself ragged as my grandmother fought and lost her battle with cancer, my brother spiraled out of control and the business nosedived had taken their toll on me. My body had learned to run on fumes and in doing so had all but shut down my libido.

But Dimitri's strong hands moving over my skin stoked the embers of my desire. When his lips touched my neck, the flames of need flared to life within me. My skin burned under his touch and I arched into him, welcoming the quicksilver flashes of excitement he evoked with his mouth and hands.

Kneeling in front of me, we were almost eye to eye. I stood only an inch over five feet and he had a good foot on me in the height department. He smiled mischievously before kissing me. I'm sure he was thinking how odd we must look right now.

When he grasped the bottom of my shirt, I lifted my arms and let him drag it up and over my head. Standing there with my bra bared to him, I was grateful I'd put on a cute pair of undies today. The bright purple print with white polka dots was more playful than sexy but at least I hadn't gone for the super comfortable sports bra and full briefs that I often slid into when half-asleep in the morning.

Dimitri tugged my jeans down my hips. I thanked my lucky stars I'd had time to shave during my morning shower. I would have died if Dimitri's hands had encountered stubble as he swept them up and down my short legs.

I gulped as Dimitri reached around behind my back to unhook my bra. He carefully peeled it away from my chest and down my arms. I started to put a hand over my naked breasts but he stopped me.

"No," he whispered. "I want to see you." He brushed his lips over my nipple. "All of you."

I gasped as his tongue slowly traced the dark bud. He suckled me gently, pulling my nipple between his warm lips and laving it with his tongue. My hands flew to his shoulders as he tormented me with his mouth. Tummy violently wobbling, I gripped his upper arms and held on for dear life.

His hands moved to my hips and he pushed my panties down my thighs. I stepped out of them and squeezed my knees together. Awash with anxiety, I tried not to focus on my hang-ups but it was so hard. He gently stroked my naked hips and legs as if petting a skittish creature. "I wish you could see how beautiful you are to me."

I stared into his pale eyes and realized he was dead serious. He wasn't trying to be kind or flattering me for some ulterior motive. It occurred to me that he didn't see all the little things that drove me crazy about my body. He saw *me*, the real me.

And he thought I was beautiful.

His lips skimmed my collarbone. "Luckily, I've got the whole night to show you."

I shivered as the weight of his words settled upon me. This was going to be a night I would never forget.

*

Dimitri was hard enough to pound through concrete as he led Benny into the shower. The urge to lift her up, wrap her petite legs around his waist and sink into her hot, willing flesh threatened his control. Somehow he found the strength to keep those primal urges at bay. She deserved something tender and easy, to be seduced and shown real pleasure. He wanted to watch her come undone and surrender to the passion inside her—and that was a thing that took time.

He still couldn't believe the night was unfolding in this way. When he'd asked her up to his apartment for dinner, he'd truly only wanted to keep her safe and help her unload some of the burdens weighing so heavily on her shoulders. He'd thought maybe he would finally work up the courage to kiss her, if the time was right. Not in his wildest dreams did he imagine she would present him with the perfect opportunity for making his move.

He'd seen the embarrassment on her face the moment she'd admitted how long it had been since she'd had a lover. In that moment, he'd recognized his chance and seized upon it. Hearing her say that she wasn't in his league had cut him deeply. He sensed that she would need reassurance tonight. Before this night was over, he would make sure she rid herself of those silly notions.

Stepping under the hot spray, Dimitri let the pounding water splash over him. Benny stayed near the glass door and wound her ponytail into a messy bun. The second she was done, he reached for her. She came willingly, sliding into his arms and pressing her cheek to his chest. His eyelids drifted together as he relished the feel of her small, soft body.

Arousal and excitement gave her silky brown skin a pink tint. With her dark hair and dark eyes, Benny favored her Hispanic mother more than her blond-haired, green-eyed father. Johnny, on the other hand, looked more like their late father. Dimitri often wondered if that was why he'd thrown himself into the Hermanos gang. The kid was overcompensating and trying to prove that he was just as Latino, if not more, than the other boys.

Not wanting to let thoughts of that little bastard ruin their night, Dimitri shoved them aside and concentrated solely on Benny. He soaped up his palms and took his time swiping his hands along her curves. Her naked skin felt so damn good under his fingers. He couldn't wait to get her in his bed so he could do more than just stroke her.

Benny's breaths deepened and her eyes seemed to darken. He captured her mouth and carefully backed her up against the tile. She whimpered when his hands moved along the gentle slope of her belly to the vee between her thighs. Almost instantly, he felt her tense. He broke their kiss and peered down into her brown eyes. There was no mistaking the glint of panic there. Not moving his hand, he asked, "Do you want to stop?"

She gulped. "No."

He nuzzled her nose with his. "But you're afraid to keep going?"

"Yes." Her whispered reply ghosted against his ear.

Understanding her mindset, he decided that perhaps it was time to take a more dominant role with her. Until she was comfortable asking for the things she wanted or surrendering to the passion blossoming within her, Benny would need him to guide her.

"We're going to play a game."

She blinked with surprise. "What?"

"A game," he said and kissed her tenderly. He felt some of the tightness leave her as he gently caressed her belly and brushed his lips across hers.

Her eyes narrowed with suspicion. "What kind of game?"

Smiling, he said, "The kind of game you're going to enjoy very much." He traced her nipple with a soapy finger, coaxing the dusky bud to a hard peak. "For the rest of the night, I'm taking away your right to say no."

She gasped with outrage but he quickly ambushed her with a kiss. He stabbed his tongue against hers. She tasted of wine and the slight sweetness of the berries he'd served with dessert. Palming her breast, he tweaked her nipple, pinching it just enough to make her moan.

When she was pliable and ready to listen, he explained, "I'll ask you how you feel when I'm touching you or kissing you or making love to you. You can say red, green or yellow and I'll adjust accordingly."

He watched the warring emotions play out across her face. For a woman who always had to be in control, this wouldn't be easy for her. He expected her to put her foot down and refuse but she surprised him by lifting her chin and nodding. A bit breathless now, she said simply,

"Green."

A smile tugged at the corners of his mouth. He let his hand slide along her hip and down to cup her backside. She had the sweetest ass, the kind of soft, supple flesh that begged to be squeezed and swatted. The image of her bouncing on his lap, of him clasping her backside to guide her up and down on his shaft, made Dimitri's balls ache.

Soon, he promised himself. But right now? This was all about Benny and her needs.

Holding her gaze, he let his hand slide lower. He forced her thighs apart and cupped her mound. She inhaled a sharp breath as he dragged his fingertips up and down the seam of her pussy. Wanting her on edge, he continued to do tease her. "Are we still green?"

"Y-yes," she stammered, her breaths coming faster now. "We're very, very green. The brightest green you've ever seen," she added with a little laugh.

Dimitri chuckled at her playfulness and gave her exactly what she wanted. He parted her tender folds and exposed her clitoris. The swollen nub responded to his swirling fingertip and left Benny shuddering. Her hands squealed against the tile as they flew back to the wall and desperately searched for purchase. He dropped his forehead to hers, their breaths mingling, and slowly circled her clit.

He watched in wonder as her expression changed. Committing the small details to mind, he studied her as she climaxed, her strangled cry echoing in the tiled stall. He memorized the way her neck flushed and her lips parted. He noted the way her upper body tightened and her breaths became almost panicked just before she came.

The sight and sound of her climax whet his appetite for more of her. He wanted to watch her come again and again. And he wanted to do it now.

CHAPTER THREE

I still hadn't regained my ability to breathe normally when Dimitri shut off the water and helped me out of the shower. Dripping onto the bathmat, I welcomed the warmth of the towel he wrapped around me. I tried not to let anxiety invade my belly but not even that shockingly quick orgasm he'd just given me in the shower could dull my crazy self-consciousness.

I think Dimitri sensed it too. He secured a towel around his waist before turning back to me. I couldn't believe he wanted to help me dry off but I wasn't about to say no having his big hands moving all over my body again. His touch soothed my raw nerves.

When I was dry, he took my hand and led me into his bedroom. My mouth went dry as I stared at his bed. The orgasm he'd coaxed out of me in the shower had been hotter than any I'd ever managed to give myself. Coming wasn't easy for me. In the back of my mind, I recognized it was a power issue. It's hard to let go and enjoy the moment when you're constantly overthinking every single second of a sexual encounter.

Back in the shower, I'd been forced off-kilter by Dimitri's commanding presence and my inability to say no. The idea that he was simply going to take what he wanted from me had made me so wet. I couldn't understand it. I started to wonder if maybe I was one of *those* girls. I'd read about them in some of my steamier books but I'd never considered that I needed or wanted to surrender control to a man.

Or maybe it was simply that I wanted to surrender control to Dimitri. Maybe *he* was the reason this experience felt so different and so exciting.

He stepped so close the tip of his cock brushed against my lower back. My clit throbbed mercilessly as his body heat wound around me. I closed my eyes as he expertly uncurled the bright yellow elastic wrapped around my hair. He ran his fingers through my dark waves, his nails scratching lightly against my scalp and making my skin tingle.

His hands moved to my shoulders and I tensed. I knew he felt it because his fingers instantly lessened their slight grip. Feeling embarrassed, I whispered, "I'm sorry, Dimitri. It's not you. Really. It's just me. I'm so—"

"Shh." His hot breath moved across my ear. He peppered feather-light kisses along my neck, causing goose bumps to break out on my skin. "I understand. I'm going to help you relax."

"How?"

He stepped away from me and yanked the covers right off his bed. They ended up in a pile in the corner. "Get on my bed, Benny." His voice was low and husky. "On your back."

Trembling now, I did as told. I swallowed hard and watched him disappear into his closet. I heard a drawer open and close. When he returned he had strange black straps in his hands. My belly did a wild dance. Restraints?

Dimitri put a knee on the bed. "I'm assuming by the look on your face you know what these are."

I gulped. "Yes."

"Have you ever used them?"

"No but I've read about them."

He laughed. "Remind me to browse your bookshelves the next time I'm at your house."

I heard the tearing sound of the hook-and-loop closure as he unlatched one of the cuffs on the restraint straps. Feeling really uncertain now, I started to protest. "Dimitri, I don't think—"

He clicked his teeth and wagged his finger. "Red, green or yellow?"

I frowned in annoyance but knew he wouldn't be swayed. Finally, I said, "Yellow."

"Good girl." Seemingly pleased that I'd followed his instruction, Dimitri let his hand drifted along my calf and up toward my knee before doubling back. "You enjoy reading stories where women are restrained by their lovers but you aren't sure you want to try it in real life."

He'd nailed it in one try. "Basically."

"Do you know what I think?"

"No but I'm sure you going to tell me."

He gave my thigh a playful pinch. "Be glad I'm not into spanking, Benny. Otherwise I might have to put you across my lap."

Even though I knew he was joking, my tummy fluttered. The idea of being spanked by a lover seemed so erotic and naughty.

"I think you need to learn to let go and relax. Your mind is constantly racing." He lowered his mouth until it touched my knee and then my thigh. My toes curled into the mattress and I held my breath. "Tonight, you're here to feel. Just feel," he added. "Can you do that?"

"No," I answered honestly. "You know I can't."

"And that's why I'm going to restrain you." He crawled over me, planting his knees on either side of my thighs, and teased his mouth over mine. My breasts rubbed against his hard chest and his stiff cock nudged my navel. I experienced a quiver of panic at being pinned beneath his massive frame but he kissed the fight right out of me, reminding me who was boss tonight.

"I'm going to restrain your legs and arms so you can't twist or pull away from me when the sensations become overwhelming. I want you to feel them all, Benny. I want to see the passion locked up inside you set free." He trailed his fingertips along my cheek. "I want you screaming and writhing and begging for mercy when I bury my face between your legs and when I fuck you."

Electric bursts zipped along my skin as he described what he was going to do to me. It should have scared me but the idea of Dimitri ravishing me left me panting and pulsing with need. I wanted it. I wanted him.

Understanding that he wanted my permission, I lifted my lips to his. He kissed me ever so gently and then I whispered, "I trust you."

His eyes widened slightly. "I will never betray that trust, Benita."

Hearing him use my real name made the statement so powerful. I understood that he wasn't just talking about here in his bed.

I held my breath as Dimitri took my wrists in one of his big hands and dragged them up and over my head. He expertly wrapped the stretchy restraints around my wrists and fastened them to the wooden slats of the headboard. Unable to help myself, I gave an experimental tug. Though the cuffs were tight, they didn't hurt but there was no way I was escaping from them.

"Oh!" I shivered and tried to twist my hips as Dimitri ran his fingers down the undersides of my arms. The ticklish sensation made me giggle. Try as I might, I couldn't pull away from him. Those strong legs clamped around my hips and the restraints binding my wrists overhead made it impossible.

My tummy swooped as he skimmed his lips over the swell of my breasts and playfully tickled his way down my body. Kneeling between my thighs, Dimitri grasped my left ankle and wrapped the cuff around it. He did the same to the right ankle and then made quick work of securing the loose ends of the restraints to the headboard.

With my feet in the air, I felt totally vulnerable and so incredibly exposed. There wasn't much slack on the restraints securing my ankles and I tensed.

"No," Dimitri instructed gently. "Don't tense up, Benny. Let the straps do the work." He massaged my thighs and calves. "Relax your muscles."

I closed my eyes and concentrated on the feeling of his strong fingers kneading my legs. By slow degrees, I let the tension leave my body. Just as he'd promised, the restraints did all the work.

"What color are we, Benny?"

I licked my lips and looked at him. He waited patiently for my answer. Without a doubt in my mind, I knew that if I said red, he'd tear away the restraints.

But I didn't want him to do that. I wanted to stay bound to his bed and completely at his mercy. I wanted him to show me all the things he'd promised. I wanted to know what it felt like to be fucked into submission and left shuddering and boneless with pleasure.

"Green."

"You can change your mind at any time." His hand

swept from my belly to my breasts and down again. His mouth curved in a mischievous smile. "But I hope you don't."

I was still giggling when he leaned down to kiss me. In that moment, as his lips sealed to mine, I surrendered totally. In the back of my mind, I couldn't shake the fear that this was only a one-night stand. If it was, I damn sure intended to get the most out of it. I wanted to walk out of Dimitri's apartment with no regrets.

A pleasured sigh escaped my lips as Dimitri nibbled and kissed his way down my body. He spent time tormenting my breasts, tugging my nipples between his lips and grazing his teeth over them ever so slightly. I shivered and arched into his sensual assault.

By the time he was done with my breasts, they felt so heavy and ached. My nipples were tight little points that seemed to buzz. His mouth made a slow trail down my belly. He kissed my navel and each side of my hips before sliding down the bed.

I bit my lower lip when his shoulders nudged my wide open thighs. My face flamed with embarrassment as he stared at that most intimate part of me. His thick, long fingers gingerly separated my folds. He framed my throbbing clitoris between two digits and brushed his lips across it in a teasing swipe. I let my head drop down to the mattress and tried to remember how to breathe.

"Do you like having your pussy licked?"

His blunt question stunned me. Even more embarrassed now, I admitted, "I've never been on the receiving end of oral sex."

His head lifted and our gazes clashed. Frowning, he asked, "But you gave it?"

I nodded. "Sure."

His lips settled into a grim line. "That sort of selfish

bullshit doesn't fly in my bed."

Before I could figure out how to reply to that, Dimitri's mouth dropped to my clit. I hissed with surprise as his soft, warm lips engulfed the pulsing bundle of nerves. He took up a leisurely rhythm, licking one side of the pink pearl and then the other. The wicked sensation of his tongue moving over me *down there* made every nerve-ending in my body tingle.

Ever so slowly, he changed his tactic. His tongue swirled around my clit a few times before he sucked it between his lips and tugged on the little nub. I cried out at the sharp pleasure. My hips lifted instinctively, pressing my hot pussy right up against his mouth.

With a hungry groan, Dimitri slid both hands under my ass and gripped my backside. He feasted on my pussy. I couldn't think and gasped for air as he lashed my clit with his skilled tongue. My fingers tightened into fists and my thighs clenched as that shudder of panic raced through my core. Any second now...

"Dimitri!" I shouted his name as the climax hit me hard. Rocking atop the bed, I moaned as the waves crashed down on me again and again. Dimitri's tongue kept up that perfect pace, licking me in just the right way until—suddenly—I came again. "*Ahh!*"

He attacked my clit and forced the orgasm right to the brink of breaking me before easing off with tender flicks. I sagged against the mattress, my body limp and my head buzzing as the post-orgasmic hormones saturated my bloodstream.

But Dimitri wasn't done with me yet.

His nimble fingers explored my pussy. "So fucking beautiful," he murmured with awe. "You're so pink and wet." His tongue swiped me. "I can't get enough of you."

"Oh!" I moaned as he penetrated me, first with one

finger and then two. My slick nectar eased his thrusting fingers. I nearly shot up off the bed when he found that spongy spot along my inner wall and rubbed it. Only the restraints kept me in place.

He chuckled ominously. "I think we've found something new to play with, Benny."

"Oh no," I pleaded. "Oh god! I can't, Dimitri. No more."

"I'll decide when you've had enough."

And then his mouth returned to my clit. The fingers inside me pumped my G-spot while his tongue circled and fluttered over the swollen bud. I shrieked as the exquisite agony of his wicked torment gripped me. My orgasm punched the air right out of my lungs and left me breathless and panting and desperate for mercy.

Dazed by the power of it, I shuddered atop the bed and only vaguely realized Dimitri had slipped off the bed. When he returned, I managed to focus on his ridiculously handsome face. He rolled a condom onto his impressive cock and scooted between my parted thighs.

He was so hard he didn't even have to guide himself inside me. The second our bodies were aligned, he thrust forward roughly, sheathing his dick deep inside my slick, hot channel. I whimpered at the sudden invasion of his massive cock. Stretched and filled, it took me a moment to acclimate to the feel of Dimitri buried inside me.

As if we had all the time in the world, he took me with long, deep and measured strokes. I wanted so desperately to touch him. My mind on the fritz, I finally uttered the only word I could remember. "Red."

Dimitri stiffened and stopped instantly. Concern twisted his features. "Are you all right? Did I hurt you?"

"No." I shook my head. "I want to touch you. Let me loose."

His face relaxed. "Not yet," he murmured and thrust up into me again.

I cried out as his hips snapped faster and faster. His hands roamed my naked body. He pinched and teased and kneaded my curves until I was practically sobbing with desire. My arousal reached a fever pitch as he gripped my ankles and fucked me harder and faster than I'd ever experienced. The bed shook beneath us and our bodies slapped together, the staccato noise of skin against skin competing with our ragged breaths.

Like a maestro plucking his violin, Dimitri reached down and rubbed my clit with his thumb. The quick stimulation sent me careening into another climax, this one so strong I thought for sure I would die.

I hadn't even come down from the heights of ecstasy when I heard the rip of the cuffs separating. Dimitri fell forward against me, our bodies making total contact, and crashed his lips into mine. His passionate kisses made my toes curl. Wrapping my legs around his waist, I pressed my cheek to his and held on tight as he drove into me with such force, his long, hard cock stroking all the right places.

"Benny!" He groaned my name, his voice pained and husky as he climaxed. Shuddering in my arms, he jerked against me, spilling his seed into the latex sheath covering him. I held tight, never wanting to let go of my big, sexy Russian, and wished the moment would never end.

*

Feeling relaxed but still trying to catch his breath, Dimitri pushed up on his palms and gazed down into Benny's gorgeous face. He captured her mouth in a loving kiss. Their tongues danced as he tangled his fingers in her hair. He couldn't get enough of her sweet pout.

Making love to her had been even better than his fantasies. Now he just had to figure out a way to convince her that things between them could work. More than anything, he feared she would pull away from him and think of a million reasons why they couldn't be together. She was a young woman who had lost every member of her family but her brother—and he was quickly disappearing from her life, too. Dimitri noticed the way she erected walls around herself to keep from getting hurt.

But it wouldn't work on him. Even if he had to do it brick by brick, he'd tear down those walls with his bare hands before he let her push him away.

Reluctantly, he separated from her. She whimpered and he worried that he'd hurt her with his rough, fast thrusts there at the end. When she reached for him, he realized it wasn't physical discomfort making her ache but emotional. Instead of taking care of necessities, he rolled onto his back and dragged her into his arms.

He stroked the soft skin of her back and brushed his lips against her forehead. "You were amazing, Benny."

She sighed and snuggled a bit closer. "*You* were amazing. I had no idea it could be like that."

He started to tell her that it would always be like this but decided he was getting ahead of himself. He'd only just managed to coax her into his bed. Ambushing her with the admission that he'd been pining for her so long was bound to make things…uncomfortable.

Rather than let their night take a turn for the awkward, Dimitri gently pressed her onto her back and examined her wrists. They were a little red because she'd twisted and pulled so hard as she came. "Do these hurt?"

"No."

"Your ankles?" He sat up to inspect them next.

"Fine."

Considering her petite frame, he said, "I'll pick up some lined cuffs for the next time."

He realized his mistake the moment he'd uttered aloud his thought. She glanced at him with a mix of wonder and uncertainty on her face. He figured it was a positive sign she hadn't immediately refused to consider a next time. Maybe she wouldn't be so averse to turning their friendship into something deeper and more intimate.

Dimitri kissed her breast and then her hip. "I'll be right back. Don't move."

With a tired but happy sigh, she rolled onto her belly and stretched out her limbs. He stood next to the bed and enjoyed the sight of her naked body in his bed. The reality was a thousand times better than the dirty dreams he'd enjoyed for the last year.

Needing to feel Benny pressed against him, he hurried into the bathroom. When he returned, she hadn't moved. He thought maybe she'd fallen asleep but she lifted her head and dazzled him with a sleepy, satisfied smile. God, what he wouldn't do to see her smiling like that every day!

Tugging on the top drawer of his bedside table, he grabbed another condom and tossed it onto his pillow. Soon enough, he would need it. He slid back into bed with Benny and swept aside the silky strands of her long hair to bare her neck. She mewled like a kitten when his mouth glided over her skin. He dotted kisses along the curve of her neck and across her shoulders.

"Dimitri?"

"Yes, sweetheart?"

"Do you always have sex this way?"

He could hear the anxiety edging into her voice and sought to reassure her. "No, I don't need bondage to find satisfaction. I enjoy it on occasion but I don't need to have my woman tied up every time." He peppered kisses down her spine. "Why? Did you not like it?"

"I liked it," she admitted softly. "I think maybe it would be too overwhelming to do every time."

"Then we'll only do it every other time."

"Dimitri!"

He smiled and nipped at her plump bottom. She gasped and tried to squirm away from him but he clamped an arm across her lower back to keep her right where he wanted her. Already his cock started to grow hard. He'd always been rather quick to recover between bouts of lovemaking but this was something of a record for him. It was all Benny, of course.

Dimitri shifted until he was half-draped across her. His hand moved between her thighs and forced them wide open. She gasped and wiggled her heart-shaped bottom as his fingers explored her soaking depths.

Breathless, she asked, "Again? So soon?"

Sliding between her thighs, he grabbed the condom he'd tossed onto the bed earlier and then grasped her hips. He dragged Benny onto her knees and let his lips dance along her lower back. "I've finally got you in my bed. I intend to enjoy every moment of it."

Once protected, he nudged her thighs apart and drove home. Her tight, wet sheath gripped him like a fist. He inhaled slowly and tried not to lose control too soon but she felt so fucking good. Taking up a measured pace, he watched his cock gliding in and out her. The sight made his gut clench and his heart race.

"You are so fucking sexy." He growled the words.

Benny made a whimpering sound and glanced back at him. Eyes dark with desire and lips parted, she presented the most erotic picture. He curled his hand in her hair and grasped a handful. With a slight tug, he lifted her head a bit higher and dropped his mouth to her neck. He gave her a tiny bite, just enough to make her gasp, before sucking hard on the spot he'd nipped.

Still holding her hair, he straightened up and began to take her harder and faster. He found a rhythm that made Benny moan. She gripped his sheets and rocked back to meet his powerful thrusts. He sensed she was on the verge of losing control and going wild. She'd shown him such passion tonight but he knew there was more hiding deep within her, just waiting to be set loose.

Unable to help himself, he planted his foot against the outside of her knee. He wanted nothing more than to crack her plump bottom with an open palm but he held back. She'd let him restrain her but spanking might be one step too far outside her comfort zone.

Thrusting deeper now, he slammed into her. The shift in angle and penetration made her cry out. The sound of his name falling from her kiss swollen lips drove him crazy.

"Dimitri! Oh! *Oh*!"

Wanting her to come and desperate to feel her milking him, he leaned forward and let his hand follow a path right down to the spot where their bodies were joined. His fingertips found the slick honey dripping from her. She sucked in a sharp breath when he located her clit. The pulsing little nub responded so sweetly to his quick circling movements.

"Dimitri! I—*ah*!"

"Come," he urged, still pounding into her. "Come on my cock, Benny. Come for me."

Like a banshee, she shrieked as her climax took hold. The strong waves of it sent her bucking back against him. The fluttering contractions of her pussy made him groan.

There was no holding back now. Balls deep, he grabbed her hips and held on tight as every muscle in his body stiffened. He shuddered against her and dragged a long, loud breath into his lungs.

When they both calmed, he carefully pulled away from her and darted into the bathroom. He exited to find her waiting near the door. Looking a bit dazed, she smiled at him before brushing by him. While she took care of necessities, he headed into the living area to shut off all the lights and recheck the door.

Back in his bedroom, he heard the rustle of clothing coming from the bathroom. He didn't even knock before opening the door. With one leg in her jeans, she glanced up at him in surprise. "Um...you ever heard of knocking?"

Frowning, he ignored her question. "What are you doing?"

"Getting dressed."

"Yes, I can see that. Why?"

She looked nervous and fidgeted with the denim clamped between her fingers "Because we're done."

His eyebrows arched. "Are we?"

"Um..."

With a shake of his head, he grabbed her clothes from the countertop and pointed at her jeans. "Take those off."

"But—"

"Now, Benny."

She didn't argue with him and handed them over. His gaze dropped to her panties. With a huff of annoyance, she slipped out of those and slapped them in his waiting hand.

Stepping aside, he gestured with a jerk of his head toward his room. "Now get in my bed."

"Dimitri, it's late. I have to work in the morning."

"Exactly," he said and took a step toward her. "The sooner you get in bed, the sooner you'll get some rest."

Their noses were just inches apart as she peered up at him. "You want me to stay here? All night?"

"Yes." He grazed his mouth across hers but didn't let her have the kiss she wanted. Rising up on tiptoes, she gave a little grunt of dissatisfaction as he denied her. He had a good reason, though, and cupped her chin. "Why do you want to leave, Benny?"

Looking so utterly vulnerable, she finally admitted, "I didn't want you to feel obligated to let me stay."

"Obligated?" He realized it was going to take more than one night of lovemaking to convince her that she was all he wanted. Capturing her mouth in a punishing kiss, Dimitri gathered her to his chest and threaded his fingers through her hair. He devoured her mouth, stabbing his tongue between her lips and tasting her until she sagged against him in complete surrender. "Does that feel like obligation?"

"No," she answered in a shaky voice.

"I *want* you to stay the night. I *want* to wake up with you." He ran his fingertip along her jaw. "What do you want, Benny?"

Her answer came swiftly. "To stay with you."

He held out his hand. "Then stay with me."

She grasped his hand and let him lead her back to his bed. Once all the lights were out and he'd set an alarm for her, he climbed in next to Benny and dragged her into his arms. She wiggled until she was comfortable and finally ended up with her head on his chest.

Remembering the way she'd tried to run away like a little rabbit, he crooked a leg over hers. He caressed the soft skin of her back and soothed her to sleep. With the hours she worked and the way he'd worn her out in his bed, Benny drifted off rather quickly.

Relaxed and content, he enjoyed the feel of her in his arms but his mind refused to be quieted. After a childhood spent in one of Russia's harshest orphanages and a military career in which he saw some of the worst humanity had to offer, Dimitri had learned to expect the other boot to drop when things were going well.

He finally had Benny right where he wanted her—but that business with Johnny was troubling. Dimitri was willing to do anything to make Benny happy but letting Johnny drag her down? It wasn't going to happen.

Dimitri pressed a tender kiss to her forehead and silently vowed he would do whatever it took to keep her safe.

CHAPTER FOUR

I came awake to the annoying wail of an alarm clock. Grumbling, I reached out to smack it but instead of hitting the cool wood of my bedside table, I whacked hot skin. A gruff grunt echoed in the darkness. The flash of panic that gripped my belly subsided as the memories of last night surfaced.

Dimitri.

Realizing I'd just hit him, I apologized. "Sorry."

He said something in Russian I didn't understand but he didn't sound upset. I figured out the alarm was behind me and rolled over to hit it. A moment later, Dimitri was pressed up against my back. Those strong arms enveloped me and the rough stubble on his cheek rasped my skin. A shiver of excitement rocked me.

I still couldn't quite believe last night had happened. After crushing on Dimitri for so long, it seemed like something out of a dream. But—*oh*—those big hands gliding over my naked skin definitely weren't from a dream. They were very real and tempting me never to leave his bed.

"Dimitri," I said softly, "I have to get up."

"It's early." He palmed my breast and brushed his thumb over my nipple. His lips moved to my neck and I couldn't squash the blissful sigh that escaped me. "Stay a little longer."

"I have to get the ovens going and check the proofing boxes." Even as I came up with excuses, I knew he was going to win.

"Let Marco handle it."

"This is one of his mornings for dialysis. It's all up to me. My customers aren't going to wait for breakfast."

Dimitri shocked me by flipping me onto my back and claiming my mouth in a sensual kiss. I could hear the smile in his voice as he said, "Then we'd be better be quick about it."

I lost the urge to protest the moment his searching mouth find mine in the darkness. Dimitri's kisses were like a drug and I craved more and more of them. His caresses set my skin on fire. Arching into him, I relished the sensation of his hard chest against my bare breasts. His hand rode the gentle curve of my belly down toward my sex. My thighs parted so easily and I gasped when those nimble fingers located my clit.

One intimate touch ignited my lust. Wanting to feel him, I reached down and grasped the hard, throbbing dick jutting against my hip. His low groan of need told me all I needed to know. I stroked his big cock, swirling my hand over his shaft before daring to slide my hand even lower to cup his taut sac.

Groaning my name, Dimitri crashed his lips to mine and kissed me with such fervor. Tongues dueling, we stroked one another until we were both panting and moaning and pumping our hips. He shoved his cock against my hand and I rocked up to meet the fingers now penetrating me. They plunged in and out of my slick heat until I hovered on the edge of coming.

A moment later, Dimitri tore his mouth away from mine and moved between my thighs. With a rough thrust, he drove into my wet, aching pussy. I cried out at the sudden invasion. After such a dry spell, my poor body wasn't used to so much sex.

Dimitri murmured gently in his mother tongue and kissed me with such tenderness. His thrusts eased up and he shifted his weight to one side. As his cock glided in and out of me, his fingertips circled my clit. "Does this feel good?"

"Yes!" My foot moved up and down his leg, my toes curling into his hard flesh as I felt that quivering tightness low in my belly. "Dimitri, please..."

"Tell me." His fingers slowed their sinful ministrations and I whimpered. "Tell me what you want, Benny."

"I want to come." I clawed at his shoulders. "Make me come, Dimitri."

He growled in Russian, the rough, rumbling sound rolling over me and making my tummy clench at its sexiness. He strummed my pulsing clit even faster and I came apart beneath him. The pleasure burst deep inside me and blazed through my belly and up into my chest. Head tipped back, I enjoyed the bright, searing waves of it.

Just before he came, Dimitri murmured something that sounded suspiciously like *my little rabbit*. I clung to him as he shoved deep and jerked in my arms.

And then it hit me.

My eyes widened with shock as I felt the spreading warmth of Dimitri's semen within me. A moment too late, he realized what I already had. In the haze of our early morning tryst, he'd forgotten to put on a condom and I hadn't even thought to remind him.

Dimitri cursed in Russian and pulled away from me, leaving a wet trail down my thigh. "God, Benny, I'm sorry. I didn't think—"

"Stop." I reached for him in the darkness and finally found his broad shoulders. "It's not your fault. We both got caught up in the moment."

His forehead touched mine. I could feel the guilt radiating from him. "I'm clean, Benny, but if you want, I'll see my doctor as soon as he opens." He hesitated before admitting, "I've never had sex without a condom."

His admission didn't surprise me that much. Dimitri had always struck me as the kind of man who never took chances—until me, it seemed.

"You're my first, too." I licked my lips and considered what we both weren't saying. Our sexual experiences had been careful up until this point and our risks of catching something were so very low. I knew Dimitri would run out to see his doctor first thing and we would have those results in a couple of days.

But there was another kind of result that would take weeks to become available.

"Are you…?"

He didn't have to finish the thought. I understood what he was trying to ask. "No, I'm not on birth control."

He didn't miss a beat. "Okay."

His calm reply soothed my anxious nerves. At least he wasn't freaking out over it. I was glad we could both be adults about our mistake.

As Dimitri slid down next to me and kissed me so sweetly, I couldn't help but wonder if calling it a mistake was the wrong word for it. It seemed such a harsh thing to call what had just happened between us. A moment of passion like the one we'd just shared? No, that definitely wasn't a mistake.

Reluctantly, I untangled myself from his brawny arms. "I have to shower."

"I'm going to start some coffee." He ran his hand along my thigh. "If I follow you into the shower, the bakery won't open until noon."

Laughing, I slid away from him and off the bed. "Would you mind running down to my office and grabbing the second set of clothes I keep in the bottom desk drawer?"

Dimitri switched on the lamp, illuminating his room and the rumpled sheets where we'd spent the night together. "I don't mind. Where are your keys?"

"With my purse in your living room," I said and quickly darted to the bathroom. He caught up with me before I could disappear and gave my butt a playful smack. "Dimitri!"

"I'm sorry," he said with a laugh. "I couldn't help myself."

Seeing him smile, with his blond hair tousled and the shadow of a beard on his face, did funny things to my belly. He pecked my cheek before heading to his closet. I slipped into the bathroom and started the shower. A knock got my attention. "Yes?"

"There are extra toiletries under the sink."

"Thank you." I knelt down and found what I needed in the cabinet. Apparently Dimitri liked to shop at the big warehouse club store a few blocks over. He seemed to be so careful with his money. I admired him for watching his pennies because I knew where he'd come from and how hard he'd worked to amass his wealth.

Sure, he'd caught a lucky break with those time share deals a few years back but he wasn't cocky about it. I'd been doing some late night cleaning downstairs in the bakery when he'd come home stumbling drunk after celebrating the deal he'd made. Helping him up to the apartment had nearly broken my back but somehow we'd managed it.

It was the first and only time I'd ever seen him like that but I understood why he'd let loose. He'd clawed his way off the streets to become a success—and it was something I deeply respected about him.

Scrubbing away in the shower, I couldn't help but feel a bit uncomfortable about our vastly different financial situations. Dimitri lived the easy life of a bachelor of means while I had days where I sat in my office praying that we'd have enough outstanding customer invoices paid to cover payroll.

Deep down inside, I feared what Dimitri thought of me. Was he like Johnny? Did he think I'd run a thriving business into the ground with mismanagement? It wasn't true, of course. By the time my grandmother had let me see the books and come clean about the creative accounting she'd been using to get by, I'd had very few options left to save the business and the people depending on me for jobs. I'd done the very best I could—but it wasn't enough.

My stomach twisted with guilt and embarrassment as I considered the very real possibility that I would fail and lose the business that had been in my family for nearly forty years. I could only imagine the kind of gossip that would blaze through this neighborhood like wildfire. I'd probably have to relocate to another city just to escape the humiliation of it all.

Not wanting to ruin what had started as such a good morning, I pushed away those ugly thoughts and dried off. I squeezed as much water out of my hair as possible and tugged Dimitri's comb through the snarls and tangles.

I couldn't find a blow dryer so I left my hair down to air dry.

Out in the bedroom, I found the jeans, shirt and clean socks from my office stacked on the foot of his bed. It only took one kitchen accident as a teenager working in the bakery to teach me a valuable lesson about keeping extra clothes at hand. If I'd known I was going to use them the morning after a torrid night with Dimitri, I might have slipped a pair of undies and a bra in there.

"I've tossed your clothes in the washer. They'll be dry before you open." With my bra dangling from his fingers, he leaned against the door frame and watched me shimmy into my jeans. His mouth curved in a wolfish grin "Although I have to admit I rather like the commando look on you."

I shot him a quick smile. "You would. May I have my bra?"

Instead of handing it over, he came into the room and slid an arm around my waist. He made sure to brush his cock against my bottom. Not even the denim of my jeans or his cotton pajama pants could stop the snap of heat between our touching bodies. His big hand cupped my breast. "Hold out your arms."

I glanced back at him. "You realize I've been wearing a bra for, like, fifteen years, right? I know how to put it on."

He nuzzled my neck and gave my nipple a little pinch that made me rise up on my toes and gasp. "Humor me."

How could I say no to that? Lifting my arms, I let Dimitri help me into my bra. His skilled hands made quick work of it but he let them linger on my bare skin. Kissing my cheek, he caressed the spot just above my navel. "I'm going to make breakfast. I'll bring something down for you."

I turned in his arms and gazed up at him. "You don't

have to do that. Go back to bed, Dimitri."

"Once I'm awake, I'm awake." His fingertip traced my lower lip. "I want to spend time with you before I head into the gym for my workout." Dimitri's hands glided down my sides before he let me loose. "It's Friday."

I smiled and patted his chest. Like many of our customers, he'd memorized the schedule we used for specialty breads and pastries. "I'll make sure to put aside half a dozen of the pineapple turnovers you love so much."

"Better make it a full dozen. Ivan and Kostya are hooked on them now." He gave my backside a squeeze. "I'm getting in the shower. If I don't, you'll never get downstairs."

Our lips met in a quick kiss. I watched him duck into the bathroom and close the door. My heartbeat finally started to slow and I slipped into the red shirt with the bakery's logo on the back. After finding my shoes in the living room, I quickly braided my still damp hair, grabbed my purse and headed downstairs.

Even though I was running a little behind my usual schedule, I was still the first one into the kitchen. Most of our morning crew started rolling in around five. I enjoyed the quiet stillness of the place and took my time turning on the lights and prepping the ovens.

After peeking into the proofing boxes and ensuring everything was as it should be, I started a big pot of coffee in the employee's locker and break room. I made a quick stop in my office to lock away my purse. The sight of the bank deposit bag made my stomach roll with unease. That was a conversation I wasn't looking forward to having with Johnny but it had to be done.

Back in the kitchen, I slipped into an apron and checked the white board for the day's baking list. Marco had long been in charge of making adjustments to it and I trusted his judgment. Apprised of the day's schedule, I started arranging work stations for Marco, Adam and Lupe, our three main bakers. I'd worked with them long enough to know exactly how they liked things arranged.

While I waited for the ovens to preheat, I punched the power button on the seemingly antique stereo system. The morning crew preferred a quiet, calm start to their mornings. The gentle plucking of a guitar and the unmistakable huskiness of Chavela Vargas echoed off the white walls. The familiar music brought back such good memories.

I had a smile on my face as I started mixing together the streusel-like topping for the *pan dulce*. Dyed vibrant colors like pink and yellow, the sweet, slightly crunchy mixture was pressed onto the dense, yeasty buns and scored to look like a shell. As a child, the delicious bread had been my favorite breakfast. Thankfully, I'd had the sense to lay off the carby goodness once I became a teenager!

As I worked, I heard the side door open and close. Certain it was Adam coming at his usual time, I called out to greet him—but it wasn't Adam who answered me back.

"Good morning, Miss Burkhart."

Startled by the unexpected voice, I spun around so quickly I knocked the metal bowl onto the floor. Sugar and flour spattered the floor and my shoes. The man standing across from me looked like trouble. He wore an expensive suit and nice shoes but I knew the type.

"Who the hell are you? What are you doing in my bakery?"

He took a step toward me. "I think it's time we had a little chat..."

* * *

Dimitri heard the music downstairs as he got out of the shower. His first few weeks in the apartment, it had driven him crazy to hear the sounds from kitchen below. Soon, he'd gotten used to it and had learned to expect it. The pangs of loneliness he sometimes felt in his new country had been eased by the noise and camaraderie drifting up from down there.

This morning, though, he heard a different sound, one that made his heart stutter. He was sliding into his jeans when the unmistakable clang of a bowl hitting the tile floor met his ears. He went still and listened. Accidents happened all the time in the kitchen but he worried that Benny might have been hurt.

"Who the hell are you? What are you doing here?"

Despite being muffled by the ceiling and floor between them, Benny's frightened voice came through loud and clear to Dimitri. Not bothering with a shirt or shoes, he zipped and buttoned his jeans and left his apartment in a flash. The metal stairs were hard beneath his bare feet but he didn't care. He'd run across broken glass to reach her.

The moment he launched himself through the side door, Dimitri spotted the dark-haired man. He didn't waste time trying to figure out the situation. With the speed and silence of his many years in elite ops, he came up behind the man. Clearing his throat, he said, "Benny, I heard a noise."

Their early morning visitor visibly stiffened and pivoted to face Dimitri. Shorter by a few inches, the man sized up Dimitri and smartly took a few steps to the side. Benny's frightened expression relaxed at the sight of him.

Wanting to ease her worries, he joined her by the big stainless steel table. The sandy sugar mixture on the floor squished between his toes. He held her gaze just long enough to telegraph a silent message. *You're safe with me.*

Dimitri turned his attention back to the man and gave him a once-over. He spotted the bulge of a weapon outlined on his right hip. Without a gun of his own, he was at a disadvantage. He slid his hand down to Benny's waist and let his fingers sit there, ready to push her behind him at the first sign of trouble.

"I think we may have gotten off on the wrong foot, Benita." The man smiled but Dimitri wasn't fooled. His weasel-like face and shifty demeanor put Dimitri's radar on high alert. "My name is Carl and I work for UpStreet Properties. I truly didn't mean to frighten you this morning. We were simply wondering why we hadn't heard back from you about our offer for the building."

"So pick up the phone and call me," Benny snapped back, her voice laced with irritation.

Dimitri's lips twitched with amusement as shock registered on the man's face. Clearly he'd come here expecting to strong arm her but this little spitfire wasn't about to be pushed around by anyone.

Changing tactics, Carl apologized with a sickly sweet smile. "You're right, Benita. It's just that the offer is time sensitive. We'd hoped to have an answer in the next few days."

"Why?" She squared her shoulders and lifted her chin. "Because you need this lot in your back pocket so you can secure approval from the city and a financing deal from that bank for the retail plaza you plan to put here?"

Carl's lips settled into a tight line. "That isn't—"

Benny lifted her hand. "You think you're the only one with friends in city offices? My customers talk to me and

I listen." With a shake of her head, she said, "Look, I told you people last week that I wasn't interested in selling."

"And your brother? Is he interested in selling his share of the business?"

Dimitri's eyes narrowed at the man's subtle threat. He didn't doubt for a minute that this guy would stoop so low as to turn a brother against his sister for the promise of a little money.

"Carl, you *really* don't want to start down this road with me." Benny's anger darkened her voice.

Not so easily swayed, Carl reached into his jacket. Dimitri tensed but the man pulled out a business card. He placed it on the stainless steel surface of the work table. "Call me when you change your mind. The generous offer Mr. Krause made expires on Monday."

Putting a hand on Benny's shoulder, Dimitri silently instructed her to stay put. He shadowed Carl to the door and deliberately knocked into him as he started down the steps. The man stumbled forward and only narrowly escaped a meeting with the pavement.

Spinning around, Carl glared but Dimitri put a finger to his own lips, warning the man to keep his mouth shut. Like Nikolai, Dimitri had mastered the art of striking fear into a person with one cold look. Carl wasn't as stupid as he looked and kept his trap shut.

"Don't show your face around here again." Dimitri raised a warning finger and pointed it at him. "If your boss has business with Benny, you tell him to pick up the phone to schedule an appointment with her. Understood?"

Carl gave a stiff nod and stormed to the black car waiting in the alley. Dimitri made sure to memorize the license plate. He had a feeling this wouldn't be the last he'd see of Carl.

Shutting the side door behind him, Dimitri returned to the kitchen. Benny had swept up the mess and stood at the sink washing her hands. Their gazes clashed across the kitchen. He read the anxiety all over her face. Hating to see her so upset, he opened his arms. "Come here."

She rushed into his arms and pressed her cheek to his chest. He kissed the top of her head and rubbed her back. "God, he scared me!"

"He won't be coming back." Dimitri intended to make that promise a reality. He'd see how Carl liked having someone show up unexpected and unannounced on his turf.

"Do you think they'll really try to turn Johnny against me?"

She already knew the answer but she wanted to hear it from him. Though it killed him to confirm her fears, he answered honestly. "Yes—and I think Johnny will take their offer."

"Oh God." Benny tried to pull away from him but he held tight. "Dimitri, what the hell am I going to do?"

He placed his hand along her cheek. The glimmer of tears in her pretty eyes made his gut twist. He made a split-second decision. "I'm going to make Johnny an offer on his half of the business."

She reeled back in surprise. "What? No! Dimitri, you can't."

He snorted softly. "I can do whatever I want, Benny. It's my money."

"But, Dimitri, if the business fails, you'll lose your money. Let's not kid ourselves, okay? I'm one bad month away from having to close the doors." She put her hands on his chest and shoved just hard enough to free herself from his embrace. "No."

He snatched her wrist and dragged her back. "You're

not going to shut me out, Benny."

"Dimitri, please..."

He tried to understand her reticence but couldn't. Trailing his fingers down her cheek, he asked, "What is so wrong with me helping you?"

Her eyes closed for the briefest of moments. When they opened, they were filled with such fear. "Because it changes things, Dimitri."

"Sometimes change is good." He brushed his mouth against hers. "Last night was very, very good, yes?"

"Yes." She ran her hands up his arms. "Last night was amazing, but if we put money between us, it's going to get complicated very fast—and then what?"

Finally, he understood. "Benny, it wouldn't be complicated. We could make it work."

"You say that now..."

Dimitri tipped her chin and teased his lips across hers. He eased into the kiss and waited for her to press up against him, deepening the gentle mating of their mouths. Tongues touching now, they clutched at one another. When Dimitri pulled back, he peered down at her for a moment before speaking. "I want to be your partner, Benny."

She swallowed. "In business?"

He realized this was one of those moments where their relationship could surge forward and grow or retreat and fester. "No, not just in business, Benny. I want you as—"

"Benny, you already in the kitchen?" Adam announced his presence mere seconds before stepping into the view. "There was a nasty wreck on the loop and..."

The older man's eyes widened as he caught sight of them embracing. Dimitri could only imagine what Adam was thinking. Naked from the waist up and with his hair still wet, Dimitri looked anything but innocent right now.

But Dimitri wasn't about to let go of Benny. He refused to let anyone make him feel shame for comforting the woman he cared for so deeply. To his surprise, Benny didn't try to jump away in embarrassment. She stepped into his embrace.

Finally, Adam laughed. "Hey, don't let me interrupt you two kids." He winked at Dimitri as he headed for the employee's locker room. "I was young once. I know how this game is played."

Benny rolled her eyes. "Adam!"

Still chuckling, Adam paused in the doorway and glanced back at them. "And about damn time too!"

"God," she said with a groan. "The whole bakery will be talking about us before we even have our first customer."

Chest constricting, he studied her face. "Does that bother you?"

She put her hand over his heart. "Not for the reason you're probably thinking, Dimitri. I spend so much time here with my bakery family that nothing is ever private." She bit her lower lip. "I wanted this to be something special, something just for me."

Feeling a bit playful, he lowered his head until his breath tickled her ear. "I've got something just for you and I promise it's very, very special."

"Dimitri!" She hissed with mock outrage but she couldn't stop smiling. "Will you get out of here?" Blushing, she glanced at the doorway leading to the locker room. "Adam will hear you and then I'll really get it from Lupe and Celia!"

He kissed her cheek and reluctantly backed away from her. "I'm going to get that breakfast I promised you."

She nodded and got back to work. They still had so

much to discuss but it could wait. After he got her breakfast squared away, he was going to dig up some information on UpStreet Properties. If they chose to play dirty with Benny, he was ready to drag them right into the mud. The kind of information he wanted wouldn't be easy to find but he knew just where to go—Yuri.

CHAPTER FIVE

"**B**enny, Lena is here."

I finished swirling bright white frosting on a chocolate cupcake and glanced up at Celia. "Tell her I'll be right there."

She nodded and left but not before shooting a silly smile my way. I fought the urge to roll my eyes. All morning, I'd been getting strange looks. Just as I'd predicted, Adam had shared his gossipy discovery with Lupe who then told Celia who told *everyone.*

It annoyed the crap out of me that I couldn't even have one day to enjoy my secret all by myself. I also couldn't shake the worry that things between us wouldn't work out and then what? I'd have the entire bakery in my business when Dimitri dumped me? The very thought made my stomach churn.

I finished frosting the tray of cupcakes and slid them down the line to be spattered with sprinkles. After tossing my gloves, I untied my apron and hung it on an empty peg. I caught Marco's attention with a little wave and let him know I was leaving the kitchen for a short while.

Out in the bakery, I spotted Lena at one of the tables closest to the door. She looked out of place in the laid-back atmosphere of the small café. With that bold, deep blue dress and nude peep-toe pumps, Lena embodied the image of a career woman on her way to a power lunch. She'd pulled her sleek black hair up and wore simple earrings. I sort of envied her polished look and upwardly mobile career path.

I marveled at the way my friend had changed since we'd known each other in college a few years back. Lena's drive to be successful, to make something of herself and rise above her impoverished beginnings in one of Houston's harshest neighborhoods hadn't lessened any. She'd blossomed with confidence and had proven herself more than capable at her job.

That blog of hers that chronicled the highs and lows of the Houston social scene had grown from a silly little pastime our freshman year to an internet hotspot that allowed her to earn advertising revenue and build her own personal brand. A social media maven, she'd recently branched into charging for tweets broadcast to her thousands of followers. She was careful to highlight only places she actually endorsed or enjoyed to maintain the authenticity of her nightlife stamp of approval.

But with that pretty face and knockout figure, Lena had to work twice as hard to get people to take her seriously. Graduating with honors and a degree in only three short years had been a good start. Snagging a job at the top Houston PR firm had been even better.

"Hey!" Smiling, I slid into the seat across from her. "How are you today?"

"Great." Lena cocked her head and studied me. "Something's different about you. Did you cut your hair?"

I shook my head and self-consciously touched the tip

of the braid dangling over my shoulder. "No."

"Hmm," Lena murmured and continued to stare at me. "You just...you look *different*."

I swallowed nervously and shrugged. "Okay."

She narrowed her dark eyes. "You know I'm not going to let this go, right?"

With a little sigh, I glanced around to make sure no one would overhear us. Leaning forward, I confessed, "I sort of spent the night with Dimitri."

"What?" Her hands flew to the table and she moved closer. With a scandalized expression, she asked, "Why am I just hearing about this now? You should have texted me this morning!"

"And said what?"

"Oh, I don't know. Maybe you could have spilled all the incredibly dirty details of your sexy night with the blond Adonis?" A bit conspiratorial, she asked in a hushed whisper, "How was it? Like so hot you almost set the bed on fire? How big is his you-know-what?" She glanced down at her lap. "Huge, right?"

"Oh God." I couldn't stop laughing as I buried my red face in my hands. "I'm really not going into specifics here."

"Then come over tonight," she said. "We'll get Vivi to cook for us and have Erin bring over a few bottles of obscenely expensive wine from Ivan's cellar. You can regale us with all the delicious little details of how it went down."

A few months ago, before crossing paths with Lena again, I would have said no. to a girls' night out. Dimitri's voice rattled around in my head. What had he said? That I deserved to have a life?

"Okay. I'll come over."

"Eight o'clock?"

"Sure but I can't stay too late. We have the Tasting Houston thing tomorrow."

"Girl, don't I know it!" With a dramatic shake of her head, she reached into her oversized leather satchel that she used for business and produced glossy red folders for me. "I've got everything ready for your station. I stopped by the print shop on my way over here. They'll make their delivery to you in a couple of hours. Just bring all the boxes down to the fairgrounds. I'll sort them out when we set up your spot."

Nodding, I opened one of the folders and examined the materials. "This is really nice."

We chatted about her plans for rebranding the bakery. She'd studied all the family-owned bakeries in Houston and discovered our little *panaderia* was something of a gem. Not that anyone knew it because we hadn't been out there, hustling to grow the brand and broadening our customer base. She wanted to appeal to foodies who sought out the authentic Mexican bakery experience and to Latinos who wanted a taste of home.

"So I think the goal is to make a splash tomorrow at Tasting Houston. We do the newspaper interview and you talk up your family history. Make sure to lay it on thick when it comes to your grandparents coming here build a new, better life. We want to play up the opportunities this place has given so many employees. We want to talk about how it enriched the neighborhood."

"I hope you're going to give me some note cards or something because I'm pretty sure I'm going to screw this up."

Lena laughed. "You won't. And, yes, I'm going to give you some talking points." She gestured to the window. "We want to make sure we talk about how this place is standing strong and fighting to preserve the history of

Houston. People like those kinds of underdog stories."

"I'm not sure if I'll be one of the successful ones."

Her expression morphed to one of concern. "Why? What happened?"

"UpStreet Properties sent this guy to talk to me this morning. He didn't threaten me outright but he insinuated that this wasn't going to end well if I didn't accept their offer. He came in through the side door, from the alley, and scared me to death. I was the only one in the place but Dimitri was upstairs thankfully."

"Ooh," Lena said, her eyes wide. "Did Dimitri get physical? Because I've seen how protective Ivan is of Erin. He wouldn't think twice about socking someone in the face for threatening her."

"No, but Dimitri wasn't very happy."

"Boy, those UpStreet guys aren't very smart. There's a giant Russian ex-soldier living upstairs and they think it's a good idea to send around one of their goons to strong-arm you?"

"They may not be very smart but they're ruthless. I'm one of the few businesses standing in their way. Carl, the goon," I clarified, "said that the *generous* offer they made would expire on Monday."

"Dickheads," she muttered.

I smiled sadly in agreement. "He basically threatened to go behind my back and buy Johnny's share of the business to force my hand."

"Assholes!" She nervously teethed her lower lip. "Do you think Johnny would sell out to them?"

"Lately, all he talks about is making money." I ran my finger over the edge of the table. "He wants that flashy lifestyle of the drug runners in his gang, you know? Cars, nice clothes, jewelry, hot girls—but that stuff costs money. God knows he's not about to lift a finger to find a real job."

"After the crap I've watched you and Erin go through with siblings, I am so glad I'm an only child." She reached out and touched my hand. "What are you going to do? Have you talked to Johnny?"

I shook my head. "I tried calling him this morning but he didn't answer. He's been hanging out with this girl and I'm pretty sure he spent the night with her."

"Uh-oh." With a wicked smile, she asked, "Does she have Sharpie eyebrows and wear lip liner this thick?"

I laughed as she drew a wide line around her mouth in the way so many of those girls preferred. "No on the lip liner but yes on the eyebrows."

"I knew it!" She giggled gleefully. "Can you believe there was a time when I thought those tough *cholas* were so cool? I wanted to be one of them."

"When did you wise up?"

Her smile vanished. "My friend, Mireya, thought that the only way she could get respect was to join one of the gangs in our old neighborhood. They beat the shit out of her as part of the jump-in ceremony but that wasn't enough. Later, they made her *pull the train*. We were in eighth grade, Benny."

Lena's anguished expression tore at me and I squeezed her hand. Pulling the train was street slang for having sex with multiple guys in a gang. I'd heard some of the girls had to throw dice for their number. It was horrific and awful and so degrading.

Inhaling a long breath, she said, "After that, I wised up and realized the only way I was getting out of there was to work hard and go to college. I was going to stand on my own two feet and make my own way."

"And you have," I said, releasing her hand. "You're amazing, Lena. Look at you! Twenty-four years old and you've got a great job. You have friends who love you. You're going places."

"Alone," she replied softly. "I guess the trade-off to being strong and independent is that it scares off a lot of men."

"The wrong men," I countered. "The right guy? He's going to see how totally wonderful you are and snatch you right up."

"Like Dimitri finally snatched you?"

I sighed as the troubling uncertainties returned. "I don't know. I'm not sure what he wants with me. Like was last night the start of a real relationship or is this just a sex thing?"

"So ask him. He's a straight shooter. He'll tell you one way or the other and then you'll know."

I hesitated before telling her about the offer he'd made. "He wants to buy Johnny's share of the business."

"Whoa!" She sat fully back in her chair. "What did you say?"

"I asked him not to do it. I don't want money between us. That's weird, right? I mean, nothing good can come from that."

Lena didn't answer immediately. Finally, she said, "Benny, it depends on the couple. Look at Ivan and Erin. She lives with him now. He supports her while she's in school but he makes it perfectly clear that she's not in any way indebted to him. He helps her out because he loves her and he wants her to follow her dreams. From the outside, it looks unbalanced but on the inside?" She shook her head. "They're on equal footing. They're partners."

"Dimitri said he wanted to be my partner before we got interrupted by Adam."

"Okay, I have to hear this. Interrupted where? How?"

I rolled my eyes. "It's not what you're thinking. We were hugging in the kitchen." I reluctantly added, "He wasn't wearing a shirt so it looked sort of—"

"Hot?" she interrupted with a smile. "Sexy? Delicious?"

I laughed. "You're not going to let this go, are you?"

"Oh, honey, you have no idea. I need something to distract me from the crap storm in my own life. This is just too yummy to pass up!"

Concerned, I asked, "What's wrong? Can I help?"

Lena hesitated before exhaling roughly, the whoosh of pent-up air carrying her frustrations. "So you know how I've been at the firm for a while now, right? I mean, I was an intern during my senior year of college and then they hired me on full-time before I'd even graduated. I took 716 from launch to Houston's best nightspot by working my ass off and giving everything I had to make it a success, but did my jerk-face manager ever give me any recognition?"

"No?" It wasn't a hard guess to make.

"Hell no!" She tapped her richly manicured nails on the tabletop. "I'm constantly out there working my contacts, surveying the readers of my blog and listening to the feedback I get on social media. I *listen* to what the people who go to clubs say. I try to innovate and come up with new ideas using that research. I knew that once Yuri Novakovsky opened his new place that 716 was really going to have to up its game to keep traffic flowing through the front door. Guess what the jackass Harry did?"

I winced. "Stole your ideas?"

"Yep." Anger laced her voice. "And he didn't just steal them and present them as his own. No, no, no. He *gave* them to the team at that Russian's new club so he could get a job. So now my club is getting spanked and I'm getting threatened with losing my job if I don't turn things around like this fast." She snapped her fingers. "And on a shoestring budget, of course. How they expect me to compete with that Russian and his endless pockets I will never understand!"

I felt awful for her. It seemed like an untenable situation. "What are you going to do?"

"I don't know." She sounded so conflicted. "On one hand, I really enjoy the firm. I feel like I've learned so much there and I had a great mentor until she moved to Atlanta. Lately, I feel like I'm floundering though. I'm not growing. I feel...stagnant."

"So make a change," I counseled. "Why not strike out on your own? Or maybe do something on a smaller scale. You have a huge advantage with your social media presence and your contacts and your network."

"It's something I've been thinking about," she admitted. "There are a handful of us at the firm and a rival place that are on the same wavelength. We're young. We're tech savvy. We're comfortable taking some risks. The idea of forming our own group has been floated but it's a big, complicated step, you know?"

"Oh, I know."

With a snort of derision, she said, "Can you believe that Russian jerk tried to headhunt me after he fucked me over like that?"

"Who? Yuri?"

Lena nodded. "Hell yeah. He had one of his drivers waiting for me when I came out of work on Monday. I'd never ridden in a car like that so I thought screw it. I met him at his skyscraper downtown. He offered me a nice salary and benefits package but the contract had some clauses in it that didn't sit well with me. I'm not that naïve!"

"I can't believe he would offer you a job after stealing your ideas."

"Right?" Her lips settled into a tight line. "Fool me once, you know?"

"So you told him no?"

"Hell yes! And then you know what he did? He came onto me and asked me out to his yacht for the weekend. Who does that? I mean, did he want to hire me because he respects my work or because he thinks I have a hot ass? How you can work for someone like that?" She shook her head. "It felt so grimy. I told him off and got out of there. I'm not stupid enough to be the next PR girl who ends up flat on her ass without a job after Yuri has had me flat on my back."

"Wow! Lena, this is like the plot to a soap opera!"

"Between you, me, Erin and Vivi, we could write one hell of a screenplay!" She checked her watch and frowned. "I have a meeting in twenty minutes. I should hit the road." She tapped the folders she'd brought me. "Remember about the delivery coming later, okay? There's a map of the fairgrounds in here. It should be easy to find your spot in the morning."

"I'll be there, bright-eyed and bushy tailed."

Lena slid her purse onto one shoulder and grasped the handle of her satchel. She eyed me critically. "Wear something a bit flirty, okay? No jeans." With a teasing smirk, she suggested, "Let Dimitri pick something out for you. I'm sure he knows what looks smoking hot on you."

I groaned and denied my desire to flip her off for teasing me so badly. Laughing, I said, "Get out!"

She snickered and headed for the door. "Eight o'clock, remember? We'll be waiting for you!"

I waved and watched her disappear around the corner

of the building. I didn't immediately get up and return to the kitchen. No, I sat there and watched the lunch time hustle and bustle.

The bakery and the small café in the front room were a meeting point for so many people in the neighborhood. The bus stop a block down drew in workers who relied on public transportation. They stopped in for an affordable hot breakfast or a quick lunch. Many of them worked long hours on their feet and seemed to enjoy a quiet rest while reading the paper and enjoying their meal.

Everything Lena said about preserving history and the integrity of the neighborhood really hit home with me. My heart ached at the idea of losing all this. I just didn't know if the business could be saved. This location, this neighborhood, was in its death throes. Even if I managed to hold off Jonah Krause for a few months, he'd find a way to push me out of the building. He'd used his contacts at city hall to bury other businesses. I would be one in a long line to fall to that ruthless, money-grubbing man.

Dimitri's offer to buy Johnny's share had been a nice gesture but it wouldn't stop the inevitable. Shooting down his offer probably wasn't the kindest thing but the idea of putting money between us made me nervous.

His mention of us being partners still intrigued me. I just hoped he didn't mean only in the business sense.

* * *

There weren't many waiting rooms Dimitri enjoyed but the one outside Yuri's downtown Houston office was one of them. His old friend had recently moved his headquarters to Texas and now owned the city's most beautiful skyscraper. His international holdings only occupied the top ten floors. The rest he rented out as office space to law firms, accounting firms and the like.

As he waited for his old friend, Dimitri chatted briefly with Jake, one of the bodyguards he'd trained for Yuri. The former Marine had been a bouncer on his roster when he'd plucked him out of that line of work and groomed him to protect Yuri. Jake seemed to like the work, especially the traveling, and the money was damn good.

Alone with his thoughts after Jake stepped away, Dimitri glanced around the waiting room. Like everything Yuri touched, he'd made sure to have the place redone with such opulence. Everything was sleek and modern with walls of glass and water features. Most of the art hanging on the grey walls confused Dimitri but the two pieces he recognized as Vivian's work drew his gaze. He stood in front of them as he waited for Yuri, just looking at the bold strokes of color and the faint human shapes in them.

"Thought provoking, yes?" Yuri strode over to join him. He tilted his head and stared at the canvases. "I'm still not sure what they are but I can't stop looking at them. Has she asked you to sit for that new project of hers?"

Dimitri nodded. "I went to her studio three weeks ago. Are you going to let her take a look at your tattoos?"

"Sure." He shrugged. "It's a fascinating concept. I'm interested to see the final collection. Everything she creates is so hauntingly beautiful."

"She's talented." Slipping into his mother tongue felt so easy and nice. It lent an air of privacy to their conversation.

Yuri hummed with agreement. "And completely oblivious to how much Nikolai cares for her."

Dimitri shot him a warning look. "You and I both know there's a reason he wants it that way."

Yuri shrugged. "It was a long time ago, Dimitri. I think it's time he forgave himself for that little accident."

"I don't think it's his forgiveness that's the issue." Dimitri grew uncomfortable talking about their friend's private business and changed the subject. "Do you have time to speak with me?"

Yuri whacked his back and grinned. "Always. Come."

He followed Yuri into his spacious office. One of Yuri's many assistants tailed them into the room. Ever solicitous, she offered him a drink that he turned down. Yuri asked for water and she hurried to bring it to him, tottering on her heels and barely able to move in the skintight pencil skirt.

There was a time Yuri would have watched her every move, his hungry gaze glued to her wiggling backside or the soft jiggle of her breasts. Today, he seemed to be completely unaware of her. Dimitri studied his friend for a long moment after the assistant exited and shut the door behind him.

"What?" Yuri sipped his water.

Dimitri leaned back in his seat and got comfortable. "You didn't flirt with her."

He looked unhappy. "I don't flirt with every woman who works for me, Dimitri."

"No? Because you have a certain reputation—"

Yuri made an irritated growling sound. "People change."

"Some do, but you?"

Yuri glared at him. "Yes. I can change."

Dimitri considered how defensive his friend was acting. "Are you changing to better yourself or to make someone else happy?" He laughed as it all started to make sense. "Who is she?"

Yuri got a far off look in his eye. "Someone who despises me."

"I find that hard to believe."

Yuri gave a little self-deprecating laugh. "Well believe it, Dimitri, because it's happened."

"Does she work for you?"

He shook his head. "I tried to headhunt her but she shot me down. She's brilliant and everyone talks about her keen eye for PR. Then she walked through that door," he gestured to entrance, "and I couldn't think. I couldn't breathe. I just gawked at her like some stupid little boy..." His voice trailed off and he frowned. "Apparently my reputation makes me the kind of man she won't work for or date."

Dimitri sensed Yuri had been hurt by the rejection. He wasn't a man used to hearing no from anyone. "I'm sorry, Yuri."

He waved his hand. "And the worst part of the whole sad affair? She's Erin and Vivi's best friend so I have to see her anytime I'm around Ivan or Nikolai."

Dimitri blinked as the pieces fell into place. "Wait. Lena? Lena Cruz?"

Yuri nodded. "You know her?"

"Sure, she's close with Benny. They're working together on a project at the bakery."

Yuri got a mischievous glint in his pale eyes. "Ah, yes. How is your sweet little landlady?"

Dimitri shot him a warning look. "She's fine."

"Still chasing after her like a puppy dog?"

Dimitri shifted uncomfortably. "Not exactly."

Yuri laughed. "Oh, I see. Did we finally work up the courage to make our move?" He waggled his eyebrows. "How was she? It's always those petite quiet ones who turn out to be the real firecrackers between the sheets."

Dimitri's jaw tightened. He would let Yuri bust his balls about a lot of things but Benny was off-limits. "Don't, Yuri."

His friend's eyes widened. "I see. That serious, huh?"

"It's complicated," he said finally. "I'm not sure we're on the same page yet."

"Well I'm sure you didn't come here for relationship advice. You'd better look to Ivan for those answers."

Dimitri snorted at the thought of seeking advice on long-term relationships from a billionaire oligarch playboy, but the suggestion to bounce ideas off Ivan was a good one. "No, I'm not here for that kind of help. What do you know about UpStreet Properties?"

Yuri's playful demeanor fled. "Nothing you'll like to hear. Why?"

"They want to buy Benny's bakery so they can put in a retail center. She said no and they sent around one of their men to scare her this morning."

Yuri's eyes narrowed and a flash of anger darkened them. Like Dimitri, he had a real problem with that particular scare tactic. Going after women was weak and cowardly.

"Jonah Krause owns the real estate development company. He has deep pockets. Not as deep as mine, obviously, but deeper than yours. It's not the money that makes him dangerous, Dimitri. It's his connections."

"To?"

"Anyone and everyone important in Houston," Yuri continued. "Make no mistake. If he wants that property, he's going to get it. He owns a lot of people in the city government. He'll put pressure on them to use imminent domain. If she beats that, he'll find a way to stop the permits she needs to do repairs or improvements. If that doesn't stop her, he'll blacklist her with contractors and make it impossible for her to get any work done. Push back hard enough and he might use some of the knee-breakers he keeps on his payroll to bring her into compliance."

Dimitri rubbed the back of his neck. His muscles tightened painfully as the picture of what Benny stood against became clear. "What do I do? How do I help her?"

"You tell her to raise the fucking price and sell out while the money is still good."

"She won't. That business and that building are her family's history."

"The business can be moved. A building is simply a building. It's bricks and drywall and wires. It's nothing." Yuri jabbed the air with his finger. "You'd better change her mind or she's going to get totally fucked on this. These are not the kind of people she wants to take on, Dimitri. This will be a nasty fight—and it's one you will not win."

Yuri's ominous warning made his stomach pitch. While he respected Benny's feelings on the matter, he worried that she was letting her emotions cloud her judgment. With enough money from a sale of the building and a sale of her home, she could start over in a better location. He'd help her with funds, if needed, to make sure she stayed solidly in the black.

Getting her to agree to that proposal wouldn't be easy. He never wanted her to feel like he didn't have her back. He feared she'd see it as a betrayal if he urged her to sell but what else could he do? Yuri never exaggerated. If he said this Jonah Krause was trouble, it was true.

"Shit." Dimitri wiped a hand down his face. "We haven't even had a full twenty-four hours together as a couple and we're going to have our first huge fight."

"Now this is something I can help you with, Dimitri! I may not be a relationship expert like Ivan but I know exactly what to do in this situation."

Dimitri eyed him warily. "And what's that?"

"You stop at the jewelry store on the way home and you buy something obscenely expensive. Diamonds are always a good choice. It softens them up and makes it less likely you're going to need a trip to the emergency room."

Dimitri scowled at Yuri. "I can't imagine why Lena thinks you're such a womanizer."

"That hurts, Dimitri." Yuri put a hand to his chest and feigned injury.

His pocket vibrated and he grabbed his phone. A text message from Benny made his chest flutter. He felt like a damn teenager as he opened the message. A grown man shouldn't feel this much excitement from something so simple—but he did.

Having dinner with the girls tonight. Hope that's okay.

Before he could type an answer, Yuri asked, "Is that from Benny?"

"She's just letting me know that she's having dinner with friends." He didn't mention Lena because he didn't want to touch that sore spot.

"Is that all she says?"

"Well…"

"Because it's probably a test, Dimitri."

He laughed. "It's a message, Yuri. That's all."

"Except when it isn't," Yuri replied. He held out his hand. "Let me see."

Dimitri pulled the phone closer to his chest but Yuri was able to bat it out of his hands. He glanced at the screen and hummed knowingly. "See? A test!"

Dimitri narrowed his eyes. "Give me the damn

phone."

Yuri slapped it back onto his palm. "She's feeling uncertain, Dimitri. I know I joked about the shy, quiet types earlier but I'm being serious now. Women like Benny need to be reassured. She's funny and sweet but she's not the most confident woman. This message?" He pointed at the phone. "That's her way of establishing boundaries."

"Boundaries?" Dimitri rarely felt out of his depth but Yuri's knowledge in the field of women trumped his.

"You have a dominating personality. Like me, like Ivan, like Nikolai," he said. "Some women love that, yeah? Some women are put off by it. Some women aren't quite sure. Benny's somewhere in the middle right now. She loves it and fears it. She's telling you that she's going to have a night with her friends to remind you who makes decisions for her. But," he emphasized, "a small part of her wants to know if you'll be bothered that she made a decision without you. She's feeling you out. She's trying to figure out how this relationship is going to work."

Dimitri stared at the screen and considered Yuri's advice. Last night, he'd been a bit forceful in getting her to stay the night with him. He'd also put her in restraints. She'd loved them, obviously, but maybe it was a bit too much for one night. Was she feeling skittish now?

He ran his thumb over the touchscreen and thought about what to type. After erasing his message twice, he settled on one that worked.

Have fun. I'd like to see you later?

With his message sent, he looked up to find Yuri eyeing him. He tucked his phone into his pocket and let loose an irritated sigh. "What?"

Yuri's shoulders bounced and he stood. "I was thinking that soon you and Ivan will be having couples-only weekends."

Dimitri shot him the finger but didn't try to deny it. For all he knew, Yuri was right. Ivan had been with Erin only a few short months but he'd already witnessed a dramatic change in his friend. It was probable he'd soon be following in Ivan's footsteps.

Yuri made his way to his desk and plucked a business card from the tray there. "Have you given any thought to the proposal I made last week?"

Dimitri thought back to their dinner at the Samovar. Yuri had blindsided him with a new business venture he wanted Dimitri to head. "You were serious about that?"

Yuri looked amused. "Have you ever known me to joke when it comes to money and business?"

"No."

He scribbled something on the back of the card. "I think you're the perfect person to head a personal security firm. We can roll Front Door Security into a bigger company. I think you have something unique to offer, especially to the heavy international clientele that's pouring into Houston." He straightened and dropped the pen back into its holder. "You and I have always stayed clean so we wouldn't have any problems there."

When he said clean, he meant on the right side of the law. Unlike Ivan and Nikolai who had both done time and had rap sheets a mile long, Dimitri and Yuri had stayed out of the criminal fray. That wasn't to say they hadn't crossed the line a time or two when it was absolute necessary but they'd been careful about it.

"Let me consider it." Dimitri rose from his chair. "When do you want an answer?"

"The end of next week?" Yuri extended the business card. "The sooner we make our move, the better."

Dimitri took the business card and flipped it over.

"What's this?"

"It's the name of a jeweler here in Houston. The only one I'll use. He's one of us."

By one of us, he meant a Russian. Dimitri tried to hand back the card. "I don't need this. I'm not going to buy Benny jewelry just to avoid an argument."

Yuri pushed his hand back. "Keep it. You might need it sooner than you think."

Dimitri started to object but nodded instead. He slipped it into his pocket. With a smile, he asked, "Do I get a discount if I mention your name?"

"Hell," Yuri said with a laugh, "he'll probably mark up the price!" He slapped Dimitri's back. "Hey, come out to the club on Saturday. Ivan and Erin are coming. It will be nice to see you and Benny together."

Dimitri wasn't so sure Benny would enjoy the wild scene at Faze, Yuri's decadent Houston nightspot, but he accepted the offer. "Sure."

"Good." Yuri walked him to the door and glanced at his watch. "I'd ask you to join me at the Samovar for lunch but I've got a helicopter coming in ten minutes. Next time?"

"Yeah."

Yuri's fingers tightened on his shoulder. "Be careful, Dimitri. I know you love this woman but don't let that love make you stupid. Ivan walked into the middle of a damn gang war for Erin and barely survived it."

"Have you ever known me to be reckless?"

"No, but I've also never seen you protect someone you love as much as Benny. I see it in your face every time you mention her name. Don't let it blind you. Tunnel vision at a time like this?" He shook his head. "Bad business."

Dimitri took the warning to heart. Yuri had a way of

cutting through the bullshit and this time was no different. They shook hands and Dimitri headed for the elevators. As he waited, his pocket vibrated again. He withdrew his phone to find Benny's reply.

Yes!

With a smile on his face, he stepped into the empty elevator. For the first time in years, he felt a quiver of hope tickling deep in his belly. Benny was finally his—and he was never letting go.

CHAPTER SIX

Later that night, when I pulled into the small parking area beside the bakery, my sides still ached from laughing so hard. I couldn't remember the last time I'd had that much fun with girlfriends. Even though I'd only known Vivian and Erin a short time, the two women had happily welcomed me into the group and made me feel a part of it. It was a really nice feeling to belong.

Dimitri's truck sat in its usual spot. I flipped down my visor and checked my reflection in the mirror. I touched up my lips and dug around in my purse for a mint that I quickly crunched between my teeth so it would dissolve faster. My tummy fluttered wildly as I slid out of my car and locked it.

I hadn't even made it to the bottom step of the metal stairs before Dimitri's door opened and he came out to greet me. "Hi."

I smiled up at him and tried to keep my knees from knocking together. "Hey."

His sexy grin made my heart dance. Barefoot and in

jeans, he looked so relaxed as he leaned back against his door and waited for me. I could tell he'd run his hands through his blond hair, leaving the ends a bit tousled. His pale blue shirt stretched across his chest and hugged his thick, muscled arms. The memory of what it felt like to have them wrapped around me made my belly clench.

The second I drew close, he slid an arm around my waist and tugged me against his chest. He cupped my face and claimed my lips in a kiss so perfectly sensuous it made it impossible for me to breathe. My heart stammered in my chest as his tongue swept mine and he sucked gently on my lower lip. God, the man could kiss!

He dragged his thumb across my mouth. "How was your night with the girls?"

"It was nice. I think Lena and Erin had the most fun, especially once they cracked open the second bottle of wine from Ivan's cellar."

A frown marred his handsome face. A bit tersely, he said, "You shouldn't drink and drive, Benny."

I bristled at his insinuation that I'd done something wrong. "I had one glass and that was right when I walked in the door. It's been more than two hours."

He looked apologetic. "I could have worded that differently. I only meant that you could have called me. I would have been happy to pick you up." He brushed his fingers through my loose hair. "I worry about you."

"Dimitri, I'm a big girl. I can handle myself."

"I know you can." He grunted softly in frustration. "I'm screwing this up. I'm trying to say that you don't always have to do everything on your own."

My annoyance fled. I rubbed my hand over his hard chest. "I understand." Wanting to show him I meant it, I added, "The next time I go out with the girls I'll really let my hair down, okay? Then you'll be the one getting a late night call from your plastered girlfriend asking you to come pick her up instead of poor Ivan."

Dimitri chuckled. "I'm sure Ivan loved that."

I smiled at the memory of Erin pawing Ivan on her way out to his SUV. "Well considering the way Erin had Ivan's shirt half unbuttoned by the time he got her to the parking lot, I'm sure he did love it."

Dimitri looked shock at my description of her lustful actions. "Erin? Really?"

I laughed. "Yes. Ivan got so flustered with her that he finally just picked her up and tossed her over his shoulder like a sack of potatoes. The last thing I saw before he threw her into his vehicle was Erin smacking him on the butt. I don't think Ivan was nearly as amused as I was."

"No, I'm sure he wasn't." Dimitri's grin brightened his face. "Come inside."

He curled his arm around my shoulders and led me into his apartment. I kicked off my flats before following him into the living area. He sat down on the sofa and I started to sit down next to him, but with one swift tug, he pulled me onto his lap.

"Dimitri!" I tried to wiggle free but he gripped my waist.

"Sit still," he urged and planted a ticklish kiss on my neck. "I missed you today. Let me hold you."

How could a girl argue with that? Relaxing, I said, "Well...okay."

He smiled indulgently but didn't point out that I wasn't exactly agreeing to a huge hardship. His fingers swirled over the bare skin just above my knee. I caught his eye. There was no mistaking that mischievous glint. His hand slid a little higher, scooting just under the hem of my skirt.

Even though I wanted the same thing he wanted, I

decided to make him wait. I wanted to draw it out and enjoy the anticipation a little longer. "Dimitri?"

"Yes?" He nuzzled my neck.

"What's the story behind Vivian and Nikolai?"

Instantly, he stiffened. Surprised by his reaction, I glanced at him. He quickly recovered and gave a nonchalant shrug. "It's not much of a story."

I held his gaze. "I'd like to hear it. I'm not comfortable enough with Vivian to ask yet but I feel like I'm playing catch-up when they talk." I ran my finger over his knuckles. "Please?"

He didn't look thrilled to do it but finally relented. "Okay."

I pecked his cheek. "Thank you."

"You know that Vivian's mother was Russian, right?"

"I sort of assumed that part. I heard her speaking Russian to Ivan earlier. It was flawless." During dinner, I'd overheard Lena and Vivian clucking at one another in Spanish, their fiery come-backs some of the funniest I'd heard in a long time. "Her Spanish is perfect, too."

He nodded. "If it wasn't for her talent with a brush, I think she might have studied languages. She would have been good at it." His hand swept up and down my thigh, pushing the fabric of my skirt higher with every movement. "Vivi's father was in a Mexican motorcycle gang. They operate on both sides of the border."

"Like the Hell's Angels or something?"

"Worse," he said, his lips settling into a grim line. "We're talking drugs, prostitution, guns and hits. Really nasty stuff and very dangerous people, Benny. When Vivi's mother married that man, her family turned their backs on her. They cut her off completely."

"Ouch."

"From what I understand, her mother was always a

little…strange. It got worse after she married and had Vivian. She had some kind of a psychotic break and tried to drown Vivi. A neighbor heard the screaming and saved her. They put Katya away in a mental institution for a while. That's when Vivi started living with her father's family—but I don't think it was much better. At that point, her father was doing time for a drug charge."

I couldn't believe what I was hearing but I sensed it was going to get much worse.

"Eventually, her mother got better and they let her leave the hospital. She got Vivi back and things were good for a while. Vivan's father got out of the pen and came home. The trouble started again. Her parents were both nasty drunks. They would beat the shit out of one another when they got going. Some of the old-timers who hang around the Samovar can tell stories that will curl your toenails. They'd go at one another with knives and broken bottles."

I grimaced. "Jesus, that's awful."

He nodded. "By the time Vivian was ten or so, her father had gone back into the pen. Her mother was more erratic and dangerous. She wouldn't stay on her medication so Vivian's grandparents, Katya's mother and father, finally stepped in and took custody of Vivi. Her mother lost all hope and she hung herself in a motel room across town."

I gasped at the horrific picture he painted. "Dimitri, that's terrible."

"Vivian's grandparents shielded her from much of the ugliness but then her father got out of prison again. He wasn't allowed to have contact with her, but he found a way to pass her notes in school, probably through a gang member's child. Somehow, he convinced her to meet with him. One thing led to another, and soon Vivi was running drugs for him."

"What?" I almost fell off Dimitri's lap. "You're joking!"

He shook his head sadly. "I don't think she realized what was happening. She was just a kid. A young, stupid kid, you know? Her father would give her a backpack and a place to meet a *cousin*. She'd take the bus, meet this supposed cousin at the mall or wherever and trade out a backpack of drugs for one filled with money."

"Oh my God!"

His jaw tightened. "Eventually, she got picked up during a narcotics bust. Her father had twisted her mind so badly she wouldn't give him up. Her grandparents were able to get her a good lawyer so she was put on probation and into counseling."

Enthralled by the tale he told, I began to wonder about Nikolai's connection. "Where does Nikolai fit into this story?"

He breathed in slowly. "Not long after Vivian was picked up during the drug bust, Nikolai was here visiting family. Vivi's father had gotten back in contact with her. He convinced her to help him do one last job so he could get enough money to take her with him. I'm sure he promised her all kinds of things to make her do it. Somehow he got Vivian to break into a house to help him steal. She was shot by the homeowner and fell out a window while trying to flee. Her father left her there to bleed to death. Nikolai was at the house next door. He heard the gunshots and the scream and saved her life."

I sat in stunned silence as the tragedy of Vivian's history washed over me. Something about the way Dimitri wouldn't meet my gaze told me there was so much more to this sordid tale but I didn't push. I trusted there was a reason I didn't need to know everything.

What he'd told me was bad enough!

"What happened to her dad?"

"As far as I know, he's still in the pen."

"So what? After that, Nikolai felt responsibility toward her?"

Dimitri didn't answer immediately. He seemed to be choosing his words carefully. "He knew her mother's family from back in Russia so he kept in touch after he returned to Moscow. I think the experience of finding a child bleeding to death after being shot and falling out of a window really fucked with him."

"It would screw up anybody."

He hummed in agreement. "When we came over here to start over, Nikolai found out her grandmother had recently died and her grandfather was in a home with Alzheimer's. He offered her a job at Samovar and made sure that everyone knew she had his protection."

"He's that powerful?"

"Yes."

I decided not to indulge my curiosity of what men like Nikolai actually did for a living. Instead, I asked, "Is that how you feel about me? That I need your protection?"

"Sometimes," he admitted. "Right now, you need me. This mess with Johnny and the real estate developer? That's not something you should navigate on your own. You need someone like me to lead the way and keep you out of trouble."

"I'm not helpless, Dimitri."

"I didn't say that."

"Well..."

"Hey," he whispered softly and touched my cheek. "I think you're incredibly smart and capable, Benny. I know how far people like Jonah Krause are willing to go to get what they want. I also know how stupid your brother can be." The corners of his mouth dipped. "Have you heard from him today?"

"Just a quick call around five," I said. "It didn't go well. He told me he would be home around midnight. Honestly, I didn't want to fight with him so I let it go. I told him we'd talk over breakfast."

His hand dipped under my top and stroked my naked skin. "Is that your way of telling me you aren't spending the night?"

I shivered as his fingers branded me with their very touch. Swallowing hard, I said, "This is my way of saying that things happened fast last night. I think we should slow down a little." Nervous, I added, "If that's okay."

His fingers went still. His pale blue eyes peered into my darker ones. "Of course it's okay. Benny, you tell me what you want and it's yours."

I got the feeling he wasn't just talking about sex. Sometimes he said things like that and I so desperately wanted to read into the double meaning. I wanted to believe that he felt as strongly as I did. Last night had thrown me for a loop. I wasn't quite sure what was happening now or where we were going. Lena's advice came to mind.

"Dimitri?"

"Yes?"

"What...what are we doing?"

His lips twitched with amusement. "I was planning to strip you naked and fuck you right here on this couch until you begged me to stop but I suppose we could watch a movie instead."

I gulped as he described the night he had planned for me before I'd given him the "let's go slow" speech. "Oh. Um—let's table that and come back to it, okay? But, really, I meant us. What are we doing? Are we a couple?

Are we just screwing around?"

His long fingers threaded through my hair. "Last night was our first date so I think that means we're dating." His eyebrows rose questioningly. "Unless you only want a sexual arrangement? Friends with benefits or whatever they call it."

"No!" I answered too quickly and he smiled. "I mean, no. I don't want that kind of arrangement. Dating sounds good."

"Then we're dating."

"Okay."

"Benny?"

"Yes?"

"Let's go back to the topic you tabled."

My cheeks grew hot. "What about it?"

His hand slid under my skirt and moved toward my panties. "You said you wanted to go slowly." His fingers inched along my inner thigh. "I can go very, very slowly, if you'd like."

Suddenly, my clit throbbed and my pussy ached for him. Trembling with excitement, I whispered, "Maybe fast is okay tonight."

He laughed and captured my mouth. Whimpering, I clutched his shoulders and prepared to be ravished by him. If my one night with Dimitri had taught me anything, it was that my big, sexy Russian was a master when it came to this kind of thing. I practically vibrated with lust and need.

He wasted no time pulling off my top and tossing aside my bra. My skirt and panties quickly followed. He dragged a soft throw down from the back of the couch and placed it under me, sparing my hot skin the cold shock of the cool leather.

Cradled in the plush couch, I watched him peel out of

his shirt and jeans. All that deliciously tanned skin beckoned. I ran my greedy hands all over his body. Giving the waistband of his boxers a little tug, I snapped them back against him. He chuckled as I pushed them down his hips.

That fat, thick cock sprang free. I clasped the steely length of him, stroking from the wide base to the blunt, ruddy tip. Dimitri sucked in a shuddery breath as my fingers moved over him. Even though I was sure I would disappoint him with my less than stellar blow job skills, I had to taste him. I started to move toward him but he stopped me. Confused, I glanced up at him. "Don't you want me to...you know?"

He pushed loose strands of hair behind my ear. "Yes, but only if you want to, not because you feel like you have to do it."

I rolled my eyes. "Of course I want to do it!"

He laughed and grasped his erection. "Then open that pretty little mouth and suck my cock."

I pushed up on my knees and put my hands on his hips. Wetting my lips, I let saliva pool on the tip of my tongue before swiping the full length of him. I dragged my tongue along the underside of his big shaft before sucking him into my mouth. His pained groan sent electric zings of excitement arcing through me. I wanted to make him feel just as good as he'd made me feel last night.

There was no way I could take all of him into my mouth. He was too damned long for that. With my lips stretched wide, I bobbed up and down on his cock. My hand picked up the slack, gliding up and down his erection. I could taste the slight tang of pre-cum as he grew more and more aroused.

When Dimitri's fingers tangled in my hair, I glanced up

at him. Our gazes met, his eyes questioning and seeking permission. I understood what he wanted and trusted him not to take it too far. Relaxing my jaw, I happily waited for him to pump his cock into my willing mouth.

Gently at first, he thrust his cock against my tongue. His nostrils flared as he slid in a few inches and then retreated. The tight tendons in his neck and his shallow breaths showed how much he was fighting the primal urge to bury his cock deep in my throat. He kept his baser needs in check and showed me just how much he appreciated my trust in him by taking my mouth with cautious strokes. I hummed around his pumping cock and made sure to flutter my tongue over the weeping crown, sucking the droplets of pre-cum glistening from the tip.

"Enough," he said with a groan and pulled free. His cock visibly throbbed as he denied himself the orgasm he clearly wanted.

A moment later, he was on his knees and shoving me onto my back. He grasped my knees and opened my legs wide. He dragged a finger through my tender folds, swirling it around my clit and then letting it slide lower to push inside my slick channel. Hearing his soft groans while I had my mouth on him had gotten me so excited.

"You're so fucking wet." He lowered his face and placed a kiss right on top of my clit. "Does sucking my cock make you hot, Benny?"

Breathless, I confessed, "Yes."

He added a second finger in my soaking channel. "Do you want me to lick you? Do you want to come with my tongue on your cunt?"

I gasped at his rough language but answered honestly. "Yes. Please, Dimitri!"

With a hungry groan, he dropped his mouth to my

pussy. As if ravenous, he attacked my clit. His tongue circled the swollen nub and flicked around it. I lifted my hips and clawed at his shoulders as he drove me crazy with that wicked, wicked mouth. The fingers buried in my wet depths moved in and out at a steady pace. He curved them up just enough—and I saw stars. "Ooooh!"

He suckled my clit, pulling the pink pearl between his lips and rolling his tongue over it. The fingers pressing against my G-spot sent me over the edge. Howling with pleasure, I cried out again and again as he pushed me higher and higher into the realm of ecstasy.

His mouth crashed to mine. We kissed frantically and groped one another. I whined like a sad little puppy when he pulled away from me to grab a condom from the pocket of his jeans. In an instant, he was back and petting my lower belly. Our mouths touched again. Lip locked, we exchanged passionate kisses while he ripped the condom wrapper.

I was panting and gripping his forearm as he sheathed himself. He grabbed my hips and dragged my bottom right to the very edge of the couch cushions. With one powerful thrust, he impaled me. "Dimitri!"

"You can take me," he said, his voice gruff and filled with intense need. His fingers bit into the soft flesh of my thighs as he pushed my knees toward my chest and started to fuck me. There was nothing gentle or tender about our coupling now. He took me hard and fast—and just the way I wanted it.

"Oh! Oh! *Ahhh*!" I cried out in sheer pleasure. Every deep stroke of his cock set my body on fire. He pinched my nipples, tugging lightly on the dusky peaks until they buzzed. The delicious ache amplified the throbbing pulse between my thighs.

Dimitri brought my fingers to his lips. He sucked on

my fingertips and got them nice and slick. He pushed my hand down to the spot where we were joined. "Rub your clit for me. Make yourself come."

My belly flip-flopped at his command. Shyness overwhelmed me, but one look into his smoky, lust-filled eyes and I couldn't find the strength to say no. Wanting to come while he pounded me with that big, fat cock, I swirled my fingertips over the bundle of nerves that clamored for attention. It didn't take much stimulation to put me on edge.

Lower belly trembling and toes curling, I found it hard to breathe. My gaze locked with his as he slammed into me again and again, his cock bottoming out before it retreated to just the head buried inside me.

Over and over, he took me, faster and harder until I screamed his name and descended into the blissful grip of orgasm. A split-second later, he followed me. A string of Russian words left his lips and he collapsed against me, shuddering and jerking as the waves of his climax ripped through him.

When we finally calmed, he left me just long enough to discard of the condom. Back in the living room, he dragged me down onto the floor with him. Our limbs were tangled in the blanket. The hardwood wasn't the most comfortable place to rest but we didn't mind.

I simply wanted to feel his hot body pressed to mine. He caressed my naked skin and peppered my face with loving kisses. Every now and then he whispered sweetly against my ear, telling me I was beautiful and amazing and so damn sexy.

In short, it was perfect.

*

Dimitri hated to ruin a perfect moment but it had to be done. Of all the times to bring it up, he figured now was as good as any. Benny rested in his arms, completely satisfied and relaxed. Surely she'd be more amenable to what he was about to say.

"Sweetheart, I've been thinking about UpStreet Properties."

"Oh?" She sounded a bit sleepy.

"I think you should raise the price on the building and sell."

She went rigid in his arms. A moment later, she pushed up on hand and glared down at him. The look on her face promised one hell of a fight. "What?"

"Benny, look," he said carefully, "I did some checking into Jonah Krause. He's a dangerous man."

"So what? I should just give him what he wants without a fight?"

He frowned at her naïve reply. "And just who in the hell do you think is going to fight this war of yours?"

"What's that supposed to mean?" She poked him in the chest. "I never asked you to fight this battle for me. *You're* the one who rode to my rescue and offered to help *me*."

"What did you expect me to do, Benny? Let you get wrapped up in something you can't possibly understand?"

"There you go again! What is with you? Why do you assume that I don't know how to maneuver through these types of business deals?"

"Because you don't," he replied tersely. "The fact that Jonah Krause sent a man into your bakery to intimidate you this morning should have driven that point home, Benny."

"So what? I cave? I sell out my family's history?"

"Better to sell out now than to go bankrupt in a month

or two and have nothing to show for it!"

She reeled back. Her eyes suddenly glistened. His gut clenched painfully at the realization that he'd hurt her so deeply with his stupid retort. "Benny..."

"Screw you." She scrambled off the floor and started jerking on her clothes. "I'm out of here."

He pushed up onto his knees and snatched away her skirt before she could grab it. "No. You aren't leaving like this."

"The hell I'm not! Give me my skirt, Dimitri."

He shook his head. "I'm not letting you fly out of here upset. You could wreck. Now sit down and listen to me." She started to tell him off again but he cut her off with a pleading look. "Please, Benny. Just hear me out."

She crossed her arms and huffed but eventually sat down. Still staring angrily, she said, "I'm listening. Talk!"

Kneeling down in front of her, he put his hands on her bare thighs and held her hurt gaze. It killed him that he'd upset her like this. "Benny, I'll support whatever choice you make. I've got your back. I need you to know that up front. Do you believe me?"

Her jaw tightened and relaxed. With a growl of frustration, she admitted, "Yes."

"Then believe that I wouldn't tell you to sell if I didn't think it was the best idea." He cupped her face and brushed his thumbs over her cheeks. "I want what's best for you, Benny. I think if you push back against Jonah Krause it's going to end badly. He has millions of dollars on the line and you are—forgive me—a nobody in the great scheme of things. He won't think twice about striking at you."

She gulped and her lower lip wobbled. "Dimitri, I can't just walk away from the business my grandparents built. You, better than anyone, should understand what it's like for immigrants to come here, to work hard and build something so successful."

"I do, Benny. But this business is failing here." She started to cry and he felt like the biggest asshole in the whole world. "It's not your fault. I've seen how hard you work. I've seen what you've sacrificed to keep this place going. You inherited a dying business in a dying neighborhood. You can't make it work here, sweetheart. Please don't let it drag you down."

She sobbed loudly, the ragged sounds tearing at his heart. Gathering her close, he moved onto the couch and cradled her on his lap. She wept in his arms, her hot tears spilling onto his chest and dripping down his skin. He ached for her, his gut twisting and his chest constricting. The knowledge that he was the one who had forced this ugly discussion made him feel so low.

Shit. Maybe Yuri was right. He should have bought the fucking diamonds.

CHAPTER SEVEN

S till feeling groggy, I gulped the last of my coffee and refilled my travel mug. I'd been up for an hour but I couldn't get moving. Last night had drained me, emotionally and physically.

After I'd finally stopped crying, Dimitri had whispered such sweet and tender things to me. He'd made love to me again, this time gentler and with such intensity that I'd had tears in my eyes again when we were done. Even though I'd protested, he'd followed me home and walked me inside the house. Apparently he took his promise to protect me very seriously.

It had been so very painful to hear Dimitri tell me the unvarnished truth. Even though I'd reacted so badly, I understood he was trying to protect me by being brutally honest. He'd said aloud what I'd been secretly dreading for so long. The business wasn't going to be profitable in this location. Something had to change.

Change? That seemed to be the only way to describe the current state of my life. I was in a constant state of flux. The bakery's future was up in the air. Johnny kept dodging my calls and refusing to come home. Dimitri seemed to want to pursue something long-term with me.

Confusion welled inside me as I dumped a hot cocoa packet and a scoop of sugar into my coffee. The spoon whacked against the inside of the mug while I tried to get a handle on my wildly vacillating emotions. I had to get a grip!

The front door opened, the hinges squealing loudly. After it was pushed closed, I heard the telltale creak of the floorboards in the living room. I rolled my eyes and cleared my throat. "Johnny?"

With a guilty look on his face, he slinked into the kitchen. Even with the island between us, I could smell the sour scent of alcohol and weed rolling off of him. I wrinkled my nose and held a hand to my face. "When was the last time you had a shower?"

He put a self-conscious hand on his chest. "Yesterday."

If that was true, I didn't even want to think about where he'd spent the night. To smell that awful, he must have been in a terrible place. I prayed it wasn't one of those low-rent whorehouses the Hermanos were purported to run.

Hoping to avoid a fight, I gestured to the short stack of breakfast burritos wrapped in aluminum foil. "I made breakfast."

"I'm not hungry."

We stared at one another. With a sigh, I said, "Okay. Let's just clear the air. Why did you steal from the business?"

"I didn't steal. That's my money, too."

"It's not your money. It's not my money. That money belongs to the business. That money belongs to our employees and our vendors."

"It was three hundred fucking dollars, Benny! It's not a big deal!"

I gawked at him. "Not a big deal? You stole from your family, Johnny! That's a big deal."

He swore nastily and reached into his back pocket. My eyes widened in shock when he pulled out a dirty envelope. Hundred dollar bills fluttered onto the countertop. "There! There's your fucking money! Happy?"

I swallowed hard as I stared at the cash on the counter and the cash still in the thick envelope. "Where did you get that, Johnny?"

"Don't ask me stupid questions like that, Benny. Just take the fucking money and shut up."

My jaw clenched. "Don't talk to me like that!"

"Or what? You'll call Dimitri to come kick my ass?"

"I've never asked Dimitri to hurt you!"

He laughed. "You're so full of shit."

"Believe whatever you want, Johnny. I know the truth."

"Yeah? Well I know you're fucking him. I saw your car there last night and the night before that. Is that how he pays his rent now?" He shouted it at me, his lips curled with disgust.

I took a step back. The disdainful look on his face made my cheeks and ears burn. "It's not like that, Johnny."

"Then how is it, Benny?"

"It's none of your business. I'm allowed to have a personal life and privacy, Johnny."

"Yeah? So am I." He waved the envelope. "My personal life. My business. You stay the fuck out of it."

Angered, I gathered up the money he'd thrown on the counter and squashed it into a tight ball. I threw it at him, hitting him in the chest with the dirty money. "Then take your money and get the hell out!"

He scowled at me and picked up the money I'd thrown at him. "I'm not going anywhere. This is my house. Why don't you go move in with your *gringo*?"

"I'm not moving anywhere, Johnny. Like you said, this is my house too."

"Not for long," he snapped back. He reached into the front pocket of his jeans and produced a folded stack of papers. My mind flashed back to the moment I'd discovered the stolen money. Hadn't my desk drawer been open?

"Is that our business contract? The one we signed just before Abuelita died?"

"I talked to a lawyer about the guy who wants to buy the bakery building. He said you can't stop me from selling my share. He's going to help me get my half of the house too."

My blood ran cold. "Johnny, what are you saying? You agreed to sell your share of the bakery to UpStreet?"

The briefest glimmer of regret flashed across his face. It vanished quickly and his expression turned hard. "It's mine. I can do what I want with it. I want the money. I *need* the money."

"For what?"

"It's none of your damn business, Benny."

"The hell it's not! You're giving away our family's history to a man who wants to tear it down and build a stupid shopping center. You're pissing on the memory of everything that Abuelita and Abuelito and Mom worked for their entire lives. I want to know *why*?"

He slashed his hand through the air. "I don't have to tell you shit, Benny."

Turning his back on me, he practically ran out of the

kitchen. I chased after him. "Johnny! *Johnny!*"

"Fuck off, Benny!" He dashed upstairs and slammed his door shut. The walls rattled when he turned on his music and blared the reggaeton beats.

Shaking and on the verge of puking, I stood at the foot of the stairs and fought the urge to run up there and smack him. How could he do this? The betrayal of Johnny going behind my back and making a decision without even consulting me cut so deeply. If we were going to sell, it should have been done together, as a unified front, so we could get the best price. I shuddered to think what kind of stupid deal he might have agreed to sign.

Every step of the way, I'd included him in discussions about the bakery and the house. Even when I knew he wasn't listening or didn't care, I'd still taken the time to sit him down and go over the accounts. When I'd stopped taking a salary, I'd talked it over with him first and shown him the balance we had to live off of in our bank account. When it came time to consider selling the house, I'd put it all on the table for him. We'd talked about real estate agents and a listing price.

I thought we were partners. Apparently, we weren't anything.

Feeling hopeless, I returned to the kitchen and pushed the lid onto my travel mug. I switched off the coffee pot and stared at the burritos I'd made for breakfast. My stomach lurched at the thought of eating so I tucked them into the refrigerator. With my purse in hand, I left the house and locked the door.

The early Saturday morning traffic was light. My mind wandered as I drove. I would need a lawyer and quickly. There were contracts in place protecting the business and delineating our rights as owners. I didn't know how long it would take to untangle all that mess but I assumed it would be expensive. If Johnny had been talking to UpStreet about selling his share, I felt certain they'd probably agreed to provide him with a business attorney.

Dimitri was right. I was going to get screwed six ways to Sunday.

* * *

After a fitful night of sleep, Dimitri slid out of bed and into a hot shower. Though he and Benny had made up and parted well, he couldn't shake the worried feeling twisting his gut. Coming home to an empty apartment felt bleaker than usual. One night with Benny in his arms and waking to her feel her pressed against him had spoiled him. Now he wanted that all the time.

What would Benny say if he casually mentioned getting a place together? If she sold her house and the bakery building, they'd both need places to stay. Wouldn't it make sense to live together?

As he got dressed, he wondered if that was a conversation they were ready to have. They'd been friends for years but this romantic entanglement was so new. She'd given him the "moving too fast" speech last night but he didn't think she really meant it. Yuri's talk of establishing boundaries and seeking reassurance made sense now.

He was drinking his first cup of coffee when he heard the bakery van beeping loudly as it backed into place at the loading dock. Certain they could use his help this early in the morning, Dimitri put on his shoes and headed downstairs. He found Marco and Adam looking over a list and discussing the best way to load in the mountains of bakery boxes.

Marco immediately put him to work. He was happy to do it, knowing full well it would ease some of the stress on the team as they tried to juggle the event and the usual day-to-day needs of the bakery. Dimitri desperately wanted this to be a success for Benny. Even if she ended up selling and moving locations, this would still be a good way to introduce herself to new customers. Lena was smart enough to get them to follow Benny wherever she moved.

Half an hour into his work, he checked his watch. Benny was running late. A quiver of concern pierced his chest. Was she simply running behind or was it something else? He wanted to whip out his phone to call her but decided to give it another ten minutes.

He was sliding the last rolling tray of cookies into the truck and latching it into place when he finally heard her sweet voice. Heat streaked through him as her silly laugh echoed in the backroom. She chattered away in Spanish, making little jokes with Marco and letting Adam tease her.

Dimitri had picked up enough Spanish during his five years living over the bakery to understand that Adam was talking about him. The two older men, Marco and Adam, treated Benny like family. He'd been expecting some push back from them but only Marco had given him the side-eye so far. Dimitri hoped his willingness to volunteer this morning would put him in Marco's good graces.

Hopping from the truck to the loading dock, Dimitri finally caught sight of Benny. Instead of her usual bakery uniform of jeans and a shirt, she wore a flirty little dress. It hugged her body in all the right places. His gaze flicked to the playful hint of cleavage. It was just enough to tease him.

One look at her face and he knew she was hiding

something. She smiled but there was such sadness in her eyes. There was only one person in the world who could hurt her that badly—Johnny.

"Lupe has breakfast for us." Marco consulted his watch. "We have half an hour before we leave. You should eat."

Benny shook her head. "I'm not hungry."

Marco caught Dimitri's gaze. He understood what the older man was silently asking. Clearing his throat, Dimitri said, "Well I am. Let's have breakfast before you leave."

Benny frowned and glanced between the two men. She seemed to realize they weren't going to let her spend an entire day on her feet without a good meal in her belly. With a dramatic sigh, she acquiesced. "Fine."

They made their way to the kitchen and grabbed two bottles of orange juice and breakfast burritos from an insulated cooler. She spoke to the ladies in the kitchen, talking to them about the day's business. He waited patiently, but the moment she was free, he took her hand and dragged her into the office.

Wanting privacy, he locked the door behind him. She raised an eyebrow but didn't say anything. He pointed to her desk chair. "Sit and eat. We'll talk when you're done."

She plopped down in her chair and dropped her breakfast on the desk. "I don't really feel like talking anymore this morning."

Putting down his food, he leaned against the desk and stared down at her. "What did Johnny do?"

Her gaze jumped to his. "How did you know?"

"He's the only person who gets under your skin like that." Dimitri steeled himself for the worst. "Tell me, Benny."

She blinked rapidly, her dark eyes shimmering with tears. "He came home stinking like booze and weed. We fought about the money he stole. He pulled out this envelope that was stuffed with cash and started throwing hundred dollar bills at me."

"Did he say where he got the money?"

She shook her head. "He told me to mind my own business."

Dimitri doubted Johnny had said it that nicely. "I'll talk to him."

"No, it's done. I'm over it. If he wants to ruin his life, let him."

"You don't mean that." She could talk tough but he knew how much she loved her brother. "You're not cold enough to turn your back on him. You have a big heart, Benny."

"A big, stupid heart," she grumbled. "He told me that he's already talked to a lawyer about selling the building. He wants the money from the house, too."

Dimitri sat back in surprise. "Just like that? He made all these decisions without talking to you?"

She nodded. "You know, if he'd come to me and talked to me about why he wants to sell or why he needs the money, I would've been happy to find a way to restructure to give him what he wants. But to do it this way? To threaten to take me to court? He's such a monster."

He'd wanted to spare her all this heartache but it no longer seemed possible. "I'll call Yuri and see what lawyer he recommends."

"Dimitri, you know I can't afford the types of lawyers he would recommend."

"Let me handle it."

"No. This is my mess. I'll clean it up."

"Benny." He said her name sternly and in a tone of voice he'd never used with her. "We're partners now. I want to help you. Please don't fight me on this."

Her determined expression softened. She gave a tiny nod. Eventually, she admitted, "I love that you're willing to help me, Dimitri. Really, I know how lucky I am. I just don't want you to feel—"

"Obligated?" he guessed.

"Yes. Obligated."

He leaned forward and put both hands on the arms of her chair, trapping her in place. "I don't feel that way. I'm helping you because I want to help you. I'm helping you because it makes me feel good to take care of you."

She drew a strange shape on his shirt. "When you put it like that..."

He grinned and pressed his mouth to hers. She relaxed under his slow, easy kiss. The taste of hot chocolate and coffee tantalized his taste buds as he swept his tongue against hers. Their foreheads touched. "Benny, don't ever hesitate to ask me for help. I'd do anything for you."

She ran her hands up and down his arms. "I know."

He felt like they were finally making some headway. It was going to be an uphill battle to get her to feel comfortable asking for his help but he was willing to fight it. "Now, eat your breakfast so you can go to this food thing and dazzle everyone."

She groaned. "I don't know how the hell I'm supposed to get through this. The business is imploding as we speak. My brother is probably dealing drugs or pimping out prostitutes to make money. Somehow I'm supposed to plaster on a smile and gush about my stupid pastries and cookies?"

A devilishly wicked idea took hold. He lowered his mouth until it teased across hers. "I know how to put a smile on your pretty face."

"Oh?"

With a quick shove, he pushed her chair back against the wall and dropped to his knees. She gasped with surprise and tried to push his hands away from the hem of her dress. Whispering hotly, she insisted, "Dimitri, we can't do that here! Someone will hear us!"

Not easily deterred, he grinned up at her. "Then you'd better be very, very quiet."

He moved her skirt out of the way and grasped her panties. She squeezed her knees together but he forced them apart. Even as she fought him, he could hear her breaths growing shuddery and excited. With her panties thrown onto the desk behind him, he made quick work of tucking her skirt up and pulling her sweet, plump ass to the edge of the chair.

"No, Dimitri! Please, don't—Oh!" She mewled like a kitten when he swiped her slit with his tongue. "*Oh!*"

He chuckled and carefully parted the pink lips of her sex. Using his fingers to outline her clit, he flicked his tongue over the juicy little bud and coaxed it out to play. He sucked it between his lips and flicked it a few times before letting it loose and finding the right rhythm.

Benny gripped the arm of her desk chair and clapped a hand over her mouth. She muffled her own moans and whimpers as he ate her pussy. He couldn't get enough of her. The nectar that flowed from her core beckoned him. His tongue dipped inside to taste her, thrusting up into her like a small cock and making her squeal with delight.

Soon, her hand left the chair arm and she gripped handfuls of his hair. He didn't mind the burning sting caused by her tugging fingers. He wanted to drive her crazy, wanted to hear her come undone as he nibbled her clit and lapped at her pussy.

When she came, it was with a long, quiet moan. She had a hand pressed tightly to her mouth, deadening the sound as it left her lips. The chair rocked, the wheels squeaking as she jerked her hips and pressed her mound against his mouth. After she sagged back against the chair, Dimitri continued to lap and flick at her. The aftershocks left her trembling and panting.

Reluctantly, he finally pulled away from her. He plucked tissues from the box on her desk and tidied her up a bit. She let him slide her panties back into place and fix her skirt. Leaning back in her chair, she smiled, her silky pout curved wide and her eyes bright. "I should sulk more often."

He laughed and caressed her bare legs. "Maybe you should hire me as your assistant."

She chortled with amusement. "I don't think we'd get much work done."

"You work too hard as it is." He pecked her cheek. "Come out with me tonight."

She started to accept but then shook her head. "I won't get done with this Tasting Houston thing until mid-afternoon. I really need to go home and clean house and mow the yard."

"Let me worry about your yard." He kissed her deeply because it was the easiest way to get her to agree. "We'll go out and have fun. Yuri asked us to join him at Faze. Ivan and Erin will be there. It will be nice."

She finally nodded. "All right. Let's go out tonight."

With their evening plans settled, he slid onto the desk and watched her eat breakfast. What he finished in three bites and four long drinks took her much longer to eat. When they emerged from her office, they got a couple of curious looks but no one dared say anything. Benny's bright red ears and neck betrayed them, of course. One look at her and anyone would know what they'd been up to in that office.

They shared a quick kiss before he wished her good luck and watched her drive away in the bakery's delivery truck with Marco and Adam. He started back upstairs but one of the dishwasher boys popped his head out the side door and stopped him.

"Yo, D!"

A smile tugged at the corners of his mouth. "Yes?"

"Benny left her keys in her car, man. They're just hanging there in the ignition." The kid, Carlos, gestured behind him. "I thought maybe you'd want to know since she's already gone."

Dimitri frowned. "Thanks, Carlos."

"Anytime, man."

Carlos ducked back into the building but Dimitri took the long way around to the parking area the employees used. He found Benny's car in its usual spot. Just as Carlos said, the keys were dangling from the ignition and the doors were unlocked.

Shaking his head, Dimitri opened the door and reached in to grab the keys. This wasn't the first time she'd done this. In the five years he'd known her, this had happened at least a dozen times.

Irritated with her carelessness, he decided it was time to teach her a lesson. He'd move her car somewhere nearby. Hopefully the shock of coming back to the bakery to find it gone would burn the lesson into her brain. Not only was she risking losing her car to theft but there was always the possibility someone dangerous could take her keys. Considering she had an address tag dangling from the chain, it wouldn't be hard for a criminal to find her home. She'd be totally vulnerable then.

He had to slide her seat back as far as it would go but his knees were still bent uncomfortably in the compact front seat. When he fired up the ignition, his gaze jumped to the gas gauge and the flashing empty symbol. No gas and keys in the ignition?

His irritation eased as he considered the stressful hell Benny had been living the last few days. Forgetting her keys and neglecting to gas up were symptoms of a broader issue. She was trying to do too much by herself. She needed to learn to rely on other people for help. She needed to grow comfortable asking *him* for help, even with something as small as gassing up her car.

Rather than prank her by moving the car, he buckled the seatbelt, backed out of the space and drove to the closest gas station. After filling up, he made his way to the full-service car wash his buddy Alexei owned. He ignored the surprised looks as he climbed out of the front seat of the tiny car. Inside the small lobby, he bought a package that included a full detail. He sat in a corner seat, pulled out his phone and answered emails and texts from the office manager and the supervisor at Front Door while he waited.

Gaze down, he kept his ears open and listened to the conversations swirling around him. He heard two men, their heads close together, whispering about something that sounded suspiciously like a human trafficking operation. It wouldn't be the first time he'd heard of such a thing. No place was immune from that kind of horror.

In this area, those operations were run mostly by a handful of Asian gangs and a contingent out of Central America who brought in young girls and boys for the most vile of purposes. No Russian with half a brain would touch that dirty action. One whiff of trafficking and the frightening side of Nikolai would rear its ugly head. It was a side of Nikolai no man ever wanted to see.

Dimitri pretended to be busy but listened intently. Even though the details bandied back and forth made his stomach pitch, he kept his focus on the two men. These were the things Nikolai would want to hear. The large and growing Russian immigrant population was terribly vulnerable to trafficking, especially the desperate young women who dreamed of a new life here.

As the two men headed for the door, Dimitri became aware of a young man talking quickly into his phone. His Spanish skills weren't good enough for him to catch every word but he was able to understand enough of it. When he heard the Hermanos mentioned, he held his breath. Even though Johnny was on his shit list, he wanted to keep him from getting hurt.

"Dimitri?" Alexei waved him over. "Your girlfriend's car is ready."

He hadn't mentioned it was Benny's car but Alexei didn't need to be told. In the same way his relationship with Benny had spread through her bakery, it would have started the rounds among his circle of friends, too.

Tucking away what he'd overheard while eavesdropping, he joined Alexei at the counter and followed him onto the sidewalk. Alexei handed over Benny's keys. "Your girlfriend's car insurance is about to expire. My boys noticed it when they were wiping down the glove box."

Not surprised that she'd overlooked that detail, he thanked Alexei and climbed into the gleaming car. He considered driving it straight back to the bakery but his discussion with Benny kept going round and round in his head. He decided it was time he and Johnny had a little talk.

Pulling into the driveway at her house, he noticed the overgrown grass and the messy flower beds. Everything needed a good pressure washing. If she was really serious about selling, all these little things would have to be taken care of to ensure she got a good price and made a positive impression on buyers. He made a mental list of all the things he would need to tackle in the next week or two to help her get ready.

He used her keys to get into the house. It was quiet inside. Uncertain whether Johnny was armed, he cleared his throat and shouted, "Johnny! It's Dimitri! You here?"

While he waited for an answer, he made his way into the living room. He spotted the stack of envelopes on the coffee table. He shouldn't snoop but that didn't stop him from thumbing through the late notices, credit card and loan statements there. He could only imagine the kind of gut-gnawing stress this was causing Benny. To come home every day and see this huge stack of reminders? She was lucky not to have cracked by now.

"Johnny!" Dimitri moved to the foot of the stairs and shouted up to the second floor. "You awake?" He paused and heard nothing. "Johnny, I'm coming up. We need to talk."

Upstairs, he pushed open the doors, standing to the side just in case Johnny did something stupid, and searched for the right room. He found a bathroom first and then an empty bedroom, probably the one their grandmother had used when she'd been alive.

The stench of pot wafting from the door on his left confirmed it was Johnny's before he even opened the door. He glanced inside and experienced a rush of disgust at the pig sty Johnny called a room. There were piles of dirty clothes and stacks of cups and empty liquor bottles on the desk and the massive speakers. In the center of the bed, still fully clothed, sprawled Johnny. He snored loudly, probably sleeping off a hangover.

Dimitri stood at the side of Johnny's bed and nudged the arm hanging over the side with his boot. "Hey!

Johnny! Wake up!"

The kid's eyes snapped open. A split-second later, he bolted upright and swung a pistol toward Dimitri. Acting on instinct, Dimitri slapped away the hand and gripped Johnny's wrist hard enough to make him cry out. He stripped the gun from Johnny's hands and elbowed him in the chest, throwing him back on the bed.

Johnny groaned and rubbed his chest. "What the fuck are you doing, man?"

Dimitri glared at him and rendered the weapon safe, popping out the magazine and clearing the round sitting in the chamber. "What the fuck am I doing? What are you doing? You could have shot me!"

"You're trespassing! It would have been my right!"

"And what if I'd been your sister? Huh? What if she'd been in here trying to wake you up and you'd shot her? What then, Johnny?"

The dumb kid didn't have an answer for that one. Dimitri tucked the pistol into the back of his jeans and pocketed the single round and magazine. "I've been shouting downstairs for you."

Johnny sat up and threw his legs over the side of the bed. He rubbed his bloodshot eyes. "What the hell are you doing here, Dimitri? You can't just come inside my house."

"I can do whatever the hell I want, Johnny. Get dressed! You've got work to do."

"You think that just because you're fucking Benny you can come into my crib and tell me what to do? She's the one sucking your dick. Order her around, not me."

Dimitri took a menacing step toward him and pointed his finger in his face. "If I hear you disrespect your sister like that one more time, I'm going to knock your teeth down your throat. You should want to protect her reputation, not cut her down in front of other people!"

Johnny dropped his head with shame. He was smart enough not to push it. Dimitri wasn't joking. One more ugly remark about Benny and Johnny was going to need a dentist.

"What do you want, Dimitri?"

"I want you to get dressed and mow the yard. Weed those flower beds."

Johnny stared up at him as if he were the stupidest man in the world. "Why?"

Dimitri sputtered with frustration. "Because this is your home and you should take some pride in it. You want to sell this house and get your money? Then get out there and make it look nice. Help your sister!"

"Oh fuck off with that shit!" Johnny waved his hand in the air. "I'm so sick of everyone telling me how Benny needs help and how much she's sacrificed for our family."

"Did you ever stop to think about why so many people remind you of those facts, Johnny? Huh?"

Johnny didn't answer.

Dimitri sucked in a long, steadying breath. Shaking his head with disgust, he warned, "One of these days you're going to finally open your eyes and you'll realize how much Benny means to you. She's your sister, Johnny, and she's all you have left of your entire family. You better hope that it's not too late and that she hasn't finally given up on you when you need her the most."

Unable to stomach another moment in Johnny's presence, he spun on his heel and headed for the door. He doubted he'd gotten through to Johnny. He didn't know if anyone could. In the doorway, he paused and fixed Johnny with a cold stare. "I heard some *vato* down at the car wash talking about some trouble kicking off with the Hermanos tonight. Be smart and keep your ass inside!"

Johnny narrowed his eyes. "Man, what you do care what I do?"

"Benny means everything to me. I won't stand by and let you drag her down into the shit you've stirred up, Johnny."

With nothing else to say, Dimitri left the room and descended downstairs. Up on the landing, Johnny shouted, "Hey, you bastard! Give me back my gun."

Dimitri stopped at the front door and smirked at Johnny. He opened his arms wide. "Come take it from me."

Johnny leaned forward but thought better of it. Acting tough, he said, "Man, fuck you. I'll just get another one."

"Do you plan to steal another three hundred dollars from your sister to buy it?"

Johnny looked taken aback. "Whatever, Dimitri. Just get out of my house."

"Gladly," he grumbled and slammed the door behind him. He slid into the front seat of Benny's car and dropped the pistol into the glove box. After he returned Benny's car, he'd grab his truck and take *that* to Kostya. If anyone could make a dirty piece disappear it was him.

His jaw clenched and his stomach knotted. Dimitri couldn't shake the feeling that his problems with Johnny were just beginning.

CHAPTER EIGHT

Exhausted but feeling incredibly accomplished, I slid out of the front seat of the bakery truck and hopped onto the pavement. The bakery had closed almost an hour earlier and the street was mostly quiet. Marco and Adam climbed out of the front seat more slowly. Together, we rolled the empty trays into the back room to be cleaned and tossed the bagged garbage into the dumpster.

I stayed behind to do a walk-through of the bakery and found everything perfectly put away and shut down. Satisfied, I headed out the side entrance. While I searched for my keys in my purse, I heard a vehicle rolling into a parking spot behind me.

A quick glance over my shoulder verified it was Dimitri's truck I'd heard. The memory of what he'd done to me in my office made my tummy swoop. I doubted I'd ever be able to walk into that room again without thinking of Dimitri on his knees with his face buried between my thighs.

I didn't think it was possible for him to look even

sexier than usual but he did. Leaning against the door of his truck, he watched me intently. I shivered under his intense stare and turned my attention back to looking for my keys. I was just about ready to dump my purse on the sidewalk when Dimitri whistled softly. When I looked over at him, he shook my keys, the soft jingling seeming so loud in the stillness of early evening.

Shit.

He walked toward me slowly and stepped onto the sidewalk. Even standing on the top step there at the employee entrance, I was still shorter than him. He stared down at me, his displeasure evident in the tightness around his mouth. "We've talked about this before, Benny."

"I know." I cringed and waited for him to ream my backside for being so careless.

To my utter surprise, he tipped my chin and kissed me tenderly. His thumb traced my lower lip. "Please be more careful, Benny. No more rushing in the morning, okay?"

Relieved, I nodded. "Okay."

With a playful grin, he dangled the keys just out of my reach. "I should make you earn these back."

I laughed and lifted on my very tippy-toes to press my lips to his. "There's no one in the bakery to hear us this time. If you wanted to take me back to my office and show me a lesson, I mean."

He groaned dramatically and gathered me in his arms. "You little temptress! If I didn't have to go in to the office to sort out some scheduling problems, I'd have you face down over that desk in the blink of an eye."

My pussy throbbed as he described what he'd do to me. I licked my lips. "Rain check?"

He chuckled softly and nodded. "Definitely."

When he handed me the keys, I took them and made

quick work of locking up for the night. Dimitri's hands moved over my shoulders and down my back. He gave my bottom a little swat. "How did it go?"

"Better than I'd expected," I said and turned to face him again. "Lena and I had a quick chat about the very real possibility of me selling the building and moving locations. I thought for sure she'd flip out because she wanted to sell the underdog angle but she took it all in stride. In fifteen minutes, she had new talking points for me and changed the background story for the reporter. She found a way to spin it to our advantage. People really loved the food. Our likes on Facebook skyrocketed and so did the mailing list signups. I'm cautiously optimistic."

He ran his finger down my cheek. "I'm glad it went well. I wanted to stop by and see you but I got sidetracked with some other business."

"It's fine. You would have been a huge distraction anyway. God only knows I can't think straight when you're around me."

He chuckled. "I know the feeling."

Down on the sidewalk, I glanced at my car and did a double-take. The inch thick layer of dust and grime had vanished. The tires gleamed. I peeked in the window and found the seats and floorboards completely devoid of the usual flotsam and jetsam. I whirled on Dimitri. "Did you wash my car?"

"Not personally," he clarified. "I took it to Alexei's and had it washed and detailed."

I thought about the empty gas tank and reached for my wallet. "What do I owe you for gas and the car wash?"

Dimitri's big hand closed over mine. He pushed my wallet back into my purse. "It was my treat."

I decided not to fight him on this one. He obviously took a great deal of pleasure in doing things like this.

"Thank you, Dimitri. I really appreciate this."

His sexy grin warmed me through and through. "I have an idea or two how you can show that appreciation later tonight."

I giggled a bit nervously. "I'm sure you do."

He slid his hand along the back of my neck and lowered his mouth to mine. Our kiss left me tingling and aching for more. "I'll pick you up around seven. Ivan and Erin want us to join them for dinner at the Samovar. Have you ever been there?"

I shook my head. Feeling a bit sheepish, I admitted, "I'm not really a huge fan of Russian food."

Amusement glinted in his beautiful blue eyes. "Have you ever had Russian food?"

"Once, at this cultural expo thing at college."

He made an annoyed sound. "Well no wonder you didn't like it! That's like me going to one of the fast food chains, eating a taco and declaring that all Mexican food is bland and gross." He gave my hair a tug. "We both know that's not true."

"Fair enough."

"The food at Samovar is amazing. You let me order for you. I'll choose things you'll enjoy."

I don't know why I found the idea of Dimitri ordering for me so hot but I did. "Okay."

He brushed that sinful mouth of his against mine. "You should go home and take a nap."

"Why?"

His hand drifted down my side to grip my bottom. Pulled against him, there was no mistaking the hard outline of his cock against my belly. "You're going to want to be well rested for the night I have in mind."

Quivering with excitement, I could only nod. He captured my lips in another deliciously sexy kiss before walking me to the driver's side. Rooted to the spot, he watched me back out of my parking space and onto the street.

I glanced in the rear view mirror to see him climbing into his truck. A pang of sadness reverberated in my chest. I didn't like being separated from him, even if only for a few hours. My sudden attachment to Dimitri worried me a little.

But maybe it wasn't so sudden? We'd known each other for five years and had been close friends for most of that time. What was happening between us now seemed to be happening so fast but unlike a lot of couples we weren't starting from scratch. We had five years of history behind us and a solid foundation of friendship.

Pondering that line of thought, I turned into my neighborhood and made the short drive to the house. For the second time today, I was stunned by what I saw. First a clean car and now a perfectly manicured front lawn!

After parking in the driveway, I took a moment to walk around the front yard and inspect the work. The flower beds had been weeded and the sidewalk edged so nicely. Now all I needed to do was buy new mulch and some pretty annuals to brighten up the front yard.

"Johnny?" I called out for him as I shut the door behind me. "I'm home."

As I dropped my keys in the bowl on the entryway table and my purse next to it, I heard him come out of his room. He appeared at the top of the stairs looking much better than when I'd seen him this morning. "Are you going out?"

"Yeah? Why?" He gave me attitude. "You want me to do the laundry and scrub the toilets and mop the floors now?"

I didn't understand why he was being so snippy with me. Was he baiting me for a fight? I decided to compliment him on a job well done. "Did you do the yard? It looks amazing! Thank you."

"Like I had a choice! Freaking Dimitri threatened to beat the crap out of me if I didn't do it!"

"What?" It took me a minute process what he'd said. "What do you mean? Dimitri *threatened* you?"

"Don't act like you didn't know!"

Aghast, I insisted, "I didn't! I asked him not to get involved."

"Well he sure as hell doesn't listen!"

That makes two men in my life who don't listen to me, I thought crossly.

"Johnny, I'm sorry that things got ugly between the two of you. I'll talk to him."

"I guess I should get used to him pushing me around, huh? Since you two are together now," he added. "Maybe I should go ahead and move out."

"Don't be ridiculous. You're not moving anywhere."

"But we're selling the house."

My stomach knotted as I remembered our fight. "If that's what you want, yes."

"And the bakery?"

"Do I have a choice? This morning you made it sound like you were ready to sign the papers. I won't fight you, Johnny."

He narrowed his eyes. "Why are you giving in so easy all of a sudden? What's your game, Benny?"

"My game? What does that mean?"

"You know what it means." Anger and mistrust flashed across his face. "I know what you're doing! You're going to let that big, stupid Russian bastard buy your half of the business! He's going to hold up my deal."

"Are you insane? I'm not letting Dimitri buy anything. *He* wanted to make *you* an offer for your share but you've already gotten cozy with those jerks at UpStreet so whatever, Johnny! Take this shitty deal and let's be done with it."

"What you mean? Why is it shitty?" He came down the stairs like a raging bull and bumped up against me. "Do you know something I don't? You think I'm so stupid you can go behind my back and get a better deal." He slammed his chest against me, knocking me into the wall. "Are you trying to cheat me?"

For the first time in my life, I shrank back with fear of my brother. I didn't know this version of Johnny. The trust between us shattered, I threw up my hands, no longer certain he wouldn't hit me. "Johnny! Please!"

He went rigid and blinked. With a visible gulp, he stepped back. For an excruciatingly uncomfortable moment, we stared at one another. Finally, he growled with frustration and snatched my keys out of the bowl. "I'm leaving."

Stunned by the turn of events, I could only watch him stomp away from me. At the door, he spun toward me and snarled, "Tell your boyfriend I want my gun back or he owes me three hundred bucks!"

The door slammed hard and I jumped. Unable to move, I kept my gaze fixed on the door and tried to make sense of what had just happened. In a split-second, Johnny had turned so frightening. I'd never been afraid of him but now I wondered who the hell he was.

Where was the brother who had been my best friend? Was this my fault? Had I done something wrong? What had I done to push him toward those thugs and monsters in the Hermanos crew?

Heartbroken and feeling depressed, I locked the front

door. Johnny's parting shot rattled around in my head. "You mean you owe me three hundred bucks..."

* * *

When Dimitri pulled into Benny's driveway, he was pleasantly surprised to see the yard had been mowed. Johnny wasn't the lost cause he'd considered him. Hopefully some of the kind, sweet-natured kid he'd once been still existed under all that gangster wannabe bullshit. The idea of moving Benny and Johnny into a neighborhood like Ivan's bubbled to fruition. Johnny could make a clean break and start over in a better place.

While he waited for Benny to answer the door, Dimitri tried to picture what she would be wearing. He hoped it was short and curve-hugging. There was nothing he liked more than seeing her tight little ass and those luscious breasts. With all the dark corners of the VIP areas in Faze, he would have no trouble finding a secret spot to show her just how much he enjoyed her hot body.

The door opened but it wasn't Benny's smiling face that greeted him. She seemed annoyed and upset. His inner alarm clanged. *Proceed with extreme caution.*

Even with that slight scowl on her face, she looked beautiful. He made sure to let her know. "Benny, you look amazing."

"Thanks." She waved him inside. "I have to put on my shoes and switch some things from my purse to my clutch. I'll be a few minutes."

"That's fine. We're in no hurry." He shut the door behind him and took advantage of the better lighting to enjoy the sight of her in that little black dress. Simple but sexy, it fit her perfectly. She'd styled her dark hair half up and half down. His fingers itched to pluck free the pins so he could tangle his fingers in the long waves while she worked her lips up and down his cock.

Later, he reminded himself. They had the whole night ahead of them.

He noticed the way she roughly jammed makeup and her phone into her smaller purse. Finding his courage, he cleared his throat, "Is everything all right?"

Her hands went still. Slowly, she pivoted toward him. The expression on her face was a mix of pain and anger. "Did you threaten Johnny?"

Ah. Now he understood.

"After he pulled a gun on me and said something rude about you? Yes." There was no use denying it. "He could have shot me. He could have shot *you* if you'd been the one to wake him up."

Her eyes closed and it was clear she was fighting tears. When she opened them again, she blinked rapidly. "But why did you come here in the first place? I thought you were going to stay out of it."

"I was but I couldn't do it. I only came here to talk to him, to make him an offer on his portion of the business so you would be in the best position to negotiate with Jonah Krause. When I went upstairs to look for him, he pulled his gun on me and things...deteriorated rapidly."

"Deteriorated?" She scoffed loudly. "Yeah, well, now Johnny is convinced we're trying to rip him off. He came at me in a rage and—"

"He *what*?" Fury burned through him at the thought of that little bastard coming at Benny. He moved closer and looked her over for any signs of bruising. "Did he hit you?"

"No."

"Benny."

"*No*. He didn't hit me." Her gaze fell to the floor.

"There was a second there where I thought he might but he got control and it was okay."

"Okay? *Okay?*" Dimitri swore a nasty streak in his mother tongue. With a slash of his hand through the air, he commanded, "You're moving in with me. Tonight."

"Don't be so dramatic, Dimitri!"

"Dramatic? Johnny shoved a loaded gun in my face this morning because I woke him up. He came at you because you pissed him off. Do you really want to see what he's going to do next?" He couldn't believe how blasé she was being about all this. "Benny, I'm not going to stand by and watch him treat you like this."

Irritated, she shouted, "Why do you care so much?"

"Because I love you!"

She rocked back on her heels at his unexpected outburst. He swallowed hard at the realization that his secret was out and there was no taking it back, even if it was too soon to tell her such a thing.

Nervousness made his voice quake but he repeated what he'd said. "I love you, Benny. When I see you hurting, it hurts me."

"You love me?"

"Yes."

"Me?"

His brow furrowed. "Yes. *You.* I love you."

"But...I mean...I'm just me."

"Just you?" Shaking his head, he tried to find the right words. "Benny, you're amazing. You're beautiful and funny. You're the kindest, sweetest woman I've ever met. Every time I hear you laugh, my stomach somersaults. Every time you smile at me, I feel like I can't breathe." He steeled himself for rejection. "Maybe I'm not the kind of man you can love but—"

"You are," she interrupted softly. With a timid smile,

she confessed, "Dimitri, I think I've been in love with you since I was eighteen years old. From the first day you walked into our bakery holding that classified ad in your hand, I had the biggest crush on you."

He grinned. "Really?"

She nodded. "Yes."

"Why didn't you say anything?"

"Why didn't you?"

"It never seemed like the right time."

Blushing, she admitted, "I thought you didn't see me."

"Oh, I saw you, Benny." He wrapped his arms around her and drew her into his embrace. "I've been watching you and waiting for you so long."

When their lips met this time, the kiss was tender and full of such emotion. The rush of happiness that surged through him threatened to knock him off his feet. Benny pressed against him, winding her arms around his waist and flicking her tongue against his. She tempted him to drag her to the couch and make love to her but he muscled down those primal urges. He'd promised her a relaxed evening with friends and intended to give her just that.

They finally broke their lingering kiss. She smiled up at him, her eyes shining with unshed tears. There was no mistaking the depth of her love for him. He could only hope that she could read the same in his expression.

He ran his thumb across her silky pout. She playfully nibbled the tip of it. Laughing, he said, "Come. Let's celebrate."

CHAPTER NINE

"Are we ready for some dessert?" Smiling sweetly, Vivi refilled my glass of iced tea and Erin's water. She stood at the edge of our table and waited for an answer. I had to hand it to her. She was one hell of a waitress. Earlier, when Dimitri had been ordering for me, she'd carefully steered him away from an entrée featuring cabbage with the tiniest, almost imperceptible twitch of her nose. For sparing me that cruciferous fate, I was ready to give her a huge tip.

Dimitri ran his hand along my shoulder. "Would you like some dessert?"

Normally, I would say no, but tonight's meal had been such a good experience, I wanted to try something from the sweet side of the menu. "Yes." I glanced up at Vivian. "What do you recommend?"

"For you? Our Lady of Pastry?" Eyes glinting with mischief, she considered for a moment. "There's this really delicious sponge cake with layers of fluffy vanilla cream and apricots and raisins. It's so yummy!"

"You've sold me. I'll have that."

"Great." She glanced at Dimitri. "And for you?"

He gave a shake of his head. "Nothing for me."

Vivi turned to Ivan and Erin who sat across from us. The hulking fighter had an arm on the back of Erin's chair and gazed at her with such tender affection. For such a big, intimidating man, he showed incredible softness toward Erin.

Ivan also shook his head but Erin studied the menu. "Which one is the marshmallow cake with the chocolate? Bird's milk something..."

Ivan's lips twitched with amusement. He rubbed his thumb along the side of her neck. "*Ptchiye moloko.*"

Erin glanced up at Vivi. "Um...yeah. That one."

Laughing, Vivian nodded and backed away from the table. Erin turned to Ivan and bit her lower lip before trying to say the words he'd just spoken. She butchered them twice before getting pretty close to pronouncing it right. Ivan's eyes glowed with such love. He leaned over and pressed a sweet kiss to her mouth. "Good enough, angel."

He said angel with that thick Russian accent and Erin practically melted into a puddle of goo right in front of us.

Out of the corner of my eye, I noticed someone approaching. Nikolai Kalasnikov slowly crossed the restaurant. Dressed in that stark black suit and white shirt, he exuded such incredible power. His eyes weren't the pale blue of Dimitri or Ivan's but a stranger, greener shade. Unlike Dimitri's straw blond, slightly unkempt and careless hair, Nikolai's darker, nearly brown hair was neatly combed. Like Ivan, he had harsh tattoos on his knuckles and the backs of his hands. No doubt his clothing hid multitudes more.

There weren't many people who could wield that kind

of quiet, disconcerting power but Nikolai did it with such ease. My heart started to race as he drew near our table. I'd been in his presence only a handful times and only very briefly, usually quick run-ins as he visited Dimitri. I knew he had nothing but friendship toward our small party but I'd heard enough rumors about him to know I never wanted to be on his bad side.

He stopped at the empty seat next to me and smiled at his two friends. They exchanged greetings in Russian and Dimitri motioned to the chair on my right. Nikolai dipped down to brush a quick kiss against Erin's cheek before turning toward me. He grinned warmly before softly pecking my cheek.

"It's good to see you again, Benita." He smiled knowingly at Dimitri. "Especially in these circumstances." Nikolai took his seat. "It's your first time at Samovar?"

"Yes."

"I hope you've enjoyed yourself tonight."

"I have. Everything was wonderful."

"Good." Nikolai sat back and shot a playful smile Erin's way. "How are the Russian lessons coming along, Erin?"

"Vivi is quite the taskmaster. She'll have me fluent by Christmas."

Nikolai laughed. "I have no doubt."

His gaze skipped to just over Ivan's shoulder. I noticed the briefest glimmer in his green eyes as Vivi approached the table with a big tray balancing on her palm. Curious, I sneaked stealthy glances at his face as Vivi placed my dessert plate and Erin's on the table.

While she set down shot glasses in front of each man and a bottle of chilled vodka in front of Nikolai, he reached into the inner pocket of his tailored suit jacket and retrieved a lighter and pack of cigarettes. I was a little surprised to see them. I didn't even know if it was still legal to smoke inside an establishment.

Before he could light up, Vivian deftly swept the cigarette from his tattooed fingers and the gleaming silver lighter from the other hand. She shot him a look of consternation and dropped the contraband into the front pocket of her starched white apron.

I held my breath in fear for her. She'd just taken something from the most dangerous man I'd ever met. As if proving the point Lena had sort of jokingly alluded to last night while we drank wine and chatted, Nikolai simply pursed his lips and let it go.

With a satisfied smile, Vivi turned to the rest of the table. "Can I get anything else for you? No? Okay. I'll be back in a bit if you change your minds."

Nikolai poured the chilled vodka into Dimitri's glass and then Ivan's before filling his own. The men shared a traditional Russian toast before tossing back the fiery contents of their shot glasses.

"So, Benny, Dimitri tells me you're considering a new location for the bakery." He touched the table near my hand. "Is it all right if I call you Benny?"

"All of my friends call me Benny and I hope we'll be friends so yes." I picked up the dessert fork on the edge of my plate. "And, yes, I'm probably going to be forced into relocating."

Nikolai shot Dimitri a meaningful look. "That Jonah Krause is a slippery man." His gaze fell on me again. "You should make sure you have a good lawyer before you sit down with him to negotiate. I'm sure Yuri can recommend someone."

"Dimitri and I discussed that last night. The situation is slightly more complicated now so I don't think I have much of a choice when it comes to involving a lawyer."

Erin's expression morphed to one of sad understanding. "Johnny?"

I nodded. "It seems he's already been in talks with UpStreet Properties."

"I'm so sorry, Benny. It's the worst feeling in the world when you realize a sibling has done you dirty."

If anyone could understand how torn I felt, it was Erin. When I'd heard the gory details of the way her sister, Ruby, had started a gang war with her boyfriend, I'd nearly died. It terrified me and left me so worried for Johnny.

"I might be able to help ease the transition," Nikolai interjected. "One of my best customers is a real estate agent who deals mostly on the commercial side of things. He has a listing for a building that would probably meet your needs. It's not far from where you are now and in a growing neighborhood."

Growing neighborhood was realtor code for high rents and high sale prices but it was the only lead I had so I thanked him. He reached into the other side of his jacket and withdrew a pen and business card. After jotting down a name and number on the back, he handed it over to me. "He'll be expecting your call on Monday."

I noticed the way the blocky style of writing so neatly mimicked Dimitri's. To be bilingual was hard enough but I couldn't imagine doing it when there two totally different alphabets at play.

"Oh. Um. Okay." I slipped the card into my clutch. Dimitri gave my thigh a reassuring squeeze under the table. His handsome smile made my tummy flutter.

As Nikolai slid his pen back into place, he glanced at a table off to the right that had been getting louder and louder as the evening progressed. The rowdy group of men stuck out among the Saturday crowd here at

Samovar. Upon arriving, I'd noticed the restaurant drew a heavy local crowd and a lot of families. It was obvious the restaurant had a great deal of loyalty among the Russian ex-pats living in Houston.

But those guys? They looked like the typical businessmen on an out-of-town trip. They'd ordered an obscene amount of caviar early in the night and seemed to be draining vodka bottles as quickly as Vivian could replace them. Where our table had sampled and savored the best the menu and the chef had to offer, those men were pounding down the delicate meat-filled dumplings and blinis as if they were cheap fast food.

Nikolai wore a tight expression when his attention returned to us. I sensed he was close to having the men tossed out of his establishment.

The conversation at our table quickly turned to an upcoming fight. Apparently it was some kind of championship match and Ivan's fighter was heavily expected to win. The men slid into Russian so easily and without even realizing it. Erin rolled her eyes at me across the table and we shared a secret smile.

While the conversation swirled around me, I tucked into my dessert. As promised, it was perfection. The sponge was ever so moist and the cream light and whipped and flavored exquisitely. I wanted to run back into the kitchen and shake the pastry chef's hand…and ask for some tips on achieving such heavenly sponge.

I was reaching for my glass of water when I spotted Vivian approach the rowdy table. She plastered that sweet smile on her face but I could read her body language. The men were getting on her nerves.

My eyes widened when one of the men dared to put his hand on her lower back. She stiffened and pushed his hand away from her body. When she bent to slide a tray of drinks onto the table, the same groping bastard reached under her skirt. I gasped loudly and drew Nikolai's attention.

In the blink of an eye, Nikolai was on his feet and striding toward the offensive man. He moved so fast and with such determination. Beside me, Dimitri swore softly and rose out of his seat. Across the table, Ivan did the same. It was as if both men anticipated a brawl.

All eyes in the restaurant seemed glued to Nikolai now. He grabbed the man by the scruff and hauled him out of the chair. Nikolai bent his head and whispered in the man's ear. Whatever he said made the drunken lout's eyes flash with fear. He winced as Nikolai's fingers tightened on the back of his neck.

A moment later, the jerk stammered, "I'm sorry. I'm really sorry I disrespected you."

Face red with the humiliation of being groped so rudely, Vivi nodded tersely but didn't say anything. Nikolai shoved the man's head down low, bending him at the waist. With his other hand, Nikolai gripped the guy's wrist and pulled it into the small of his back. Contorted in a stress position, the man walked awkwardly in the direction Nikolai steered him. He used the man's head to whack open the double doors leading to the kitchen.

Slowly, the restaurant returned to normal. Dimitri and Ivan shot one another concerned glances but slid back into their seats. The kind, elderly gentleman who served as the host stormed over to the table where the other men sat in stunned silence. He slammed down their ticket and spoke a few harsh words. They practically jumped out of their seats and ran toward the front to settle their bill and leave.

When Nikolai reappeared a few minutes later, he ran a smoothing hand down the front of his shirt. His square jaw visibly clenched as he crossed the restaurant. Stopping near Vivian, he spoke softly to her. She nodded and the tiniest smile ghosted across her lips. I caught Nikolai wink at her before he made his way back to our table. Vivian followed a few steps behind him.

Erin reached for her hand. "Oh, honey, are you okay? Do you want me to send Ivan after him? He hasn't punched anyone in a few weeks. I'm sure he's dying to get it out of his system."

Vivian laughed and glanced at Ivan who playfully put up his fists. "No, thank you. I'm okay."

Her gaze skipped to Nikolai who looked calm and cool despite having just thrown a man out the back door of his restaurant. Apparently he'd earned some brownie points because she reached into her apron and withdrew the cigarette and lighter she'd confiscated earlier.

The grim line of his mouth lifted slightly as he allowed the barest hint of a smile to brighten his face. He accepted her gift but didn't light up. Instead, he held her gaze as he returned the lighter and cigarette to the pocket where he'd earlier stashed them.

Erin and I made eye contact. Her eyebrows rose ever so slightly and I knew she'd be on the phone to Lena the moment we walked out of the restaurant.

"Vivi, what time do you get off work tonight?"

Before Vivian could answer, Nikolai said, "She's off now."

Vivian frowned at him before glancing back at Erin. "Apparently, I'm off now."

Erin laughed. "Come out with us."

"Where are you going?"

"To Faze," she said. "It will be fun."

Vivi made a face. "You know Lena won't go there. Tonight's her only night off in weeks. I don't want her to be alone."

Erin made a frustrated sound. "I'll call her. She'll come."

"Well…"

"Vivi!"

"Okay. I'll come." She checked her watch. "It's going to take me a while because of the bus schedule on Saturday."

Nikolai said something to her in Russian and Vivian frowned. She started to reply but Nikolai gently cut her off. Annoyance written all over her face, she nodded. "Fine."

I glanced at Dimitri who slid closer as Vivi and Erin made plans. His hot breath tickled my ear. "Nikolai told her to have Sergei drive her. She didn't want to take a car but he wasn't asking."

Clearly I wasn't the only one dealing with a bossy Russian man in my life!

* * *

Half an hour later, Dimitri gripped Benny's smaller hand and led her along the edge of the sidewalk lining the night club. Ivan walked a few feet ahead of them, his arm securely wound around Erin and hugging her tight to his side. The line outside was so long it curved around the building. Frustrated would-be revelers were crowded tightly into the space between the velvet ropes.

When it became clear that their small group would get to jump the line, loud grumbling erupted from the crowd. Some jostling near the front caught Dimitri's eye. Quickly, he swept Benny in front of him and stepped to her right, putting his body between hers and the irritated crowd. Even with his best bouncers working security, fights often kicked off over the dumbest things. He didn't want Benny anywhere in the danger zone.

Kelly Connally, a former Marine and one hell of a bare-knuckle fighter, hopped the velvet rope and ran interference. The big bull of a man drove the rowdy, slightly drunken crowd back into line. They backed up quickly and quieted down. Dimitri caught the younger man's eye and nodded his approval.

At the door, Big V, the first bouncer he'd ever hired, held court. With his shaved head and barrel chest, Vincent didn't have to put much effort into intimidation. No one argued with him when he turned them away from the door. Beneath that frightening exterior, he was a damn good guy.

But he had a reputation as something of a lady's man. And there was one type of woman that Big V absolutely loved.

Grinning wolfishly, he grinned down at Benny. "*Oye, mamacita*, you're looking fine tonight."

Obviously uncomfortable, Benny stiffened but smiled up at the giant bouncer. "Um, thank you."

Fully aware the massive giant had a penchant for tiny, curvy women like Benny, Dimitri scowled at Big V. His conquests were legendary but he wasn't about to try his game on Benny. He held the bouncer's gaze and made sure the man understood that Benny was off-limits. He didn't want to spend the whole night worrying about Big V sending free drinks and swag Benny's way. She'd be flustered by it and wouldn't be able to enjoy her night.

Big V's eyes widened as he realized Benny was his. The bouncer lifted his hands in understanding. "Sorry, boss. We cool?"

With a stiff nod, Dimitri slid a protective arm around Benny's waist. She glanced up at him but he just shook his head and indicated she should follow Ivan and Erin.

When they stepped into the bustling, noisy club, Benny instinctively pressed closer to his side, seeking his heat and his protection. He dipped his head and brushed his lips across her temple. The club scene wasn't her scene but she'd never experienced it the way she would tonight as Yuri's guest.

With his arms guarding her, Dimitri expertly guided her through the sea of hot, gyrating bodies. The loud, thumping music reverberated off the walls. It was nearing ten and the place was on fire. The waving ocean of bodies throbbed with sexual tension and drink-induced lust. He didn't envy the security team tonight. They'd be earning their salaries for sure with this excited crowd.

Gauzy partitions and frosted glass marked off the VIP areas on the second floor. Yuri held court from the largest section, his hands on the iron railing as he stared out over his dancing, drinking clientele. He might have made his billions through ruthless acquisitions and sales of mining operations and oil and gas deposits but his first love had always been this.

Even when they were kids, he'd dreamed of owning an entertainment empire. Now with clubs in Moscow, London, New York City, Los Angeles and Houston he was doing just that. Yuri wanted to expand into other European cities and Asia but he'd take it slowly. Always cautious, he never over-extended himself and gave careful, deliberate consideration to every business move. Dimitri deeply respected Yuri's intellect and shrewd financial sense.

As they climbed the stairs up to the second level, Dimitri let his hand slide from Benny's lower back to her plump bottom. She glanced over her shoulder at him but didn't try to push away his hand. He gave her butt a little pat and winked at her. Her lips curved under as she tried not to grin but there was no way she could deny her reaction to his playful groping.

At the top of the stairs, he dragged her back against him and lowered his mouth to her neck. He placed a noisy kiss in the spot where her vein jumped wildly and touched his lips to her ear.

"Promise me one hour. If you're not having a good time, I'll take you home." He gently caressed her lower belly through the soft fabric of her dress. She shivered slightly and turned into his seeking kiss. "Then I'll make sure you have a *very* good time."

.

CHAPTER TEN

"So how are things between the two of you?" Erin slid closer to me on the sleek white couch so we could talk without shouting. Ivan, Dimitri and Yuri had moved to the other end of the VIP area right after Nikolai had arrived. Heads together, they seemed to be talking about something serious. The nosy side of me really wanted to know what it was.

Feeling totally comfortable with Erin, I confessed, "Dimitri told me he loved me tonight."

Excitement crossed her face. "Oh my gosh! That's wonderful. What did you say?"

"That I love him."

She threw her arms around me and gave me a hug. "I'm so happy for you. This has been a long time coming from what I understand."

"Apparently," I said a little sheepishly. "I didn't realize Dimitri felt that way about me and he didn't realize I was practically dying for him either. Talk about a hot mess of confusion!"

Erin giggled. "Sometimes relationships go that way."

She glanced back at Ivan and smiled. "Sometimes they happen hot and fast, and there's nothing to do but grab on tight and hang on for the ride."

"Do you ever worry that things happened too quickly? Even though I've known Dimitri for years, I keep second-guessing myself."

"Ivan and I happened fast. Probably too fast," she admitted, "but when you know, you know. I wouldn't change a thing. Is it always rainbows and ponies? No. We have our arguments but we love each other so we figure out a way to make it work." She squeezed my hand. "You love Dimitri. He loves you. Just communicate and compromise and you'll be fine."

From what I'd seen of her relationship with Ivan, they were totally open with one another. It seemed like good advice and I tucked it away for later.

"So...um...about your brother," Erin said nervously. "What are you going to do about that?"

I exhaled slowly. "God, I don't even know."

"You think he's making a mistake selling out his share?"

I played with the hem of my dress. "No. Honestly, he's the smart one in that situation. He's not letting his emotions drag him deeper into the shit. He wants his money while there's still money to be had. I don't blame him for that—but I worry. Constantly. I worry that he's going to do something really stupid with this money or that he's going to sign some ridiculous deal with that developer and lose everything."

"It's not easy when you have to assume a parent role with a sibling. Believe me." She rolled her eyes. "Ruby and I have gone around and around for years. At a certain point, though, you just have to stand back and say enough. You've made mistakes. I've made mistakes. We survived and we learned from them. Johnny will do the same."

Like Dimitri, she offered wise counsel. It was just so hard to think about stepping back from Johnny and letting him make his own decisions. I wanted to spare him all the hardships possible but maybe he needed to experience them.

"How is your sister?"

Erin made a face. "She's struggling with sobriety. I mean, you'd think being in jail would make sobriety easy, right?" With a sad shake of her head, she said, "I never realized how damn easy it is to get drugs in jail. She's been able to hold off so far but I'm really worried about what will happen when they move her out of the treatment area of the jail to the general population."

"I'm sorry, Erin."

She shrugged. "There's not much I can do but let her know I love her and support her. This is a battle she has to face on her own. I just pray every night that she stays strong and remembers why she's trying to stay clean. She has a whole life ahead of her, if she can just kick the pills."

Something startled Erin. She reached for her purse and withdrew her vibrating phone. She glanced at the screen and signed dramatically. "It's Vivian. Lena is outside but refusing to come in now that she's here." She rose and patted my arm. "I'll be right back. I have to go diffuse this situation."

Laughing, I reached for my drink. I'd had some wine at the restaurant and didn't feel like having a cocktail here. I'm sure the waitress thought I was nuts to turn down all the free top-shelf liquor at my fingertips in lieu of a cold, crisp lemon lime soda but whatever.

Erin made her way to Ivan's side and ran her hand up

and down his beefy arm. He lowered his head so she could speak to him. With a laugh, he slid off his barstool and followed her out of the VIP area. Like Dimitri, he could be terribly overprotective. Of course, after what the pair had survived, I couldn't blame him.

Though I was totally fine sitting alone and enjoying the sultry ambience of the closed-off section of the club, I didn't mind when Yuri joined me. The sinfully sexy billionaire had an easy-going smile and friendly air.

"I realize I'm no substitute for Dimitri but he's a little busy at the moment with Nikolai. You're having a nice time?"

"Yes. Very."

"This is probably very forward of me but I wanted to let you know that I'm simply a phone call or email away if you ever have any questions about your business."

My jaw dropped at his incredible offer. This man, one of the world's wealthiest, shrewdest businessmen, was extending a huge helping hand. "I don't know what to say, Yuri. Thank you."

"I'm happy to help. I remember what it was like to be thrown into my first business without very much experience. I made so many mistakes. I went bankrupt, actually. Did you know that?"

"No."

"Well I did. It was quite a humbling experience but it taught me something. What you're experiencing now? This contraction of the business and the cash flow issues?" He shrugged as if it was nothing. "It happens. You'll survive this dry spell and come out stronger."

"I wish I had your confidence."

He grinned. "You will someday."

Feeling more at ease with him, I gestured around the place. "You're quite the renaissance man, Yuri. Oil, gas, minerals and night clubs? That's a very impressive array of interests."

He smiled and waved his hand dismissively. "I'm not really that hands-on with any of my ventures anymore. I'm more of a project manager these days. What I truly excel at is hiring the best and the brightest to join my team. That's how you find real success."

I remembered Lena telling me all about her superior at the PR firm who stole her work and used it to get a job with Yuri. "I bet you have a lot of people try underhanded tricks to get on your payroll."

"Unfortunately," he agreed. "I don't often misjudge a person's character but it happens. Lately, though, I seem cursed when it comes to acquiring real talent. Take your friend, Lena, for example."

I narrowed my eyes, silently warning him to watch his step where she was concerned. "What about her?"

"I hired her old manager not long ago. He tried to work with the team I'd assembled but they don't gel. Apparently, he needs Lena at his side. She was his sounding board for coming up with brilliant, innovative ideas." He slid a little closer. "What do you think it would take for me to persuade her to come join me?"

"Yuri," I said his name carefully. "I don't think I'm the right person to ask about that, but if you want Lena so badly, you'll want to start off with an apology."

"For what?" He looked taken aback. "Did I offend her in some way?"

He seemed so genuinely distressed. I figured Lena would be upset with me, but knowing how hurt she was by the betrayal of her coworker, I decided to get in a little retribution for her.

"Yuri, don't you think it's a little strange that this PR guy you hired came to you with all these amazing ideas but hasn't been able to produce anything new since he joined your team? Did you ever wonder why he wanted you to hire Lena specifically? I mean, come on! His *sounding board*?"

Yuri's cheek tensed. "What are you saying, Benny?"

"You know exactly what I'm saying. You're a smart man, Yuri." Spelling it out for him, I explained, "That guy stole her ideas, the ideas she'd put together for 716 to keep them competitive with your new club, and brought them to you. He wanted to jump ship and he used Lena's hard work to get him there."

Yuri sat back and gazed at the far wall. Eventually, he said, "Have I really become that out of touch?" He swore in Russian. "No wonder she told me to go fuck myself when I offered her a job!" He cringed. "And then I really stepped in it by inviting her out for a trip on my yacht for the weekend."

I made a sympathetic face. "Yeah, she was pretty upset about that."

"Shit." He wiped a hand down his face. "You probably won't believe this but I panicked when she declined my job offer. I thought I could entice her to join the team if I showed her the perks of being in my employ." He grimaced. "Instead of treating her like the brilliant professional I know her to be, I fell back on my usual game. I tried to win her over by flashing money."

His body language spoke volumes. He seemed really disgusted with himself.

Touching his arm, I drew his attention. "Yuri, maybe you shouldn't try so hard."

His brow knitted. "What do you mean?"

"The yacht, the wining and the dining," I clarified. "That might impress a lot of women but it won't impress Lena. If anything, it's going to make her wary and suspicious. Where she comes from, men offer big, fancy gifts when they want one thing and one thing only."

"*Shit.*"

"Look, you two come from very similar backgrounds. Why not start there?"

Yuri considered me for a moment before nodding. "But first I owe her an apology." His gaze skipped to the entrance of the VIP area where Vivian and Lena had appeared with Ivan and Erin. "And I think this is my chance. If you'll excuse me?"

I shot him an encouraging smile. "Good luck."

Sitting back, I watched Yuri greet them. He cautiously approached Lena and extended his hand. She reluctantly shook his hand but jerked back a little when he lowered his mouth to her ear. Still holding her hand, Yuri kept her from retreating. Her scowl slowly faded. When she pulled back and gazed up at him, I watched her expression soften. She nodded and Yuri gestured to a private area where they could talk.

"What in the world is that about?" Vivian wondered as she slid onto the couch next to me.

"I think Benny has been playing matchmaker," Erin said with a laugh.

"No!" I spread my hands out in front of me. "Not matchmaker in the romantic sense. There was a disagreement of the business variety between them and I helped smooth it out. That's all."

"Sure," Erin replied teasingly. She glanced over at the pair, now deep in discussion. "They wouldn't be a bad couple."

"Definitely not," I agreed.

"I don't know," Vivi said cautiously. "Yuri has a certain reputation. She's not looking for a guy like that. More importantly, Lena can be *difficult*. She has a lot of issues with trust."

"Can you blame her? Her mom walked out when she was a kid and never came back. That dad of hers is something else."

Vivian agreed with me. With a smile, she added, "But if Yuri is anything like Ivan or Dimitri he'll be too stubborn to let her walk away from him. You know how these guys are. They catch the scent of something they want and they never let it go."

As if on cue, Dimitri and Ivan joined us. Nikolai remained at the private bar and nursed his drink. I didn't miss the way his gaze lingered on Vivian before flicking away to survey the small crowd rubbing elbows around us. Erin stood just long enough for Ivan to slide underneath her before plopping down onto his lap.

Dimitri took the spot Yuri had occupied during our talk. He curled some of my hair around his finger and gave it a little tug. "Having fun, sweetheart?"

"Yes."

"You want to stay?"

"A little longer," I said, thoroughly enjoying myself. Though I really wanted to get home and see what kind of exquisite pleasure Dimitri had in store for me, I liked spending time with our friends. After living like a social hermit for the last few years, I realized how much I'd missed this.

When Lena finally joined us, she sat down next to me and pinched my thigh. I yelped softly and met her narrowed gaze. She wasn't mad but I sensed I would hear an earful about this in the very near future. She wagged her finger. "You are a very naughty girl."

I feigned ignorance. "Am I?"

With an arm around Nikolai and Lena's drink in his hand, Yuri made his way to the couches where we sat and chatted. I spotted the way Yuri so expertly manipulated Nikolai into sitting right next to Vivian before he perched on the arm of the couch next to Lena and handed over her drink. I wasn't sure what to make of the relationship between Nikolai and Vivian. From the looks of it, neither did they.

Sitting there, surrounded by Dimitri's friends and mine, I felt so incredibly lucky. All the laughing and the smiling and the little jokes—we were slowly becoming a cohesive unit. I wasn't sure how it was all going to play out but I felt optimistic.

Dimitri nuzzled my neck. His soft lips tickled me. "One dance and then I'm taking you home."

He clasped my hand and led me out of the VIP area. I stuck close to his broad back, relishing the heat and strength of him. A glance over my shoulder confirmed that Erin, Ivan, Vivi and Lena were close on my heels. It seemed Nikolai wasn't the dancing type and Yuri stayed behind to keep him company.

Down on the dance floor, Dimitri carved out a space for our small group. It was Lena who started dancing first. Sultry and sexy, she swung her hips and threw her hands in the air. That long, dark hair swished around her shoulders. She owned that beat and made it look so easy.

Grabbing Vivian by the waist, she dragged her close. My eyes widened slightly at the sensual display put on by the two friends. Lena rocked against Vivian, her hand still on her friend's hip. Vivi laughed and visibly relaxed. When a guy tried to grind up on Lena's ass, Vivi put one hand on his chest and shoved him back. With one move, she established the boundaries. He was smart enough to stay put.

For a big guy, Ivan moved with surprising finesse. He held Erin close and cupped the back of her head. As they swayed together, he claimed her mouth in a demanding kiss. She clutched at his arms and rose up on tiptoes to tangle her tongue with his.

The music slowed to a thumping, thudding beat. Not really comfortable on a dance floor, I glanced up at Dimitri. He smiled knowingly and spun me around so that I faced away from him. Hands on my hips, he controlled my movements. The way he held me now reminded me of other, more intimate times we'd shared.

Closing my eyes, I relaxed under his strong, commanding hands. The low lighting and the packed dance floor afforded me enough anonymity to shed most of my inhibitions. When Dimitri's hands moved over my body, I inhaled shaky breaths. The rigid outline of his cock pressed against my back. Like him, I grew more and more aroused.

Hands skimming my curves, Dimitri nipped my earlobe. His mouth touched my ear. "I can't wait to get you home. I'm going to strip you naked and tie you up."

I gulped and tried to squeeze my thighs together to ease the pulsing heat between them but somehow Dimitri's hand had snaked under the back of my skirt. His hand prevented it. Those long, skilled fingers brushed the skimpy lace of my panties. I nearly came right there.

"Your pussy is so fucking hot already."

"Dimitri, please," I begged and silently prayed the dimmed lights wouldn't brighten. If we stepped out of the shadows, anyone would be able to see where he'd hidden his hand.

"Please what, Benny? Please take you home and strip you? Please tie you up? Please fuck your tight, wet cunt until you come so hard you pass out?"

"Yes. All of it. Please," I pleaded breathless. Turning my face, I touched my lips to his. "Take me home,

Dimitri."

*

Dimitri couldn't get Benny out of that club fast enough. Familiar with the layout, he took her out a side entrance that opened to the street closest to the parking lot where he'd left his truck. She scurried along beside him, her fingers tight around his. Craving her sweet mouth, he stopped every few feet to kiss her. She whimpered against his lips and pressed her breasts to his chest. The temptation to pick her up and take her right there against the wall of the building nearly toppled him. Somehow he managed to find the strength to keep it together.

At his truck, he wasted no time unlocking the door. When he picked her up, she squealed with surprise and giggled. The high-pitched sound traveled right to his aching balls. He'd heard her make that noise before, usually when he had his tongue on her clit.

"Wait," Benny panted and pushed at his chest, stopping him from dropping her on the passenger seat and buckling her belt. "How much have you had to drink tonight?"

He frowned at her question. "Not much."

She narrowed her gaze and studied him. "I think we have different definitions of what is or isn't too much. You had vodka and beer at dinner. I saw you drinking more vodka with your boys."

He started to argue with her but realized she was right. He *had* imbibed more than usual. It had been so long since he'd been out with his brothers, all of them together and surrounded by their beautiful women. He'd gotten too relaxed and had accepted too many free drinks.

Benny playfully walked her fingers down his stomach and slid her small hand into his pocket. The little temptress made sure to glide her fingertips over the rigid length of his cock before removing his keys. Biting back a groan, Dimitri let Benny have her fun.

"Put me down. I'm driving. You're riding in this seat."

He didn't put her down. Showing her who made the rules, he carried her around to the driver's seat and placed her in his seat. While he adjusted the chair's position, he informed her, "I'm *letting* you drive."

She rolled her eyes. "Uh-huh."

Laughing, he pecked her cheek and shut the door. She started the truck as he climbed onto the passenger seat. Even tipsy, he recognized that he was incredibly lucky to have a woman confident enough to tell him no. If she'd let him drive, he probably would have made it home safely but it wasn't a risk he was willing to take.

Watching Benny drive his oversized truck made him smile. Here in Texas it wasn't uncommon to see petite beauties like her sitting behind the wheels of jacked-up trucks. She looked good there, like she belonged—and she did. In his truck, in his arms, in his bed, Benny belonged with him.

At the bakery, Benny pulled into the parking spot he preferred. The moment she killed the ignition, he flicked off his belt and reached for her. If there had been enough room in that front seat, he would have flipped up her skirt and unzipped his jeans to have her. She burned him up, left him panting and aching with need so strong it rendered him insatiable.

Somehow, they finally made it out of the truck. The horn chirped when she pressed the lock button on the key fob. He was on her in a second, pinning her between his body and the truck. She gripped the front of his shirt in both hands as he devoured her mouth, stabbing his tongue between her lips and tasting the slight hint of lemon and lime still clinging to her.

"Inside," she panted. "We have to get inside, Dimitri."

With a growl of agreement, he swept her up into his arms and dropped her over his shoulder. She giggled loudly and smacked his ass. "What are you doing?"

"Taking you inside." He slid his hand up her bare thigh and under her skirt. With a hand clamped on her bottom, he hurried to the metal staircase and took the steps two at a time to reach his apartment. Remembering Benny had his keys, he reached back and wiggled his fingers. "Keys, sweetheart."

She slapped them into his hand. He fumbled with the lock and finally got them inside. Kicking the door closed, he flipped the deadbolt and carried her to the nearest flat surface—the dining table. Mouths mating, they tore at one another's clothing. He toed off his shoes and socks and pushed her pumps out of the way so he wouldn't trip over them in the semi-darkness.

The lamp he'd left on lent a soft glow to the room. With his shirt gone and his jeans on the floor, he tugged at her dress, ripping it over her head and throwing it behind him. Her lacy panties and strapless bra soon joined the dress. Naked and trembling with desire, she reached for him. Dimitri crushed their mouths together and kissed her until she whimpered.

Cradling the back of her head, he guided her down to the table top and dropped to his knees. In only his boxers now, he knelt at the table's side and dragged Benny's ass right to the very edge. She cried out when he attacked her sweet pussy. "Dimitri!"

He groaned against her clit and lashed the swollen bundle of nerves with his tongue. Already, she dripped for him. He could spend the rest of his life just like this, with his mouth latched onto her clit and her slick honey coating his chin, and never tire of it.

She thrashed on the tabletop and smacked the wood with her flattened palms. He swirled his tongue over the tiny nub and penetrated her with a finger. She moaned with such desperation and lifted her hips. Loving the way she responded, he slid a second finger into her slippery channel and started to thrust fast and shallow. Her keening cries grew higher and higher in pitch as he drove her wild with his tongue and fingers.

When she came, he held her down, forcing her to take even more of his tongue lashing. She shrieked and rocked her hips but he didn't let go. Tonight, he wanted her limp and breathless and hovering on the verge of passing out before he was done with her.

He sensed when she'd had enough, maybe too much, and slowed to a gentle flicking rhythm. She purred like a kitten and scratched her nails across his scalp while he lapped slowly at her tender folds. Petting her lower belly, he finally abandoned her pussy and peppered noisy kisses up her thighs and along the slope of her stomach. He captured her mouth in a long, hard kiss and pinched her nipple. Gasping, she arched into him. "Dimitri..."

Chuckling, he soothed her nipple with his tongue. "Bedroom?"

"Yes." She caressed his cheek. "I seem to remember you promising to tie me up tonight."

He spotted the glint of excitement in her dark eyes. His chest tightened with anticipation as he thought of the surprise he had in store for her. Grasping her hands, he hauled her into a sitting position and lifted her off the table. Without saying a word, he led her into his bedroom. Instead of the harsher overhead light on the ceiling fan, he chose the two lamps on either side of his bed. Their dimmer, softer bulbs kept the mood just right.

Still holding her hand, he dragged Benny over to the wide, deep closet. He knew the moment she spotted the contraption he'd installed that afternoon. Her feet faltered and she bumped into his side. "Is that—? Did you—? A *sex swing!*"

He couldn't help but laugh at her scandalized tone. Sliding his arms around her waist, he buried his face in the curve of her neck and inhaled the sweet scent of her perfume. The silky ends of her hair tickled his skin. "The first night we were together we played a little game. Do you remember?"

She nodded. "Red, green or yellow."

"Yes." He reached out and gave the kinky contraption a swat. The metal hooks and rings jingled as it swayed back and forth. "What do you say, Benny?"

She didn't even hesitate. Glancing back at him, she grinned with excitement. "Green."

CHAPTER ELEVEN

My tummy fluttered wildly as I stared at the black swing dangling in Dimitri's closet. A quiver of fear struck me but my curiosity was stronger. I'd read enough steamy romances to have an idea of how these worked. It always seemed like something that I would only be able to fantasize about, but like Dimitri's restraints our first night together, this was another fantasy about to come true for me.

He caressed my breasts and nibbled my earlobe. "What are you thinking, sweetheart?"

I loved the way he called me pet names. Smiling, I confessed, "I was thinking that you're making all these wicked fantasies I never spoke aloud to anyone come true."

"That reminds me," he said quietly. "I still need to poke through your bookshelves to see these dirty books you've been reading. I could use some inspiration."

Giggling, I melted into his warm embrace. Dimitri's hot, hard body felt so damn good pressed up against me.

Lust began to overwhelm me. Before I became dizzy with need, I asked, "Is this thing safe?"

He snorted and kissed my neck. "I made sure to reinforce the spot in the ceiling where it's attached. I also tested it myself. If it will hold me while I'm bouncing up and down, it will definitely hold you."

My concerns allayed, I asked, "So, like, how do I get onto it?"

"Like this," he said and swept me up in his arms. Gathered to his muscled chest, I relished his strength. There was something so intoxicating about Dimitri and this primal male side of him.

I tensed as he placed me on the scoop-shaped seat. Because I was so petite, it cradled me rather nicely. I relaxed as my fear of falling faded. A little flinch of panic gripped me at the sight of the cuffs dangling near my head and the stirrups with cuffs down below. Being trussed up in this sex swing would be quite a different experience than being restrained to his bed—but I couldn't wait to get started.

Dimitri, on the other hand, seemed happy to draw things out and leave me quaking with anticipation. He crossed to his bed and retrieved the supplies he'd set out there. Condoms, a hand towel, lubricant...and two things I couldn't quite see before he swept them up into his hand.

Eyes narrowed with suspicion, I gripped the cold chains supporting the swing and asked, "What do you have in your hand?"

"What? These?" He flashed me a smile and the contents of his closed fist so quickly I didn't see it all. "They're just some things I picked up this afternoon."

I gulped nervously. "What kinds of things?"

"Patience, sweetheart." He placed his armload of

supplies on top of his dresser so they were within easy reach. "Before I show you what I bought today, I want you to understand that I'm more than happy to tuck them away in a drawer for some later date. If the swing is all you want tonight, that's fine. We're in no rush, Benny."

I pulled my upper lip between my teeth and tried to still my racing heart. When he finally opened his hand, I nearly had a heart attack. The slim, short anal plug was simple to identify. Even though I'd never used one, I'd seen them online. A few times I'd been curious enough to surf sex toys on the internet but I'd never been brave enough to buy them.

The set of silver clamps connected to chains gave me pause. I knew what nipple clamps were, of course, but I counted four clamps and a strange clip attached to the long, thin chains. Where did all of those go?

He must have read the confusion on my face. Stepping close to the swing, Dimitri tucked my feet into their stirrups. With my thighs now wide open, he brushed his knuckles down the seam of my exposed pussy. "Two of these clamps go on your nipples. Two of them go *here*." He traced the lips of my sex. "This clip?" He delicately parted the petals of my sex to reveal my throbbing clit and gently rolled the swollen bud between his fingers. "It goes right here."

"What?" I squeezed my knees together in a flash, trapping his hand. "I don't think so!"

Dimitri chuckled. "Benny, it won't hurt. It will feel very, very good."

"And you know this because you have a clitoris?"

He granted me that one with an amused smile. "Fair enough."

An irritating thought popped into my head. "Have you used clamps on your other girlfriends?"

"Yes."

Jealousy burned through me. Suddenly gripped by the need to be just as cool as those girls, I lifted my chin. "Okay. I'll try them."

Dimitri tilted his head. "Benny, are you jealous?"

"No."

He tossed the clamps onto the dresser and slipped arm between my back and the swing. Pulling me up into a sitting position, he threaded his fingers through my hair and gazed deeply into my eyes. "Benny, I'm only going to say this once so listen carefully. Whatever I had with other women in my past, it means nothing to me now. You? This thing we share? It's eclipsed everything."

Seared by his intense gaze, I gulped and nodded. Hearing him say that demolished whatever bits of jealousy remained within me. He viewed me in the same way I viewed him. No other man could ever compare to Dimitri and he believed no other woman would compare to me. The heady realization filled me with such happiness I had to fight back tears.

After a sensual kiss that made my toes curl and my pussy ache, I drew my initials on his naked chest. Lifting my playful gaze to his, I murmured, "I want to try the clamps but not the other one. Not tonight, at least."

My decision made, I relaxed into the swing's embrace. Dimitri continued to tease me with his kisses and his masterful hands. His callused palms rode the curves of my body while his lips dotted my bare skin. He stroked and caressed, stoking the passionate fires within me until I felt sure they'd consume me.

When he sucked my nipples between his supple lips, I moaned and arched my back. The sharp, swift tugs drew the puckered points to tight peaks. He reached for the clamps and my belly flip-flopped. Oh, Jesus, what had I gotten myself into now?

But he was so gentle with me. Using his mouth and hands, he brought me such immense pleasure. When the first clamp bit my nipple, I inhaled a noisy breath. My pinched peak throbbed mercilessly at first but Dimitri distracted me from the slight discomfort by sliding his thick fingers through my slick folds to tease my clit.

Head thrown back, I groaned when the second clamp squeezed my nipple. My breasts ached now. Heavy and so incredibly sensitive, they begged for attention. The chain attached to the clamps dangled between my breasts. Another, longer chain arced off from that one and slapped against my belly.

Knowing what was coming, I closed my eyes and tried to breathe. Dimitri didn't apply the labia clamps or the clitoris clip immediately. The dirty bastard knelt down and used that wicked mouth of his to bring me right to the edge of a climax. He flicked and fluttered his tongue over my pulsing clit until I was nearly delirious.

I hissed when he applied the clamps to the tender lips of my pussy. It wasn't painful really but it felt...weird.

"What color are we, Benny?" Dimitri peppered ticklish kisses around my navel.

"Green."

"You're sure?"

"Yes." I stared down at the strange jewelry now adorning my most sensitive bits. The Y-shaped chain looked so pretty against my skin.

Dimitri stroked my inner thighs. "God, I wish I had some ribbon."

"Ribbon? Why?"

"I could tie some around each of your thighs and hook these clamps to the ribbon." He flicked the metal pincers squeezing my labia. "You'd be so perfectly open to me then."

I quivered at the very idea of such a thing. His fingertip swirled in the wetness leaking from my core. He smeared the slick nectar around my aching clit and then framed the tiny pearl between his fingers. I had only a split-second of warning before the clip slid down over the bundle of nerves. "Oh!"

His concerned gaze skipped to my face. "Benny?"

"Gr-green," I whispered. "It's just...it's more than I was expecting."

"Is it painful?"

"No."

"We won't leave this on long tonight." He bent low and brushed a teasing kiss against my clitoris. "You're so fucking sensitive here."

"*Ah!*"

Chuckling, Dimitri grasped my ankles and lifted them out of the stirrups. He brought my feet high in the air and cuffed them to the chains on either side of his broad shoulders. My wrists were quickly captured in his big hand and bound above my head.

Restrained and throbbing with desire, I whimpered. "Dimitri, I need you. *Please.*"

"Patience, little one." He stepped back and finally shed his boxers. That magnificent cock I loved so much stood erect. Droplets of pre-cum adorned the very tip of it. Like me, he was beyond excited. He snatched a condom from the dresser but didn't apply it immediately.

Holding the package between his teeth, he used both hands to stimulate himself. One fist moved up and down his ruddy shaft. He cupped his balls with his other hand, supporting the taut, heavy sac in his long fingers. In awe, I watched him stroke and fondle himself. I wet my lips and wished I was kneeling at his feet and opening my mouth wide to receive that massive tool.

As if sensing my lust shoot into overdrive, Dimitri finally rolled on the condom and moved closer. He stroked me lovingly before grasping the base of his dick and pressing the fat crown of it to my soaking entrance. The clamps and clips squeezing strategic erogenous zones left me shaking and pulsing. I felt more aware of my body than ever.

Instead of a fast, hard thrust, Dimitri entered me inch by excruciatingly delicious inch. The clamps tugging my nether lips apart made the experience one I would never forget. "Oh! *OH!*"

He growled in Russian and began to take me with deep, measured thrusts. Cuffed and overcome with arousal, I surrendered totally to Dimitri. Whatever he wanted from me, I would gladly give it.

And, God, did he give it to me!

An endless stream of cries left my throat. From long, slow thrusts, he gradually switched to shallow and fast strokes. His cock glided in and out of me, hitting all the right spots. The clamps holding me open and the clip compressing my clit kept me right on the edge of coming. My belly tensed and wonderfully panicky shudders rocked me.

Dimitri ran his fingertip over my clit and I moaned raggedly. Holding the chains in both hands now, he used the swing's momentum to take me harder and deeper. This coupling was unlike any other we'd shared. With the help of the swing, Dimitri was free to snap his hips and grind into me. He could use both hands to tease and torment my body because he wasn't using them to support his own body weight.

On and on it went until I felt sure I would just die from the sheer pleasure of it. A moment too late, I realized where Dimitri's fingers were headed. The clamps were both removed from my nipples. The sharp tingle of blood rushing into the depressed tissues made me shriek.

A millisecond later, the clamps down below were unclipped. He pinched my dusky lips between his fingers and soothed the raw burn with gentle petting. When he pulled his cock free from my body, I groaned in protest and rocked my hips, lifting my backside from the swing in a desperate attempt to draw him back inside me.

With a devilishly wicked smile on his face, Dimitri knelt down and carefully removed the clip. My poor clit pulsed unceasingly. It verged on painful but then Dimitri's soft tongue swirled over my throbbing flesh—and I lost it.

Screaming his name, I came hard. The rapturous waves of my unending climax crashed into me and dragged me down into the thrashing undercurrents of bliss. I couldn't think. I couldn't breathe. My brain on the fritz, I could only feel. Pleasure. Pain. More pleasure. So much pleasure.

As I trembled with strong aftershocks, Dimitri cooed lovingly. In that rough, rumbling voice I craved so much, he said, "My sweet, beautiful Benita."

Quickly and efficiently, he freed me from the restraints and lifted me up into his brawny arms. I wound my shaky legs around his waist, trapping his stiff cock between his belly and my slick sex. With fast, powerful strides, he made his way to his bed and sat.

Straddling his lap, I scooted along with him as he shifted on the bed until he was totally stretched out and comfortable. He grasped my bottom with both of his hands and lifted my backside. One rocking motion later, his rock-hard dick slipped inside me.

Impaled on him, I put both hands on his chest. I

breathed his name on a languorous sigh. "Dimitri..."

"Ride me, baby. Make me come."

As if he had to ask twice...

*

Dimitri didn't think Benny had ever looked as strikingly erotic as she did in that moment. The post-orgasmic blush turned her honey brown skin a lovely shade of pink. With her mussed hair and red, swollen nipples, she looked thoroughly debauched. She licked her lips and started to sway on his lap.

That tight, hot sheath enveloped his cock like no other. It was a ridiculously sentimental and romantic thought but Dimitri couldn't shake the idea that she'd been made just for him. They fit together so perfectly. Surely that wasn't mere coincidence.

She sighed his name again. Her sultry pout drew his attention. Rising up on one elbow, he tangled his fingers in her long tresses and stabbed his tongue into her mouth. She purred as he ravaged her, fucking her with his tongue and branding her as his.

Falling back to the bed, he enjoyed the view of her luscious, bouncing breasts. He cupped the supple flesh and brushed his thumbs over the tender peaks. She inhaled a rough breath but didn't ask him to stop. He felt her pussy flutter around him, confirming what he'd come to suspect about his woman. The sex kitten lurking within her loved a little kink—and he was happy to show her the way.

Watching her ride him with such passion stunned Dimitri. Just a few short days ago, she'd been so shy and uncertain with him. She'd learned to embrace her vulnerability and trust in his love. Seeing how she'd blossomed filled him with the strongest sense of pride.

"God, I love you." He tugged her down for another kiss. The moment their lips met, he planted both feet on the mattress and started to fuck her. He pounded into her, hammering her snug pussy as she clawed at his arms and let her tongue dance with his.

"Dimitri! Oh! *Oh!*"

"Come for me, sweetheart." He pleaded with her to let go, to give into the raging inferno threatening to sweep her away. "Come one more time."

Her grip tightened. Her breaths grew shuddery and shallow. Even though his stomach muscles burned, he didn't let up his breakneck pace. One more. He just needed to hear and feel her coming one more time.

With a shriek that could shatter glass, Benny climaxed. The feel of her sweet little cunt rhythmically milking him sent Dimitri flying off the edge of the cliff. He growled like a damn bear as cum rocketed through his shaft. The white-hot frissons of pleasure left him gasping and limp.

Benny fell forward against him. Her hair was plastered to his cheek but he didn't have the energy to push the ticklish ends away from his skin. Panting hard, he wrapped both arms around his woman and embraced her. The whole world could be ending right now and he wouldn't care. He had Benny and that was all that mattered.

She shifted slightly and pressed her forehead to his. Her gentle breaths buffeted his face. "Dimitri Stepanov, I really, *really* love you."

Smiling, he whispered, "Benita Marquez Burkhart, I really, *really* love you."

Giggling, she fell off him and onto her side. He rolled so he could gaze into those big, beautiful brown eyes. There was so much he wanted to tell her. He simply didn't know where to start.

But their perfect moment was shattered by the sudden, unexpected pounding of a fist against the front door.

CHAPTER TWELVE

In a flash, Dimitri sat up and moved his body between the woman he loved and the open doorway of the bedroom. The incessant pounding never let up at the front door.

"Please! Help!" A man's voice, muffled by the door, echoed in the quiet stillness of the apartment.

Dimitri jumped off the bed and grabbed Benny by the waist. He carried her into the bathroom and put a finger to her lips, preventing her from asking the million questions probably racing through her head. Voice barely a whisper, he instructed, "Lock the door. Get in the tub. Keep the light off. Do not make a sound."

She nodded and he kissed her, his lips lingering on hers. Tearing his mouth away, he pushed her inside and shut the door. The *snick* of the lock came a heartbeat later. He put a hand to the wood and prayed she wouldn't need its thickness to defend her from whatever was waiting on his doorstep.

He grabbed his flashlight and pistol from the bedside

table and quickly loaded it. After snatching up and hopping into his boxers, he shut off the light and moved with stealth into the living area. He killed the lamp there, too, just in case.

Flashlight in hand and pistol at the ready, he cautiously approached the front door. The desperate knocks hadn't stopped. He peered through the peephole but couldn't make out the shape on the other side. His gut twisting with anxiety, Dimitri flipped the deadbolt and opened the door.

"Dimitri, please..." Johnny's pained voice met his ears. A moment later, the young man fell into his arms. Something wet and hot spilled onto Dimitri's skin. The scent of blood filled his nose, the smell causing flashbacks to uglier days.

"Shit." Cursing roughly, he dragged Benny's little brother into his apartment and kicked the door shut. Putting down his weapon, he locked the door, smearing blood all over the silver fixture, and slapped on the light.

His face pale and drawn with pain, Johnny clutched his left arm. His shirt and jeans were soaked with blood. Dimitri pushed the kid's hand out of the way and inspected the nasty bullet wounds on his upper arm.

"Benny! Bring towels. *Now!*" Dimitri lifted Johnny up and carried him into the kitchen area where the tile would be easier to clean. After turning on the brighter lights in there, he placed the kid on his back and jerked his shirt out of the way to examine his belly. "Are you hit anywhere else?"

"My side," Johnny said with a groan. "Fuck. It *hurts.*"

"Of course it fucking hurts," Dimitri snapped back. "This is what happens to stupid little punks who play gangster."

"Johnny!" Benny arrived on the scene wearing one of

his shirts. Thankfully the shirt hung down to her knees and kept her modest. Not that any of that mattered right now. "Oh my God. Oh my God."

"Calm down, Benny." Dimitri hated to be short with her but the last thing he needed was for her to fall apart on him. He jerked the towels from her hands. "Go get my phone. It's in my jeans. Find Kostya's number. Dial it and bring the phone here."

She glanced at Johnny and hesitated only a moment before rushing off to follow his instructions. While Dimitri waited for her to return, he applied pressure to the wounds he found on Johnny's body. He had a bullet lodged in his bicep and multiple grazes down his arm and along his ribcage. Glass shards were embedded in some of the wounds. He had gashes and scrapes everywhere. Some were deeper than others. All of them needed medical attention.

As if sharing his thoughts, Benny slid down next to him and held the phone to his ear. "We have to get him to the emergency room."

"No!" Johnny spoke first but Dimitri agreed with him.

"No, Benny." He shook his head. "It wouldn't be safe."

"But—"

"No." He didn't like being firm with her, but like Erin who had stumbled into the middle of a damned gang war, Benny had no idea how this shadowy world worked.

She clenched her jaw but didn't fight with him. Not now, at least. There was no doubt in his mind that she would give him the tongue-lashing of a lifetime later.

Kostya finally answered. Sounding sleepy, he quickly perked up as Dimitri gave him the bare details in the language only they could understand. As always, Kostya came through for him. "Ten minutes."

Dimitri pulled his ear away from the phone as it went dead on the other end. "Kostya is on his way. He'll stay with you, Benny, while I take Johnny to see the doctor."

She gulped as she moved to her brother's side and cradled his sweaty head in her hands. "The doctor?"

He nodded and kept pressure on Johnny's wounds. "He's on Nikolai's payroll. I trust him to fix Johnny and keep his mouth shut."

"But why?" Benny looked so terribly conflicted. "Why do we have to keep our mouths shut? Why can't we just call 9-1-1 and get the police and an ambulance over here?"

"They'll kill us," Johnny interjected, his voice weak and breathless.

"Who?" She gently rubbed her brother's cheek. "Who did this to you?"

He shook his head, refusing to answer.

"Johnny, please—"

"No, Benny. You don't need to know. The less you know, the safer you are."

Dimitri found some respect for Johnny. For the first time in a long time, he was finally putting someone else before himself. If he told Benny details, she wouldn't be able to lie to the police who would be sniffing around soon enough. She'd cave under pressure and put a target on her own back. If the people who shot at Johnny thought she could finger them, they wouldn't hesitate to take her out to protect themselves either.

"Benny, hold these towels on his wounds. I need to get dressed."

She moved next to him and put her hands over his. He tugged his hands free and brushed a kiss against her cheek before standing. Hurrying into the bedroom, he grabbed clothes from the closet and shut the door, hiding the evidence of their amorous night.

He was pulling on his shoes when there was another knock at the door. Certain it was Kostya but refusing to take any chances, he picked up the gun he'd set down near the door and glanced through the peephole. Kostya's familiar shape greeted him. He unlocked the door and ushered his friend inside.

Kostya's gaze fell to the bloody smears on the floor. His jaw hardened but he said nothing. A man of few words, he didn't need to ask what had happened or what needed to be done now. He'd come prepared, wearing blue hospital scrubs and surgical coverings over his shoes.

His friend trailed him into the kitchen where Benny talked soothingly to Johnny and pressed hard on his oozing wounds. Kostya took one look at the bloody scene and nodded stiffly. "No problem, Dimitri. I'll take care of this."

Relieved to have Kostya's help, Dimitri grabbed trash bags and duct tape from the pantry. He secured the makeshift trauma dressings in place and wrapped the trash bags around them to keep blood from leaking out all over the place. Kostya addressed him in their shared language and asked for Dimitri's keys. After swiping them from the pile of clothing on the floor, he left the apartment, no doubt to secure a shower curtain or tarp over the front seat of Dimitri's truck.

Alone with Benny and her brother, he slid a bloodstained hand along her waist and pulled her close. He could practically smell the fear spilling off of her. "Kostya will keep you safe while I'm gone. Do whatever he tells you, Benny. I'm going to get Johnny patched up and stow him someplace safe." He glanced at her brother who seemed to be hanging on fairly well. "I swear to you, Benny. I will keep him safe."

With a terrified sob, she threw her arms around his neck. "Please be careful. Both of you," she begged. "I can't lose you both."

"You won't." He kissed her then, pressing all his love for her into it. His lips moved to her forehead. "It will be all right, *lyubimaya moya.*"

She sniffled and nodded weakly before turning to her brother. She gripped his bloody hand in hers. Tears dripped down her face. "Johnny, I love you."

He rolled his eyes and tried to make light of the situation. "I'm okay, Benny. It's nothing. You'll see."

Kostya returned to the apartment. Dimitri didn't want to prolong the awful parting of the two siblings so he lifted Johnny off the floor and carried him out of the kitchen and across the living room to the door. He didn't pause at the threshold to his apartment.

No, he kept moving. He moved with stealth and silence, hurrying to the open door of his truck and placing Johnny on the seat. The kid groaned in agony but didn't fight him when he buckled the belt around him. Checking both ends of the street and the parking lot, Dimitri saw nothing out of the ordinary. Hopefully Johnny hadn't been followed. If he had...

"No one knows I'm alive, man."

Dimitri threw the truck in drive and hit the gas. "You're sure?"

"Yeah, man. Benny's car? It's fucking toast."

"Toast? What do you mean?" He shot Johnny an annoyed look. "You were driving your sister's car?"

"I took it this evening, after our fight."

Reminded of how Johnny had come at Benny during their argument, Dimitri informed him, "You're lucky you've been shot. If you ever slam your sister into a wall again, I'll shoot you myself—and I won't fucking miss."

"I'm sorry." Johnny's whispered apology wasn't enough but it was a start. "I really screwed this up, Dimitri."

"Yes, you did."

"I saw the other car too late." Johnny's voice had a far-off quality. "You were right, man. I should have stayed inside."

"What happened?" Unlike Benny, he needed to know every single detail. "Tell me everything. I can't help you and I sure as hell can't keep Benny safe if you lie to me."

"This upstart crew is trying to push into our territory. They want to take the whores and the booze and the cigarettes we run. Our captains told us to go out and be seen. Street presence, you know?"

Dimitri grunted as he merged onto the interstate and his truck gained speed. For some reason, these street gangs wanted to be so damn flash and showy. There was a reason they had such a hard time rising above their small-time thievery and whore-running. Running a successful illicit business took finesse and secrecy, something Johnny and his cohorts lacked.

What they didn't lack? Violence.

"A white SUV turned down the street, passed right by us, and then they were shooting at us. The bullets were tearing through the glass before I even realized what was happening. I tried to get us out of there but another SUV blocked me in. I jerked the wheel and took the curb. I didn't make it far before I slammed into a building. The car caught on fire or maybe the building was on fire. I don't know." He sounded so confused. "All I know is I managed to climb out the windshield and get out through one of the big windows on the side of the building."

"And you left the car behind? And your friends?"

"They were dead. Dead!" Scared shitless, Johnny

started to cry. "I couldn't save them."

Dimitri wasn't about to console him. He'd warned Johnny countless times that this was the life of violence that awaited him. Now the dumb kid had seen firsthand the kind of destruction and hell the gang life created.

He sniffed and wiped at his face with the back of his hand. "Are you really taking me to a doctor?"

Dimitri frowned. "Why the hell would you ask me that?"

"Maybe you're thinking you can finally get rid of me and have Benny all to yourself. You just pop me in the back of the head and tell Benny I died in surgery."

Enraged that Johnny would even suggest something so dishonorable, Dimitri reached over and slapped the little bastard on the back of the head. "What do you think I am? A monster? I've never killed anyone outside the battlefield. I don't intend to start with your sorry ass."

"Okay! All right! I'm sorry."

"Sorry? You're an ungrateful little shit." Gritting his teeth, Dimitri fought the urge to smack him again. "Do you have any idea what I'm risking to help you tonight? Huh?"

Eventually, Johnny said, "Yes."

"And do you know why I'm doing it?"

"Because you're in love with my sister."

"Yes. I love Benny. I'll do anything for her, even if it means getting knee-deep in this Hermanos bullshit you've stirred up tonight."

"I didn't start this!"

"It doesn't matter, Johnny. You chose to be part of it. No one put a gun to your head and made you join this gang. You could have had a different life. You chose this one."

"I just wanted to belong to something."

"Now you do belong to something," Dimitri coldly replied. "You belong to a brotherhood of men who have watched their friends be gunned down by animals. You belong to a group of men who get to live every day with the guilt of knowing that they survived when their friends didn't."

Johnny sank into silence. Dimitri didn't care if he'd hurt Johnny's feelings. The kid had to learn there were serious consequences to his stupid choices.

"Did you see the men who shot you?"

"Yes."

"You'd recognize them?"

"Yes."

"When the doctor is done with you, I want their names. I want their descriptions. I want to know everything you know about them."

"Why?"

"If I'm going to keep Benny safe, I need all the intel I can get. You're going to give it to me."

"They won't come after her. She doesn't know anything."

"And if you're wrong?"

Johnny considered his query. "I'll tell you everything."

* * *

Kostya wouldn't tell me anything and I hated it. After Dimitri and Johnny left, he gently prodded me out of the way and got to work cleaning. I spotted the hastily discarded clothing on the floor and became so embarrassed. Not only had my brother seen the evidence of the wild sex I'd had with Dimitri but now Kostya knew. I hurried to pick up everything and carry it back to

Dimitri's bedroom. I found a pair of shorts with a drawstring that fit me fairly well. They were too long but I didn't mind. I just wanted my bottom covered.

The frustratingly silent man brought in a small red bag from his vehicle. I watched with a mixture of fascination and horror as he emptied the contents onto the kitchen table. Gloves, surgical booties, bleach, solvents, paper towels, microfiber cloths, trash bags, toothbrushes, grout-cleaning tools—the homemade "cleaning" kit had everything an underworld soldier might need to make evidence disappear.

Though Dimitri seemed to put a hard wall between his life and the shadowy, criminal world that Nikolai inhabited, he obviously knew where to go for help when things got ugly. Kostya was a mystery to me. I thought he was Ivan's driver but I wasn't sure. Maybe, like the doctor Dimitri had spoken of, Kostya worked on Nikolai's payroll.

Down on all fours, Kostya started to mop up my brother's blood. The sight of the dark, congealed mess made my stomach pitch. Desperate to do something, I asked, "Can I help?"

Kostya's gaze jerked to my face. His expression was almost comical. He shook his head. "This isn't work for pretty, young girl like you. Go to bed. Let me work."

"Go to bed? Are you crazy? I can't go to sleep. My brother and the man I love are out there somewhere. They're in a dangerous situation."

Kostya studied me for a moment. Finally, he gestured to the box of gloves and booties. "Put those on and come here."

It was hard, dirty and hot work. I tried not to think about how Kostya had become so proficient in rendering blood evidence neutral. The tricks he showed me left me a little cold and frightened of him.

Would he hurt me? No. Dimitri wouldn't have left me in this man's care if he was even the slightest bit unstable. Had he hurt other people? That seemed to be a certainty.

While I finished the last round of mopping with a microfiber cloth, Kostya took a black light, cleaning rags and a spray bottle outside. I could only imagine how much blood Johnny had dripped on the steps. I was too afraid to poke my head through the door to watch Kostya work in the dark of night. Instead, I attacked the bloody smears Dimitri's fingers left behind on the door and the light fixtures.

When it was done, Kostya rolled out a few feet of white butcher paper to make a large square and taped it to the floor in front of the door. He grabbed the package of wet wipes, gestured me over and pointed to the paper. "Everything off."

I blinked at him. "What?"

"Take it all off. I leave nothing to chance."

I hugged my arms across my chest. "I'm not getting naked in front of you."

He looked taken aback. "No! I didn't mean—I would never—I'll turn my back."

Kostya spun quickly away from. I hesitated before doing as instructed. He cleared his throat. "Wipe your feet and your hands."

Cold and naked, I picked up the wet wipe package and cleaned my fingers and toes. I dropped the soiled wipes on the paper. "Now what?"

"Go into the bedroom. Get dressed. Wait until I tell you it's safe to come out."

I scurried off the crinkly paper and dashed to the bedroom. I closed the door halfway and hurried to Dimitri's closet. The sight of the kinky sex swing where he'd ravished me made my cheeks burn. Had I really done that? The slight ache between my thighs from being thoroughly fucked by him reminded me just how good it had been.

I found another shirt and shorts to wear. It occurred to me that if this staying overnight business was going to be a regular theme I needed to keep a better selection of clothing downstairs in my office.

"Benny? You can come out now."

I left the bedroom and discovered Kostya wearing jeans and a t-shirt. His scrubs were piled on top of the clothing I'd just removed. Curious, I wondered, "What do you do with all this when you're done?"

"It's destroyed."

"But why do we have to do all this? I don't understand the need for such secrecy."

Kostya considered me for a long, uncomfortable moment. Finally, he asked, "What do you think is going to happen tomorrow?"

I gulped and shrugged. "I don't know."

"I do. The cops will be here. They're going to ask questions. They're going to want to know where you brother has gone. They're not the only ones who will want to know where he is. The people who shot him? They'll want to clean up that loose end. His own gang? They're going to be afraid that he's going to rat them out."

"But—"

"This is how we make him disappear. He was never here tonight. He vanishes. It's done."

Kostya's words scared me to death. My heart leapt into my throat. Vanish? Make him disappear? Surely Dimitri hadn't meant that he would send Johnny away when he'd promised to keep him safe. Ivan had managed to keep

Erin's sister alive and safe and in her life. Why shouldn't it be the same for Johnny?

Deciding that Kostya was crazier than I'd first suspected, I put some space between us and went into the kitchen. The biting scent of cleanser burned my nose. Desperate to stay busy, I opened Dimitri's refrigerator and cabinets and stared at the contents. The urge to cook or bake something couldn't be denied.

Kostya slid onto one of the stools at the small island. "What are you making?"

"I'm not sure yet. Are you hungry?"

"I wouldn't say no to breakfast."

I mentally inventoried the ingredients on hand. "Do you like *migas*?"

"I don't think I've ever had them."

I gawked at him. "How long have you been in Texas?"

"Seven years."

"And you've never had *migas*?"

My incredulous tone coaxed a smile from him. "No, but there's a first time for everything, yes?"

With a nod, I got to work. It didn't take long to slice and fry up the corn tortilla strips. I cracked eggs into the heavy cast iron skillet and scrambled them with the crispy tortilla bits. Dimitri still had half a jar of the delicious salsa verde Lupe had given out to everyone last week. I'd always preferred my *migas* with yummy *queso fresco* but Dimitri only had a small block of sharp cheddar. Either way, they would still be delicious.

I dropped a heaping spoonful of salsa on my plate but let Kostya decide how much he wanted. Not surprisingly, he let only the tiniest dribble of the rich, green sauce on his. I could see the uncertainty on his face as he prepared to take his first bite. I grinned when I watched surprise and delight color his expression.

"They're good, right?"

"So good," he agreed and dug into his late-night snack. "I've always liked breakfast for dinner."

I chuckled softly and stabbed my fork into the gooey mess of cheese and salsa and eggs. "This is actually supposed to be a hangover cure. It's pretty common on the late-night menus at diners and food trucks around here."

We fell into a comfortable conversation as we ate. In the back of my mind, constant worry for Dimitri and Johnny reigned supreme. The sound of footsteps on the stairs interrupted our chitchat. Kostya flew off his stool and moved to the door. He looked tense and ready to strike. The door opened—and it was Dimitri who stepped inside the apartment.

I relaxed at the sight of his handsome face but my stomach pitched wildly at the sight of so much dried blood on his hands and clothing. "Oh my God."

His tired gaze met mine. "He's okay, Benny. The doctor patched him up nicely. He's resting at a safe place. You don't need to worry. I've taken care of it."

Kostya spoke softly to Dimitri, the Russian words rushing from his lips so fast they sounded blurred to me. Dimitri listened and finally nodded. He started to strip out of his clothing. My eyes widened at the realization he was going to get naked right there but I remembered what Kostya had said about no loose ends.

"Let me get you some clothes."

Dimitri shook his head. "I'll shower first."

"Okay." I noticed his gaze lingering on the food we'd been eating. "Are you hungry? I can fix something?"

Totally naked now, he ran his fingers through his disheveled hair. "I'm more tired than hungry but thank you for offering, sweetheart."

Kostya wasted no time in cleaning up the entryway. He rolled everything up inside the paper square and secured it with tape before dumping the whole mess of soiled items into a bigger heavy-duty trash bag. The smaller bags we'd filled while cleaning went into that one.

Armed with his cleaning supplies, he headed for the bedroom. Apparently, Kostya was going to be very thorough tonight. When the shower shut off, I started to tidy up the kitchen. I could barely hear the two men talking. Every now and then, I'd hear the unmistakable squeak and whoosh of the smelly cleaning solvent Kostya kept in that bottle.

When Dimitri finally emerged, he wore only pajama bottoms. He took the dish scrubbing brush from my hand and shook his head. "It can wait. Let's go to sleep."

"But Kostya—"

"Knows what he's doing," Dimitri gently interjected. "He's almost finished in there. He'll do my truck and leave." He pressed a concerned kiss to my forehead. "We need to talk."

With a nod of understanding, I grasped Dimitri's strong hand. We made our way to the bedroom, passing Kostya in the hallway. The serious look on the other man's face told me his night was just beginning. Making him a hot meal seemed like the very least I could do for him.

When we were safely ensconced in Dimitri's bedroom and the front door had been closed and locked, I asked, "How much do we owe Kostya?"

"Nothing." Dimitri slid onto his bed and tugged me down with him. The glimmer of moonlight coming through the wide slats of the wooden blinds painted his skin with bluish stripes. "This is a personal favor."

"It's a huge favor, Dimitri."

"I know." He slid his arms around me and cradled me against him. I pressed my ear to his chest and closed my eyes. The sound of his heartbeat eased the tension gripping my gut. With a rough sigh, Dimitri said, "The police will be here soon. I'm not telling you the details of what happened tonight. I want you to be able to be as truthful as possible with the police."

My head throbbed as anxiety took hold. "What am I supposed to tell them about Johnny being here tonight? Kostya made it sound like I'm supposed to pretend I didn't see him."

"You didn't see him tonight. You haven't seen him since your fight. He took your car and he left. End of story."

"I don't like lying, Dimitri. It's not right. The police aren't the enemy."

"No, they're not. The people who shot your brother? They're the enemy and they don't play by the rules. Your world view is colored by right and wrong, black and white, but that is not the real world, Benny. The real world is shades of grey and sometimes, to survive and protect the people we love, we have to lie our asses off. Do you understand?"

"Yes." I snuggled closer as a chill of fear coursed through me.

Dimitri must have sensed my fear because he caressed my arms and kissed my cheek. "You're safe with me, Benny. I'll never let anyone hurt you."

"I know you'll protect me."

"But you're worried about Johnny?"

"Yes."

"Listen to me, I can't promise you that I'll find an elegant solution to this mess, but I'll do whatever it takes to keep him alive."

I shivered at the stark reality Dimitri presented. My eyes burned as tears began to well up and spill onto my cheeks. I tried to cry silently but I sniffed a bit too loudly and Dimitri stiffened.

In the darkness, his rough fingertips stroked my wet face. He rolled me onto my back and gazed down at me, his face only just visible in the moonlight. "*Lyubimaya moya.*" He kissed me lovingly. "Don't cry."

"I'm s-sorry." I felt like such a child as I wept but I couldn't make it stop. The fear and the pain and the uncertainty clawed at my heart. "I'm losing the bakery. I'm losing my brother. I'm losing everything, Dimitri."

After the awful turn our wonderful night had taken, I wasn't taking any chances. I slid my arms around him and held on tight. He shifted onto his back again and dragged me onto him. His fingers threaded through my hair and his hand swept up and down my back.

"Not everything," he whispered lovingly and kissed me. "You'll never lose me."

I silently prayed that was true.

CHAPTER THIRTEEN

A loud, insistent knock ripped me from the deep sleep I'd been enjoying. For a split-second, I didn't know where I was. The feel of Dimitri's big hand sliding up my arm brought back the night's best and worst memories.

"Easy, Benny," he urged. "It's only the police."

I rubbed my face and cleared my throat. "How can you tell?"

He laughed. "That's a knock they teach at the academy." He squeezed my thigh. "I'll go deal with this. You should probably get up and make yourself presentable. They won't want to wait long."

The pinkish orange hue of early morning sunlight colored the room. Dimitri didn't even bother grabbing a shirt. He left the bedroom, closing the door behind him, and answered the incredibly loud knocks. My belly trembled with nerves but I forced myself out bed.

In the bathroom, I quickly ran through my morning

routine. My hair was a wild mess but I managed to tame it into a low, sloppy bun. For the first time, I noticed the light scratches on my neck and the unmistakable love bites Dimitri had given me. I probably should have been embarrassed by the evidence of our lust-filled night but no longer cared who saw them. We were two adults. We loved one another. End of story.

Dimitri tapped on the door. "Sweetheart, when you're ready, there are two detectives here to see you."

I opened the door and stared up at him. "I don't know if I can do this."

He gripped my hand and kissed my cheek. "You can."

Dimitri practically dragged me out of the bedroom. My stomach somersaulted as I trailed after him into the living area. I felt sure I would puke—until I saw a familiar face.

"Santos?"

Detective Eric Santos stood just inside the door. He smiled at me. "Hey, Benny, it's been awhile."

"Yes, it has." I felt Dimitri's fingers tighten around mine. I glanced over at him but he wore that unemotional mask so I couldn't tell if he was jealous or curious about my history with the detective.

"Your girlfriend and I grew up a few doors apart," Santos explained. "I used to work downstairs in the bakery during high school and while I was at the academy." He looked a little sad. "I hear you're selling."

"Oh? Where'd you hear that?"

He shrugged. "People talk."

"At the moment, the plan is to relocate. We'll see how it plays out."

"Miss Burkhart," the other detective interrupted, "we've been here over a minute and you haven't asked us why we're here. Any reason for that?"

I managed to school my expression and muscle down the panic fluttering in my belly. "Detective...?"

"Carson."

"Well, Detective Carson, I have a young brother who thinks he's a gangster. When two police officers show up at my boyfriend's door this early in the morning, I just sort of assume he's done something really stupid."

"Where is he, Benny?" Santos arched an eyebrow. "We need to talk to him."

"I haven't seen him since yesterday. We had an argument and it got ugly and he left. He stole my keys and took off."

"Got ugly?" Santos' lips settled into a grim line. "Did he hit you?"

I shook my head. "No, it didn't get that far. It was an argument over selling the house and the building. That's all."

He didn't look convinced. Dimitri brushed his lips against my temple before he headed toward the kitchen to start coffee. He kept an eye on me as he worked and reassured me he was right there if I needed him.

Detective Carson pulled his cell phone from his pocket and tapped at the screen. "Is this your car?"

I moved closer and gasped. "What the hell happened to my car? Is that—was it on fire?"

Santos nodded. "It's lodged in an empty storefront ten blocks over, Benny. It's been shot up and, yeah, it caught fire. It's a total loss."

His information stunned me. Johnny walked or ran ten blocks after being shot and surviving that gnarly crash? "My brother was driving that car last night. Is he okay?"

"We don't know." Santos narrowed his gaze in suspicion. "You're sure you haven't seen him?"

"No. You would have found me in the emergency

room if he'd come to me." The fact that I found it so easy to mix truth and lies made my stomach churn. What the hell kind of person was I becoming? "Did you check the ERs around town? Is he in one of them?"

Santos shook his head. "No one with his name or fitting his description came into any emergency room in the city." He hesitated. "I checked the morgues, just in case. He's not there either."

"Well where is he?" I didn't know the answer so it was an easy thing to ask.

Santos shrugged. "That's why I got you out of bed at six on a Sunday, Benny. I figured if anyone knew where he was, it would be you."

I shook my head. "We aren't as close as we used to be, Santos."

Detective Carson turned to Dimitri. "And you, Mr. Stepanov? Do you know where Juan Burkhart is?"

Dimitri didn't miss a beat. He finished rinsing out the cast iron pan from last night and tugged the dish towel from his shoulder. "Johnny and I don't get along. I don't agree with the kind of life he leads. He wouldn't come to me for help. You'll probably want to ask some of the thugs and lowlifes he calls his crew."

"He's not the only one who has friends who are thugs and lowlifes," Santos grumbled as he jotted something down in his notebook.

Dimitri heard the snotty remark. Holding Santos' gaze, he said, "I'm sure you meet all kinds in your line of work, Detective."

Santos issued a short laugh and stuffed his notebook back into the pocket of his jacket. "Benny, I don't have to tell you how serious this is. This shooting? It could tip off a gang war. If you see Johnny, you've got to call me. He's not safe on the street."

"If he contacts me, I'll call you."

Santos stared at me. I could tell he didn't believe me. With a jerk of his head, he indicated his partner should head for the door. Dimitri got there first and smiled at them as he ushered them out of his place.

Pausing at the door, Santos extended one of his business cards to me. "You should be getting a call about the car soon. There's going to be a lot of paperwork so brace yourself, Benny. This isn't going to be a pleasant experience. Honestly, you probably need a lawyer. That building owner is going to want to sue."

I groaned and took the card from him. Could this morning get any worse?

Santos and Dimitri exchanged a look. Finally, Santos said, "You're friends with Ivan Markovic, so I know you're fully aware of the kind of shit these street gangs are willing to pull to save face. You better keep a close eye on Benny."

"I don't need anyone to tell me how to protect the woman I love."

Santos left without another word and Dimitri shut the door. As soon as I was sure the two detectives couldn't hear us, I hissed, "Did you know about my car?"

Dimitri rubbed the back of his neck and grimaced. "Yes."

"Why didn't you tell me?"

"Because you can't fake surprise, Benny. The way you looked when that detective showed you the picture? They know you're in the dark now."

"But I'm not totally in the dark, Dimitri." I exhaled raggedly and wiped at my face. "I just lied to the police. The police! I'm going to go to jail!"

He clicked his teeth. "You're not going to jail. You don't know anything. You haven't done anything. Hell, even Johnny didn't do anything truly criminal last night. He drove his car into a building but he was also trying to escape a barrage of bullets. He wasn't drinking. He probably wasn't doing drugs. And I know he wasn't carrying a weapon because I confiscated his yesterday. At most, he could get charged with reckless driving."

"Then why can't we bring him in, Dimitri? You heard Santos. He can keep him safe."

"Where? In protective custody? If Johnny survives to testify at a trial, what then?"

"I don't know!" I threw up my hands and shouted at Dimitri. "I. Don't. Know!"

His expression softened and he embraced me. "Come here, baby. I'm sorry. I didn't mean to upset you."

"It's not you. I just—I don't know what to do. I always have a plan. Lately, I feel like I'm screwing up everything. First, it was the business. Now, it's my brother."

"You didn't screw up the business. What's happened with the bakery is a combination of factors beyond your control. Are there things you could have changed? Maybe, but that's how you learn, Benny. We'll move the bakery and start over and you'll apply these lessons to the new venture." He swept his fingertips down my cheek. "And Johnny? He did this to himself. He's old enough to know right from wrong. Now he's paying the consequences."

"It's not just Johnny I'm worried about, Dimitri. What about you? What about Kostya? You two stuck your necks out last night. You helped Johnny because you love me. What kind of girlfriend am I to drag the man I love into my brother's gangster bullcrap?"

"Don't," Dimitri chided softly and traced my lips with his thumb. A teasing smile curved his sexy mouth. "You're the best girlfriend in the whole world."

I chortled and rolled my eyes. "Be serious."

"I am."

"No, you're being silly."

"I thought we could use a little silliness. The mood in this room has grown way too serious."

"There's a reason for that."

Cupping my face, he nuzzled our noses together. "Benny, everything I've done for you, I'd gladly do all over again." Before I could protest that he'd done too much and risked too much, he silenced me with one of those sensual kisses that made me a little loopy with desire. "Now, we're going to take a shower and have breakfast. Then I'm taking you home so you can get some clothes."

After being kissed like that, I couldn't think of a single reason to argue with him. Inside the steamy confines of the shower, Dimitri used those skillful hands and that sinfully talented mouth of his to make me forget all about the problems plaguing me. I slipped back into my dress from the night before but didn't have any clean undies. Of course, Dimitri loved the idea of me going without panties every day...

When we finished breakfast, I waited for Dimitri to grab his keys and wallet and phone. In the rush to make out last night, I'd left my clutch in his truck. As we came downstairs, I could hear the morning crew opening up the bakery for our short Sunday hours. I fought the urge to duck in and greet them. By now, they would have heard the news about Johnny. I didn't think I could face them right now.

Dimitri seemed to understand my hesitance so we took the long way around the building, ducking around the back. As we rounded the corner to the parking lot, my steps faltered at the sight of five Hermanos gang members loitering near a dark blue SUV. Always strong and so courageous, Dimitri didn't even slow down. He interlaced his fingers with mine and gave me one of those reassuring smiles that made everything better.

"Hey, uh, Benny?" One of the tattooed guys stepped forward but didn't dare get any closer. His nervous gaze jumped to Dimitri who smoothly moved just in front of me, ready to block whatever might come. "Uh, you don't know me, but I'm friends with your brother."

"And?" I didn't know this guy from Adam but the amount of ink on his neck and arms told me he was bad news. I probably should have been a bit more diplomatic but I didn't want him to know how much he frightened me.

"Have you seen Johnny?"

I shook my head. "No."

"You sure?"

"Are you calling my girlfriend a liar?" Dimitri took a step forward and they all stepped back. He towered over them by half a foot and had the bulk of so much lean muscle on his frame. These gang members were all thin and wiry. They couldn't take Dimitri in a fist fight but he'd be defenseless against a gun. I gripped Dimitri's hand tighter, afraid he would get badly hurt.

"No way, man." The Hermanos member put up both hands. "We're just trying to find our guy. We don't want any trouble with any of Nikolai's friends."

"Then get the hell out of here!" Dimitri gestured to the road. "You don't need to worry about Johnny. He's been taken care of."

The gangbanger's eyes widened. Dimitri's statement could be interpreted many ways. The guy didn't stick around to ask which one it was. He whistled and his men piled into the SUV and sped out of the parking lot.

Dimitri grasped my arm and tugged me toward his truck. He unlocked the door and basically tossed me onto the front seat. His gaze moved around the parking lot, as if he expected trouble. When he got into the driver's seat, he didn't even bother buckling his seatbelt before he gunned it and got us out of there.

It wasn't until we were idling at a red light that he buckled his belt and glanced at me. He reached for my hand and brought my knuckles to his lips. He kissed them softly. "I'm sorry I was so abrupt back there. I wasn't sure how to read that crew. I couldn't be sure they weren't going to circle around and shoot at us."

"God, Dimitri, is it ever going to be normal again for us?"

"Soon," he promised and eased on the gas as the light switched to green.

"What did you mean about taking care of Johnny?"

"What I said," he answered matter-of-factly. "He's taken care of. They don't need to worry about him. Hopefully, they'll tell the other gang the same thing."

"But you made it sound like he was, you know, dead."

Dimitri's hand tightened around mine. Regret filled his voice. "Benny, for all intents and purposes, Johnny will be."

My heart stuttered, and my eardrums throbbed. "What do you mean?"

Dimitri winced at my squeaked question. "I mean that Johnny probably has a hit out on him. Both sides of this mess will want to shut him up before the cops find him. They already know Detective Santos and his partner were at my apartment. You can bet on that. They'll watch you and hope you lead them to him."

"I wouldn't!"

"Not on purpose," he replied, "but it's easy to

accidentally let something slip, especially if he stays close by." With a shake of his head, Dimitri said, "No, Benny. He has to go away."

"For how long?" The thought of losing Johnny left me feeling so empty. My heart ached so badly.

"Forever."

My jaw dropped. "No, Dimitri!"

"Benny!" He said my name in that forceful, calm tone of his. "You have two choices here. Johnny stays nearby or he leaves. If he stays, they're going to find him and clip him. So you need to decide, *lyubimaya*. Do you want to visit your brother in another town or in a graveyard?"

When he put it like that, there wasn't really a choice to be made. Lower lip wobbling, I whispered, "Send him away, Dimitri. Save his life."

* * *

Hours later, Dimitri sat at one of the corner tables in the bakery's small café. He sipped iced tea, put out fires at Front Door and worked on scheduling conflicts. His gaze moved from his paperwork and laptop screen to café's interior.

His stare lingered on a framed photograph of Benny and the bakery employees taken after one of last year's summer softball league games. He'd watched her play a few times. She was actually very good. For someone so small, she could hit a softball like a powerhouse. It wasn't surprising that she'd gone to school on a softball scholarship those first two years.

His gaze skipped to the door and windows. Coming out to find Hermanos thugs in the parking lot that morning had rattled him. It drove home the point that it was time to move. Though he'd been toying with the idea for months, he'd delayed pulling the trigger because of Benny. He'd liked being so close to her and the thought of moving away from her had gutted him.

Now that they were a couple, he saw no reason to delay. Benny would probably be selling the building sometime in the next few weeks. He'd be evicted as soon as the new owners got the keys.

But more importantly he wanted a place he could easily protect. When he worked nights or if he accepted Yuri's offer to go into business together and had to travel, Dimitri wanted to know that Benny was safe and secure in their home.

Last night, he'd spoken to Ivan about the upscale, cloistered neighborhood where he'd built his impressive home. Despite that brazen home invasion, Ivan's neighborhood still ranked among the safest in the city. There were now more paid guards patrolling the grounds. Dimitri was familiar enough with the area to feel comfortable moving there.

Would Benny move in with him? That was the big question. She'd probably say no the first time he asked. He had some pretty good ideas for coaxing her to accept.

His gaze drifted to her sweet face. Her eyes were tired but she smiled and chatted with every customer that came through the front door. The Sunday draw seemed busier than usual. Maybe it was the growing sense that the end of an era was upon them. Or possibly it was the desire to come down to get the best gossip.

After they'd dealt with the nightmare down at the police department and her insurance agent, he'd tried to convince her to take the day off but she couldn't be persuaded. She'd made the point that working would keep her busy and her mind off Johnny. He'd given in finally but only on the condition that she let him take up residence in a corner of the café to work and keep an eye on her.

Their gazes met and held across the café. He smiled at her. She grinned, the sexy curve of her mouth a smile for him alone. He'd meant what he said earlier. He didn't begrudge Benny anything. He'd made the decision to help Johnny knowing full well that the blowback could engulf him. To protect her? To keep her happy and safe? Dimitri would brave those flames without a second thought.

Her gaze jumped to the door. An annoyed frown deflated her smile. He glanced over and spotted none other than Jonah Krause entering the establishment. Fighting the urge to jump out of his chair, Dimitri cast a wary eye on the man. Though he wanted to run to Benny's aid every time she faced something upsetting, he knew better than to undermine her in that way. She was a capable young woman. She could handle this.

And if she did need his help, she'd let him know.

CHAPTER FOURTEEN

I plastered a smile on my face as Jonah Krause crossed the bakery but inwardly I groaned with despair. Of all the days for him to come see me, it just had to be today!

He didn't have the slick look of his hired muscle, Carl. No, Jonah Krause looked like a soccer dad. His striped polo shirt and khakis lent him a friendly air but I knew better. I'd talked to my neighbors as they slowly sold out to this man. They'd fallen like dominos, each one taking a slightly lower price for properties than the next. I wasn't quite that desperate—yet.

"Miss Burkhart!" He grinned like a fool and extended his meaty hand. "I'm sorry to drop in on you unannounced but I wondered if we might have a chat."

"You do seem to love trying to catch me off guard, Mr. Krause."

His smile slipped fractionally but he quickly recovered.

"About that—I wanted to apologize for Carl. He misunderstood my directions. I assure you I don't conduct business in that way."

I fought the urge to roll my eyes. With a flick of my fingers, I stepped away from the counter. "We can talk in my office."

My gaze skipped to the table where Dimitri kept his vigilant watch. His eyes narrowed as I led Carl toward the kitchen doors. He lifted out of his seat but didn't follow immediately. I sensed he was at war with himself.

On one hand, he wanted to ride to my rescue and protect me. On the other, he wanted to let me do this on my own. In that moment, I realized how much he truly loved and respected me. Knowing it wouldn't be easy for him to wait out here, I made a quick gesture toward the kitchen. I hoped he'd understand what I meant.

Jonah glanced over his shoulder and spotted Dimitri rising out of his chair. "Is he your business partner?"

"You could say that." I led him through the kitchen. All eyes were on us as we traversed the space. Marco shot a nasty glare Jonah's way. It was instantly clear to the real estate developer what kind of a reputation he'd earned with his strong-arm tactics.

Inside my office, I pointed to one of the chairs across from my desk. I didn't shut the door all the way, leaving it half open, just in case. I wasn't sure if he would threaten me or not.

Jeanne Crane, the woman who had owned the knitting and wool shop on the corner had given me a play-by-play of her meeting with this man. He'd basically threatened to use her estranged son's recent sex crime charges to smear her and drive away her business. Considering the way things were going with Johnny, I wasn't going to take any chances.

"So," he said while plucking a pen and small notepad from his pocket.

"So," I replied and sat in my chair. "This is where we play nice and trade selling prices, right?"

"It's time you accept the inevitable. By the end of the week, I'll own the rest of the buildings on either side of this street. You've made your stand. It's time to go quietly."

"Or?"

Something dark flashed in his green eyes. "You wouldn't like the *or* option, Benita."

I refused to let him scare me. "Luckily, your two options aren't the only ones available to me."

His pen scratched across the paper as he glanced up at me. "Have you had other offers?"

"Yes." It wasn't a total lie. Dimitri had offered to buy Johnny's share.

He made a throat clearing noise. "I suppose I have the deep pockets of your *tenant* to thank for that."

I heard the way he added that lilt of emphasis to tenant. My private life wasn't his concern so I didn't open the door to discussing it. "Where the offer came from doesn't matter. It just matters that it's on the table."

"You know, this doesn't have to be adversarial, Benita. You give a little. I give a little. We come to an agreement and make this work."

I narrowed my gaze. "Don't you mean I give a lot and you give almost nothing? I've heard the way your *negotiations* worked out for my friends on this street."

"They weren't as tenacious as you are." He ripped the top sheet of paper from his notepad, folded it in half and tossed it onto my desk. "Let's start here."

My tummy clenched as I reached for the paper and unfolded it. The number written there was less than half what he'd offered me during his earlier overtures. Underneath the insultingly low offer was an address. "What is this?"

"It's the address of a building I think you'll like."

I lifted my gaze to his smarmy face. "A building you own, I'm sure."

"It's a nice fit for your business needs."

"And probably a nice fit for one of those kickbacks the city is giving out to real estate companies who foster friendships with minority businesses," I guessed.

He touched his chest. "You wound me, Benita. Don't you know how much I support the minority community?"

The slight sneer of contempt on his face made me want to hurl my ceramic cupcake paperweight at him. "Oh, Mr. Krause, if you only knew how much we think of you. I mean, you have been such a *good friend* to our community."

He snorted with amusement. "I'll give you a good deal on the lease."

I tapped the paper and threw it down onto my desk. "If you consider that offer a good deal, I'm not interested. And, anyway, I already have a lead on a new building. Nikolai Kalasnikov has put me in contact with a friend."

I saw his lips tighten at the mere mention of Nikolai's name. I'd name-dropped for that reason alone.

With a sigh, I mentioned, "I'm not the only one who has to agree on the terms of selling this building. My brother owns part of this business."

"Only thirty percent," he replied. "Little Johnny was kind enough to bring over a copy of the partnership contract. You let me worry about settling up with him. That price is for your share of the building."

I shook my head. "That's not the way I work. I want a fair price for the entire building. Johnny and I will settle up on our own."

"I'll give you a better deal if we do this separately."

"Why? Because you plan to screw over my brother by offering him peanuts?"

Jonah shrugged. "From what I hear, he's not going to need money where he's headed."

"You should check your sources. You've obviously heard wrong."

"Have I?" He settled back into the chair and propped his ankle on his knee. "Because I heard that your brother got caught in a drive-by last night and drove your car into an empty building a few blocks down the road. I also heard that the real estate company who owns the building plans to sue the shit out of you both."

The icy burn of dread spread through my chest. Mouth dry, I stated the obvious. "You own the building."

"Why, yes, I do! Bought it on Friday, actually. Hell of a coincidence and the damnedest luck, wouldn't you say?"

I wanted to smack that shit-eating grin right off his face but stayed in my seat. "I suppose this means you don't intend to move on this price."

"Oh, I intend to move down if I don't walk out of here with a deal."

"So what? If I take this deal, you won't sue me?"

"Probably not."

"Probably?"

"That building sustained quite a bit of damage," he replied. "I'd be lying if I said I wasn't tempted to sue you just to prove a point." Any pretense of friendliness disappeared from his face. "This game of yours? It's cost me a lot of money."

"Game?"

"Your principled stand? It infected more than one of your neighbors and forced me to go over my acquisitions budget. A nice, fat lawsuit might be a good way to inoculate myself against this sort of stupidity in the near future."

"I did what I thought was right, what I still think is right. This neighborhood could have been saved but you and those vultures on the city planning committees made damn sure none of us could get any kind of support for improvement."

"That's your problem, Benita. People like you? You're all stuck in the past. You think anyone gives a shit about buying homemade tortillas or hand-dyed wool or handmade furniture? Fuck. No." He practically guffawed at me. "People want their Starbucks and their Targets and their McDonalds. I'm here to give it to them."

Before I could even respond, he sat forward. "You should have been a good girl, Benita. You should have fallen in line, taken my first offer and gotten the hell out of my way. Instead, you chose to be a stupid, little brat about this—and now I'm spanking your ass to teach you a lesson."

Incensed, I crumpled up his crappy offer and threw it in the trash. "Get out."

He didn't move. "Take the deal, Benita."

"No."

"I'll take you to court."

"Go ahead."

"I'll take every last fucking penny you have. I'll ruin you. I'll make sure no one will rent to you and I'll blacklist every single one of your employees. I've got Immigration on speed dial." As if his ugly, racist threats weren't enough, he added, "And your brother? I'll get my private investigators to smoke him out so fast your head will spin. I'm sure the guys who shot at him last night would love to get their hands on him."

The door to my office slammed into the wall. Dimitri appeared in the doorway, filling the wide space with his broad shoulders and impressive height. His furious stare fixed right on Jonah Krause. "I think you're done here."

"I'll say when I'm fucking done."

My eyes widened at Jonah's brave reply. Dimitri actually cracked a smile—but it was a dangerous one. "I can assure you, Mr. Krause, that if I leave this doorway, you'll be screaming that you're done in less than ten seconds."

Visibly flustered, Jonah rose from his chair. He pointed a finger at me. "If I walk out that door, I'm calling my lawyer."

"I guess it's a good thing I have mine on speed dial." I didn't but it was the snappiest comeback I had at the moment.

He glared at me and then Dimitri. "You two are playing with fire. You won't like the way this ends."

Dimitri stepped aside just enough to clear a tiny space for Jonah to exit my office. His stony stare unsettled the real estate developer who moved so quickly I thought his ass was on fire. Dimitri's gaze remained trained in the hallway. I saw him lift two hands to his eyes and make a gesture. I could only assume that one of the guys in the kitchen was going to follow Jonah out of the building.

With a long, slow inhale, Dimitri turned to face me. Rage was etched into his handsome face but the harsh lines faded when our gazes met. "I'm sorry."

I blinked. "What? Why?"

"I shouldn't have slammed open the door like that and thrown him out. You were handling it so well but I simply—I lost it when he started to talk to you like that."

I stood and crossed the distance between us. Sliding my arms around his waist, I pressed my cheek to his chest. "It's fine. I'm glad you threw him out." Disgusted, I asked, "Can you believe that crap? Threatening me with Immigration? Like everyone who is brown in this town is illegal or something! What a jackass!"

"We have to get a lawyer. Immediately."

"I have to get a lawyer," I corrected.

Dimitri cupped my face and tipped my chin. He peered down at me with such love in his pale blue eyes. "I told you we're partners. *We* need a lawyer. I'm going to see Yuri right now. He'll steer us in the right direction."

"Do you think Jonah will really do everything he threatened?"

"Yes." He didn't even hesitate before answering. "I think he's going to make your life a living hell."

I groaned and buried my face against him. "I should have just taken the lowball offer and sucked it up. I've really screwed everything up again."

"No amount of money is worth that abuse. He's a pig." Dimitri sounded like he wanted to spit on the very floor the man had walked.

"A well-connected pig," I clarified. "I'm worried about Johnny. What if he really does have a private investigator that can find him?"

"You don't need to worry about that. Johnny's safety won't be an issue after tonight."

I reeled back in shock. "Tonight?"

Dimitri reluctantly nodded. "I have plans in motion. If everything works out, he'll be out of Houston and far, far away by sunrise."

Emotions overwhelmed me. "Will I get to see him again?"

"Of course, sweetheart." Dimitri kissed me. "I wouldn't rob you of the chance to say goodbye." His lips lingered on mine. "Kostya should be here any minute.

He's going to keep an eye on you while I run some quick errands. You are not to leave this bakery, understood? Kostya is going to be your shadow."

"I understand."

"He'll bring you to me later."

"And I'll see Johnny?"

He nodded. "You can say goodbye."

* * *

Dimitri slipped out of the back seat of the private car Yuri had arranged for him. On habit, he checked the area around the upscale marina. The driver had assured him they weren't being followed, but with Johnny's location so desired by so many people, Dimitri didn't want to take chances.

Certain he was in the clear, he closed the door and headed for the private slip at the far end of the marina where Yuri kept one of his so-called baby yachts. This one was only one hundred feet or so long but no less ostentatious than the mega yachts Yuri kept moored in various parts of the world. This one he used to entertain locally and to make short trips around the Gulf of Mexico and the Caribbean. Sometimes he even rented or loaned it out to friends of friends.

Last night, when Dimitri had been desperate to find a place to stow Johnny, Yuri hadn't thought twice about offering his boat. He'd arranged it all, sending a driver and guard to bring Johnny down to the private marina outside Galveston. Dimitri hoped Johnny had been a good guest and not caused any problems. Yuri had gone above and beyond the call of friendship this time.

One of the crew members spotted and welcomed him onto the yacht. He was led down into the luxurious living space. Yuri sat in a comfortable chair and listened to the news. There were two laptops and three cell phones surrounding him. How he could concentrate like that, Dimitri would never understand.

"I thought the whole point of having a yacht was to relax?"

Yuri laughed and closed his laptops. "The world markets never really close, Dimitri." He shifted the cell phones to a side table. "Have you come to visit the prisoner?"

"Has he been difficult?"

Yuri shook his head. "He's been a model captive. I haven't heard one single complaint." He stood and gestured for Dimitri to follow. "Of course, that could be from all the pain killers they're pumping into him."

He trailed Yuri to one of the roomy cabins. Propped up in bed, Johnny rested on his right side and watched a movie on the flat screen mounted on the opposite wall. Someone had rigged up a temporary hook to hold the bag of clear fluid attached to his IV.

Johnny looked relieved to see him. "How's Benny?"

"She's fine." Dimitri came into the room and sat in the empty chair next to the bed. "She misses you but I promised her she could see you tonight. How are you feeling?"

"Like shit, man." Johnny grimaced as he pointed to his bandaged arm and side. "They really fucked me up, Dimitri."

"You were lucky, Johnny. They could have killed you."

Wearing an embarrassed expression, he asked, "Does Benny know about the car?"

He nodded. "Two detectives were at my door around sunrise. One of them knows you two well."

Johnny's eyebrows drew together. "Wait. Eric Santos?"

"That's the one."

"Was he hard on Benny?"

"No."

"Is she really mad about the car?"

Behind them, Yuri snorted. Dimitri ignored his friend's subtle outburst. "She wasn't happy about it. There's a bigger issue now. That building you damaged? It belongs to Jonah Krause."

Johnny paled. "You're joking."

"I wouldn't joke about that. He came by the bakery to try and force Benny to sign an awful deal for the building. When she turned it down, he threatened to sue over the building and ruin her chances of ever opening the bakery again. He says he's got a private investigator looking for you."

Yuri swore softly. "Then we'll move him tonight."

Dimitri glanced at his friend. "Agreed."

"Move me? Where?" Johnny's worried gaze jumped from Dimitri's face to Yuri's and back again. "How long are you sending me away?"

"This isn't the kind of thing that blows over in a few months, Johnny. Your crew was at the bakery this morning trying to get answers out of Benny. I told them you'd been taken care of, Johnny."

"So you're sending me away forever?"

"Do you want to take your chances on the streets? Think carefully, Johnny. If you leave this boat, you're on your own. I'll do whatever it takes to protect Benny, even if that means taking her out of Houston to some place where she doesn't have to look over her shoulder."

"I don't want Benny to get hurt. I never wanted Benny to get in trouble." Johnny rubbed his face. "I don't know what to do, Dimitri."

Yuri cleared his throat. "Can you swim?"

Johnny frowned. "What?"

"Can you swim?"

"Yes." He pointed to the sling supporting his arm. "When I'm not in this."

"Are you a hard worker?"

"I can be."

"Can be or will be?"

Johnny swallowed. "I will be."

Yuri caught Dimitri's eye. "I'll give him a trial run on the yacht."

"You want me to work on your boat?" Johnny looked taken aback. "I've never worked on a boat. I wouldn't know what to do."

"You'll be on the bottom rung, Johnny. Think lots of housekeeping and errand running. If you do a good job, there's room for advancement." Yuri lifted a warning finger. "If I get one report of any theft or criminal bullshit, I'll have them throw you overboard. Understood?"

Johnny nodded weakly. "Yes, sir."

"Good." Yuri turned for the door. "I'm going to see if we can get someone out here to cover up that shit on his neck."

As Yuri disappeared, Johnny touched the gang tattoo marking him as an Hermano. Regret flashed across his face. "You think I'll ever be able to leave this behind?"

Dimitri felt such strong compassion toward Johnny in that moment. For the first time in such a very long time, he sensed Johnny actually understood the enormity of his unwise decisions.

"Listen, you know Ivan, right? He's like you. He did some really stupid shit when he was younger. He paid for those mistakes. Hell, in some ways, he's still paying for those mistakes but he made a clean break, Johnny. He said no more and he stuck to that. Even when it came to defending and protecting Erin, he didn't cross that line. He toed right up against it but never stepped across."

Johnny blew out a noisy breath. "I don't know if I'm that strong."

"You are. You have to be. There's no other choice." He gripped Johnny's hand and drew his full attention. "This is a once in a lifetime chance. You get to start over, Johnny. You're getting out of a gang without having to kill someone. Don't fuck this up."

"I won't." He said it as if he were swearing to it.

Dimitri released Johnny's hand. "This won't be so bad. You'll get to travel and see the world and make money doing it."

"Unless I get picked up on an outstanding warrant," Johnny interjected. "What if Santos gets the district attorney to put out a witness warrant for me? I knew a guy who had one of those. He got picked up crossing the border at Laredo."

"Yuri and I talked about this last night. If something like that happens, you'll have to stay away from countries with extradition treaties." Dimitri waved his hand. "Don't worry about it. The crew will take care of you. Believe me. You're not the first person to choose a life at sea to outrun a shady past."

"And what about keeping Benny safe? Ivan managed to keep Erin and Ruby alive because he was able to give back what was taken and negotiate a peace. If you send me away, you won't have anything to offer."

"I don't need to offer them anything. They know who stands in my corner—he's a hell of a lot more terrifying than anything they could possibly use to threaten us."

Johnny's face showed some surprise. "So it's us now?"

Dimitri's stare didn't waver. "I love Benny. I'm not

going anywhere unless she tells me it's over."

Johnny returned his stare. "She won't. She's loved you a long time." His jaw tightened and he narrowed his eyes. "You better not do her wrong, Dimitri. I swear to God I'll swim my ass back to Houston if you hurt her. She needs one man in her life she can count on and that obviously isn't me."

He heard the pain in Johnny's voice. It was good that Johnny's newfound self-awareness allowed him to see how badly he'd managed things over the last year. Dimitri hoped this was the start of a new outlook for the kid.

"You don't have to worry about Benny. I'll take care of her."

"Get her out of that house, *cuñado*."

Dimitri laughed. "Oh, we're family now, huh?"

Johnny gave a one-shouldered shrug. "Let's be real, Dimitri. You're going to marry her. I may as well get used to calling you my brother-in-law, right?"

Dimitri nodded. "Yes."

"I'm serious, Dimitri. Get her out of that damn house. It's nothing but memories. It's not healthy for her. She's got to learn to move on from all that. Mom's gone. Dad's gone. Abuelito and Abuelita are gone. That house is full of ghosts—and the bakery building, too."

Dimitri sat back. "Is that what this is all about? You wanted to force her to sell to save her from—what?"

"She's going to work herself to death." Johnny shook his head. "She's so fucking stubborn. When Mom and Dad were killed in that wreck, she wouldn't let anyone else do the funeral arrangements. She was *fifteen*! Grandpa dropped dead of a heart attack in the bakery and who was there doing CPR to try to save him until the paramedics showed up? Benny! And then when Abuelita was dying of cancer, it was like Benny thought if she just prayed harder and worked harder and researched more, she could save our grandma. But she couldn't, Dimitri. That bakery? It's going to kill her."

"I'm trying to get her to cut back. I got her to go out for dinner and dancing last night."

His eyes widened. "Benny? You got Benny to go to a club? Damn! She must really love you."

Dimitri chuckled. "Apparently so."

Serious now, Johnny said, "Promise me that if you help her restart the business, you won't let her work these eighty and ninety hour weeks. Make her rest. Make her *live*."

"I will, Johnny."

The kid extended his hand and Dimitri gripped it tightly. "I know thank you isn't enough for all you've done for me, but it's all I got."

Dimitri squeezed Johnny's hand and nodded. "It's enough."

CHAPTER FIFTEEN

I'd always wanted to snoop around on a luxury yacht but I'd never thought it would be like this. Under the cover of darkness, and after two car and driver switches, Dimitri slid his arm around me and hustled me toward the gleaming white yacht on the very end of the exclusive marina slip. I was quickly led onto the ship and into a beautifully decorated living area.

"Benny!" Yuri grinned and opened his arms as he came toward me. He engulfed me in a bear hug and pecked my cheek. "It's good to see you again. I'm sorry the circumstances are less than ideal."

I held tight to his hand. "Thank you for this, Yuri. I don't how I'll ever repay you."

"Don't worry about it. I owed you."

I frowned. "Owed me? For what?"

"You helped me smooth things over with Lena."

My eyes widened with surprise. "She accepted your job

offer?"

He laughed. "No, but she did follow me back on Twitter this morning. That's progress."

"Um...sure." Was this how romantic overtures began in the era of social media?

He smiled and gestured toward a slightly ajar door. "Johnny's waiting for you. Why don't you take a moment with him before the lawyer gets here?"

I glanced at Dimitri. "What lawyer?"

"Johnny wants to sign over his interests in the house and bakery. We need to get that taken care of before he leaves."

I didn't like being in the dark about the lawyer situation but wasn't going to argue with Dimitri here. Later, in private, I'd let him know that while I enjoyed him taking care of things, I also wanted to be kept in the loop when it was this important.

Stepping away from Dimitri and Yuri, I entered the other room. Johnny sat in a low chair near a big, wide window. The view of the night ocean was stunning, especially with the moonlight reflecting on the smooth surface. He smiled at me and beckoned me closer.

I knelt in front of him and hugged him carefully. "You look so much better."

"I feel better."

My gaze moved over him slowly. I wanted to reassure myself that he truly was all right and would make a full recovery. I spotted something new on his neck. "What's this?"

He winced as he pointed to the spot where he'd once had that ugly Hermanos tattoo. "Yuri wanted it covered up. He says the clients he brings onto the yacht don't mind tattoos in general but the obvious gang tats make them nervous."

I studied the dramatic angel wings the tattoo artist had applied over the numbers and letters. He'd skillfully hidden the gang mark. I glanced at Johnny with some surprise. "Angel wings?"

He shrugged. "Yuri saw my full name on my license and passport when Dimitri brought them earlier this afternoon. The guys I'm going to work with are already calling me Johnny Angel."

I squashed a smile. "Sorry."

"I think this is karma."

I moved to the empty chair next to him and held his hand. "Santos came by this morning. He wants you to come in, presumably so you can finger the shooters who killed your friends." I hesitated before asking, "Are you sure you want to run?"

"I don't want to, Benny, but I know it's the only way to survive. I've done some stupid shit in the last year or so but I've never done anything violent. Last night? Getting shot and watching my friends get their brains blown out right next to me?" He shook his head. "I can't live that way anymore. I can't put you at risk either. My crew will expect me to pick up a gun and go after those bastards. The other gang? They're going to want to kill me to keep me quiet."

He wasn't saying anything I hadn't already considered. I'd hoped it would help to hear him say it but it didn't. "I'm really going to miss you, Johnny."

"Yuri says you'll be welcome to visit whenever you want. If I do well on this ship, he'll move me to the crew on his big yacht. They sail the Mediterranean with that one. That would be a nice vacation, right?"

"Sure." I nodded, teary-eyed now. "I just wanted so much better for you."

His dark eyes shimmered. "I did this to myself, Benny.

This wasn't your fault. God knows you tried to keep me in line."

Holding my brother's hand, I tried to keep my grief at losing him in check. If I started sobbing, I might never stop. Beside me, Johnny shifted in his chair. He gently tugged his hand free from mine and reached into the pocket of the new jeans he wore. I realized someone had picked up new clothes for him. Dimitri? Yuri? Kostya? I wasn't sure who I owed a thank you.

Johnny darted a nervous look at the doorway. Assured it was clear, he thrust a phone into my hands. "Keep this hidden. Give it to Santos when you see him."

I shoved the phone into the pocket of my jeans and lowered my voice to a whisper. "Why?"

"It's Diego's phone. He was making a video of some hot girls right before that SUV pulled up next to us. He caught all of it." He grimaced. "Don't watch it, Benny. Just give it to Santos. He'll know what to do with it."

I licked my lips and considered what I knew of police procedures from TV shows and books. "I don't think they can use it as evidence, Johnny. I'm pretty sure they require someone who was there to validate it."

"It's the best he's going to get. Ain't nobody gonna talk, Benny. At least this way, the cops will know who did it. They'll be able to watch them and maybe catch them before they hurt someone else."

Movement near the door caught my attention. I nodded at Johnny, letting him know I'd do as he'd asked. Dimitri entered the room with a couple of men I didn't recognize a few steps behind him. Dimitri stood next to my chair and put his hand on my shoulder. He gently rubbed my back and smiled down at me.

Yuri came into the room and shut the door firmly behind him. He clapped his hands together and grinned.

"Let's get down to business. Peter, I'd like to introduce you to Benny and Johnny Burkhart. Benny, Johnny, Peter is a lawyer I trust a great deal. This is his associate, Hank. He's a notary. They've agreed to help us out with this sticky little situation."

I caught Yuri's use of the word *us*. "And who exactly is us?"

"You, me and Johnny," Yuri said while gesturing between the three of us. "You are going to sell me that building."

"What?" I looked at Johnny who seemed just as surprised.

A glance to Dimitri revealed the same shock on his face. He frowned and addressed Yuri in Russian. I caught Jonah's name but nothing else. It occurred to me that I might need to seek out Vivi's services in the same way Erin had.

Yuri just shrugged and said, "I'm bored. The idea of rattling his cage amuses me."

I didn't know whether to laugh or scold him. "Yuri, you don't want to get involved with this guy. He's a jerk. Anyway our building isn't worth that much now. That whole area has been zoned for this retail development. You wouldn't be able to sell it to anyone but him."

"I know. That's what makes this whole thing so entertaining. Can you imagine the look on his face when he realizes he has to negotiate with me?" He grinned evilly and laughed harder. "But it's not about the money to me. It's about reminding someone who has been very lucky in business that he should remember where he started." Yuri pointed to the floor. "At the very bottom."

"How much?" Johnny asked rather indelicately.

I gawked at him. "Johnny!"

"What?" He shot me a look like he thought I was

crazy. "It's bound to be more than Jonah Krause offered. You need that money, Benny. If you're going to start over, you need cash. If he's going to sue you because I drove into his building, you'll need money so you can settle out of court. I'm just asking how much Yuri's putting on the table."

The lawyer, Peter, cleared his throat and turned a notepad toward us. The number written on it was a fair price. It was only a few thousand less than I would have asked as a starting point in negotiations with anyone else.

Before I could even consider it, Johnny stated, "We'll take it."

I snapped my gaze to him. "No, we won't. We have to discuss this."

"Benny, for once in your damn life, will you just take the money and run? You don't have to think everything to death. Say yes and let's be done with this. Let's cut Jonah Krause out of our lives for good."

I swallowed hard. Maybe Johnny was right. Was there anything to consider here? Yuri was offering me a decent price for the building. It was enough to clear all of the debt and get us set up in a new place. A better, more vibrant neighborhood where our bakery and the deliciously authentic food we created would be appreciated.

Finally, I nodded. "All right. We'll take it."

I felt Dimitri's sigh of relief. His hand relaxed on my shoulder. He bent down and kissed my cheek. I could tell he was just as happy as Johnny to see this chapter closed.

"You can stay in the building until you get a new location ready." With a teasing smile aimed at Dimitri, he added, "But your rent just went up."

As Yuri and Dimitri joked with one another, Johnny and I read through the contract and the legal papers giving me control of Johnny's shares of the building, the business and the house. Even though I trusted Yuri not to cheat me, I read the pages of legalese twice. It was straight-forward and I understood everything clearly.

We signed our names, and in twenty minutes, it was all done. The lawyer and his notary left. Yuri's crew brought in a nice dinner. The kind gesture let me spend more time with Johnny—but it wasn't enough.

Soon, it was time to go. The yacht was leaving Texas waters that night for the Caribbean. As much as I didn't want to leave Johnny behind, I wanted him safe and happy more.

"I love you, Johnny."

He squeezed me so hard I couldn't breathe. "I love you, Benny."

"Be safe."

"I will."

"And call me."

He laughed. "I will."

Reluctantly, I pulled away from him. Dimitri shook his hand and gave him a clap on the back before sliding an arm around my waist. Our tearful parting tore at my gut and left my heart aching and empty. Only Dimitri's strong arms wrapped around and supporting me kept me from collapsing onto the pier and sobbing.

Safe inside the private car, Dimitri tugged my seatbelt into place and dragged me as close to him as possible. I buried my face in the warm crook of his neck and cried softly as he stroked my hair. He whispered sweetly and assured me that this was the best thing for Johnny. It was his chance to start over, to see the world, to grow up and become a man. I prayed that was true.

By the time we reached his apartment, it was nearly two in the morning. All cried out, I experienced such sadness now. For nineteen years, Johnny and I had been joined at the hip. Lately, things had been tense between us but there had still been good times. The idea of never seeing him over the breakfast table or playing video games until we passed out on the living room floor left me nearly breathless with grief.

Dimitri sat down on the bed and pulled me between his thighs. His hands caressed my back as he peppered tender kisses along my cheek and neck. "Tell me what you need, Benny. Tell me how to help you."

I cupped his face and ran my fingertips over the hard angles of his cheeks. He'd already helped me so much. "I feel like I'm the one who should be thinking of ways to help you and to repay you for everything you've done for me."

He dragged his lips along the edge of my throat and nibbled a sensitive spot there. "Helping you makes me happy." He ran his hands down my back and gripped my bottom through my jeans. His mouth teased against mine. "Let me put a smile on your face, Benny."

"Dimitri..." I moaned as his masterful hands stoked the flames of my desire. His palms glided along my hips and down my legs. A moment too late, I remembered exactly what I'd stuck in my pocket.

He went still as his hand moved over the bump there. "What is this?"

"Um..."

His long fingers dipped into my pocket. He retrieved the phone and stared at it. "Where did you get this?"

"Johnny gave it to me."

"This isn't his phone. I destroyed that one."

"No, it belongs to a friend of his. Wait." I frowned with confusion. "Why did you destroy Johnny's phone?"

"It's a temptation and way to track him. I got him a

new, clean phone so he can contact you." Dimitri didn't look happy about the phone he'd taken from me. "Why did Johnny give you this?"

"It has video on it of that night. He wants me to give it to Santos."

An irritated expression crossed his face. "I thought we agreed you weren't going to get involved."

Now it was my turn to be irritated. "Did we? Because I feel like you're the one making all the decisions and I'm the one standing here, nodding my head and saying, 'Yes, Dimitri.'"

His eyes widened. Clearly taken aback, he hurriedly said, "Benny, I never meant to make you feel like I was running roughshod over you."

"I know you're trying to protect me but dropping that bomb about the lawyer tonight at Yuri's yacht? You should have told me on the drive over, Dimitri. I felt totally blindsided."

He flinched. "I'm sorry. You're right. I should have mentioned it. I swear I didn't know Yuri was going to offer to buy the building from you."

"I know you didn't. I could see it on your face."

Dimitri tossed the phone aside and slid his hands up and down my arms. "Listen, Benny, when it comes to you, I can be a bit overzealous. If I'm crossing the line, tell me. I'll try to be more self-aware but don't hesitate to tell me if I'm making you feel this way. I never want you to feel like I'm trying to be controlling." He looked sick at the very idea of it. "That's not the kind of man I am and that's not the kind of relationship I want us to have."

"It's not the sort of relationship I want either." I brushed some of the soft, stray strands of blond hair behind his ear. "I realize you're better at navigating messes like these than me and I appreciate your guidance,

Dimitri. Please don't think I'm being ungrateful."

"I don't."

"Good because I want us to be partners, like you said. I get that when it's something big and scary like this I'm better off letting you take the reins but maybe you could slow down a bit and clue me in so I'm not wandering around in the dark?"

"Definitely," he agreed. He traced my lower lip and I playfully nipped at his thumb. Smiling so sexily, he asked, "Are we okay now?"

"Yes."

"Then come here and let me make love to you." He wrapped his arms around me and dragged me on top of him as he fell back onto the bed. He sifted his fingers through my hair and tugged me down for a kiss. Straddling him, I melted into his commanding kiss. The slight hint of lemon from dessert still clung to his lips. I swiped my tongue against his because he just tasted so damn good.

With one swift, easy move, Dimitri flipped us. Crawling over me, he captured my mouth in a punishing kiss. I gripped his shoulders and rocked my hips, arching into his steely, hot body. Pinned beneath him, I let go of all the worry and emotional pain plaguing me. I surrendered to the feel of his skilled hands and that wickedly erotic mouth.

My shirt was shoved out of the way and his lips pressed searing kisses to the swell of each breast and then my belly. Dimitri unbuttoned and unzipped my jeans and jerked them down my legs. Lifting my hips, I helped him rid me of my jeans, panties and shoes.

Naked from the waist down, I shuddered with anticipation. He slid off the bed onto his knees and dragged me right to the very edge. Pushing my thighs open, he gripped the backs of my knees and held me right where he wanted me. His tongue probed my pussy and I cried out his name. He chuckled lightly, the slight vibrations rattling my throbbing clit.

With a low groan, he swirled his tongue around the little nub. I clutched at his shoulders, my nails digging into the soft flesh of his back as he drove me crazy. Flicking and suckling, Dimitri pushed me closer and closer to the edge. The things this man could do with his tongue!

"Dimitri!' I moaned and thrashed atop his bed. "Oh! *Oh*!"

He growled hungrily and lapped at me. The merciless speed of his tongue fluttering over the swollen kernel of my clit sent me skyrocketing into a stratosphere of ecstasy that left me trembling and panting.

When the last few jolts of climax rippled through me, Dimitri pried his mouth away and sat back on his heels. Boneless and floating on air, I watched him strip out of his clothing. I still couldn't believe this big, delicious man was all mine.

Pushing up onto my knees, I peeled out of my shirt and threw my bra on to the floor. I motioned for Dimitri to come closer. He grinned wolfishly at the realization of what I wanted to do.

Down on all fours, I reached for that magnificent cock. I stroked his hard length with just my fingertips and then curled my fingers around him. Dimitri inhaled a shaky breath and pulled his lower lip between his teeth. I leaned down and licked the fat crown of his cock. He groaned loudly and threaded his fingers through my hair.

Loving the ways I could make him react, I sucked the tip of him. The wide girth stretched my lips. I hummed quietly as I worked my mouth up and down his shaft, slicking his hot skin. I didn't have enough experience in this department to deep throat him—and he was way too long for me to even give it that old college try. He didn't seem to mind one bit.

"Benny." He murmured my name with such affection. He brushed his knuckles down my cheek before tangling his hands in my hair. I relished the tug of his fingers and the tingling heat on my scalp. He was barely in control now. To know I had that kind of power? What an aphrodisiac!

He thrust into my welcoming mouth, rubbing the length of his cock along my tongue. I tightened my lips around him, sucking him hard as he retreated. Over and over, I teased him until he'd had enough.

With a desperate growl, he popped free from my mouth. I gasped as he grasped me by the waist, flipped me over and dragged me back against him. He issued a frustrated sound before stepping away just long enough to grab a condom from the top drawer of his bedside table. In record time, he'd sheathed himself.

I glanced over my shoulder and watched him guide his cock into me. The muscles of his chest and arms were tight as breached my entrance. Overwhelmed by the delicious ache of his huge dick gliding into me, I dropped my forehead to the bed and wiggled my bottom. A split-second later, Dimitri's palm cracked my backside. "Oh!"

He chuckled and rubbed the spot he'd just smacked. "Sorry, sweetheart. I couldn't resist. You have the prettiest little ass."

After being tied up and put in his kinky sex swing, I started to wonder what other dirty penchants Dimitri might have. Pushing back to meet his thrusts, I silently showed him that having my bottom whacked in the heat of passion was a-okay with me.

He gripped my hips and pounded into me. Embracing the wanton girl inside me, I let go of my inhibitions and decided to enjoy every single second of Dimitri's wild, intense fucking. It stunned me how he could be so incredibly tender and sweet one moment and nearly feral the next.

I cried out with every forceful thrust. My lower belly wobbled with excitement. My nipples formed taut peaks that ached and throbbed. I wanted to reach down and touch myself to ease the pulsing ache between my thighs but I didn't think I could withstand the force of his rough coupling on just one hand.

As if reading my mind, Dimitri pulled free from my body and tossed me onto my back. He pounced on me, crawling between my open thighs and sliding home with one easy thrust. Head thrown back, I moaned with pure delight. He nibbled my neck and rocked into me, his big cock hitting all the right places.

"Dimitri!" I nearly lost it when his fingertips found my swollen clit. He drew tight circles around the bud while taking me with slow, deep strokes. "God!"

Holding my gaze, he brushed his mouth to mine. "Come," he urged. "Come with me."

Hearing the need in his voice sent me over the edge. My thighs gripped his waist as I rocked and shuddered beneath him. The wonderful waves of pleasure were intensified by the way he groaned my name and jerked inside me. Our tongues danced as we trembled and clutched at one another. We interlaced our fingers above my head and gazed at one another in wonder and awe.

Eyes closed, I reveled in the way Dimitri nuzzled my neck and kissed me with such love. He didn't pull away from me immediately but seemed content to stay buried inside me and joined so intimately.

"I never thought I'd have regrets when it came to you, Benny." He claimed my mouth with a kiss so thorough I was nearly dizzy when he broke away from me. "But, my God, I regret waiting so long to make my move."

I ran my fingers through his hair and cupped the back of his neck. "Maybe it wasn't the right time for us until now. Maybe we weren't ready for one another."

"Maybe." He kissed me again. "I'm glad we're together now."

"Me, too," I whispered. "I love you."

"I love you." He smiled and kissed the tip of my nose. "I'll be right back."

After he pulled away from me, I rolled onto my side to watch the sexy view of his naked ass as he made his way to the bathroom. The door closed and I let loose a long sigh.

Relaxed and happy, I rubbed my hand over the soft bedding and let my mind wander. With the bakery building sold, I would have to find a new place quickly, install all the necessary equipment, get permits and handle all the other tiny details to get us open quickly. Yuri's offer to let me stay until the new location was ready eased my worries.

Still, there were other things to consider. I had to figure out a way to keep—

A strange sound interrupted my thoughts. I held my breath and listened. I felt certain the noise had come from down below in the bakery. My heart raced when I heard another, clearer noise. There was no mistaking that sound. Shattering glass!

"Dimitri!"

The door opened a moment later. Wiping his hands on towel, he asked, "What's wrong?"

"Did you hear that?"

He shook his head. "Hear what, sweetheart?"

"I heard glass break downstairs."

He went still. "You're sure."

I nodded. "I heard a noise and I listened hard. Then I heard another noise. It was breaking glass."

Frowning, he tossed the hand towel on the counter and strode into the bedroom. He snatched up his jeans and grabbed his shirt. As he jammed his feet into his shoes, he pointed to the second drawer of his table. "Grab my gun."

I did as he asked, gripping the cold, metal piece with extreme caution. It was the first time I'd ever touched a weapon. I handed it over quickly. Dimitri shot me an amused glance before kissing my cheek. "We'll work on that. You need to be comfortable with a handgun."

"No, thank you."

"I wasn't asking." He headed toward the bedroom door. "It's probably nothing, Benny, but just in case, lock up behind me. If I'm not back in two or three minutes, call the police. Tell them we have a prowler."

Nodding, I slipped off the bed and trailed him to the front door. He slipped out into the night and I quickly locked the door behind him. I hurried back into the bedroom and tugged on my jeans and shirt.

But when I went into the bathroom to search for an elastic band for my hair, I caught a scent that stopped me cold in my tracks.

Smoke.

CHAPTER SIXTEEN

He heard the shrill screech of the smoke alarms before he caught the scent of burning drywall. A moment later, he discovered the side entrance propped open with heavy crates. Dread squeezed his chest. Was it a kitchen accident or arson?

A brief hesitation ensued. If the fire was small enough, he could put it out with one of the many fire extinguishers bolted to the bakery's walls. Knowing it was probably a bad idea, he ducked inside the building anyway.

The smoke wasn't bad in the back rooms where they kept stock but one step into the kitchen and Dimitri coughed. Thick and heavy, the smoke rolled out of the front café space of the bakery. He caught the scent of accelerant. The acrid tinge of fuel hung ripe in the smoky air. With an arm over his face, he backed out of the kitchen and turned toward the side entrance. This place was going up and it would be fast. He had to get to Benny.

As he stepped through the open doorway, a baseball bat slammed into his gut. "*Oof!*"

Dimitri collapsed forward as pain unlike anything he'd experienced in a hell of a long time gripped him. Movement out of the corner of his eye spurred him to action even though the pain was intense. He blocked another blow with his arm and grunted at the burst of agony as the bat made contact.

Swearing loudly, he drove his fist into the stomach of the man still hidden in the shadows. He hit something paunchy and soft and knew he'd be able to take the man, even with a burning belly and probably broken arm. His attacker doubled over and Dimitri struck. Grabbing the man's shirt, he drove his knee into the attacker's face, crunching his nose and bloodying his mouth. One good punch to the temple put the gasping man down for good.

The bat hit the pavement and rolled into the shadows. With his injured arm held tightly to his aching gut, Dimitri pushed the man over onto his back with the tip of his boot. One of the lights mounted along the building's roof illuminated the familiar face of Carl, the goon Jonah Krause had sent to scare Benny that morning.

"Dimitri! I smell smoke!"

He glanced up to see Benny coming out of the apartment with her purse in her hand. "Hurry!"

She paused halfway down the steps. "What happened to you? Are you hurt?" Her gaze dropped to the ground and Carl's unconscious form. "Who the hell is—*Dimitri!* Look out!"

Frantic, she pointed over his shoulder. He spun just in time to see three men coming at him. These punks wore the uniform of a gangbanger. With their sagging jeans, baggy shirts and gold chains around their neck, they looked ready for a fight. One of them held a bottle of lighter fluid in his hand. Another had a knife. The other one, the bigger one, was only armed with his fists—unless he had a gun hidden on him.

"Benny! Run!"

"I can't." Her weak reply stunned him.

He glanced over his shoulder and spotted another man coming from the opposite end of the alley. Benny had slowly backed up the steps toward the apartment as the other would-be attacker advanced on her. Soon the fire would break through to his apartment and the flames would be licking at her feet.

In that moment, he knew fear. Four against two wouldn't have been bad odds if he'd had Ivan or Yuri or Nikolai at his side but Benny? She was barely five feet tall and had no idea how to handle herself in a street fight. Add to that his injured arm and they were fucked.

But he'd die before he let anyone harm his Benny.

Wincing, he reached back for the gun he'd tucked into the waistband of his jeans. In the fight with Carl, it had been dislodged. He glanced around but couldn't see it. The shadows were heavy in this area and the smoke now rolling from the door made it difficult to see.

"Where the hell is Johnny?"

Dimitri lifted his gaze to the guy holding the knife. He tried to gauge the situation. "He's gone. I sent him out of the country."

"Liar."

"It's true. He's out of here. You'll never see him again."

"That's not what he said." The guy gestured to Carl. "He promised us Johnny was here, in the apartment." He turned his attention to the man stalking Benny and spoke to him in rapid-fire Spanish.

Dimitri didn't catch everything he said but his Spanish was good enough for him to understand most of it. "NO! You're not taking her back into that apartment to look for Johnny. He isn't here. He's gone."

"*Pinche guero*, you don't tell me what to do." The knife-wielding gangbanger stepped forward to stab him and Dimitri took advantage of the opening.

Using his wounded arm, he blocked the knife blade. He hissed as the steel sliced his skin, but years of training and conditioning and the experiences of war suppressed the pain and panic a normal person would have felt at being cut.

No, Dimitri embraced the battle-hardened instincts he'd honed in *Spetsnaz*. If these bastards thought they were going to hurt Benny, they had another thing coming.

*

I fought the panic surging through me and tried to breathe as the menacing thug inched up the stairs. Down on the ground, Dimitri faced three men, all of them probably armed and ready to kill him. I wanted to scream for help but no one would hear us. Every building in the vicinity was totally empty. We were on our own.

There was screaming from down below as Dimitri swiped the bottle of lighter fluid from one of the men and sprayed him in the face with it. Clawing at his eyes and shrieking in pain, the man fell to his knees. The other two rushed Dimitri. Already bleeding and injured, he moved sluggishly but valiantly.

Certain Dimitri was going to die if I didn't help him, I dug deep and pushed away the terror trying to grip my belly. The man coming toward me looked so damn smug.

His overconfidence was my only advantage. Adrenaline surged through my veins as I quickly gripped the railings on either side of me. With as much force as I could muster, I slammed both feet into the man's chest. He grunted and tipped backward. His eyes widened with fright as he lost his balance.

When he tried to grab the railings, I kicked him again, throwing everything I had at him. He stumbled backward and fell. I cringed at the sound of his heavy body smacking and rolling and tumbling down the metal steps. He hit the pavement hard and didn't move.

Was he dead? God, I hoped not. The idea of killing a man made me sick.

The grunts and the slap of skin on skin as Dimitri defended himself spurred me into action. I ran down the steps, hopped over the unconscious man on the ground and searched for something, *anything*, to use a weapon.

The sight of a bat shocked me. *Where the hell did that come from?*

Not caring about the details, I picked it up and rushed into the fray. Two of the men held Dimitri's arms while another one came at him with a knife. Already he had blood dripping down his arm and neck. The sight of the man I loved bleeding enraged me.

With the familiarity of a girl who had played softball since second grade, I swung that bat like a champ and connected with the back of the man nearest me. The scent of lighter fluid saturated the air. This was the one who had sprayed my bakery and the one Dimitri had squirted with his own weapon of destruction. The man lurched forward in pain. I hit him again, this time taking out his knees and dropping him like a sack of rocks.

Dimitri stared at me in shock but didn't hesitate. He grasped the jeans of the man on his right and swung him toward the guy holding the knife. The dude I'd taken down with the bat tried to get up so I hit him again. Groaning in pain, he got smart and kissed the pavement.

Facing off against both men, Dimitri showed exceptional skill. Even so, I knew he needed help. I reared back with the bat, ready to swing at a moment's notice. My chance came when Dimitri kicked one of the men my way. I slammed the bat into his shoulder. The knife he'd been holding clattered to the ground near my foot.

I kicked it out of the way and put the bat against his jaw. "One move and you'll be eating out of a straw for the next six months!"

The pop of gunfire shocked me. I glanced up to see the only gang member standing aim his weapon at Dimitri. Clutching his arm, he dipped forward. Blood oozed between his fingers. My body slackened with horror at the realization he'd been shot. "Dimitri!"

Always a damn hero, he stepped into the line of fire, protecting me with his huge body. "Benny, run!"

"No!"

"Benny!"

"Houston PD! Drop that weapon!" Detective Eric Santos burst into the alley, just behind the shooter. Gun aimed at the man trying to kill Dimitri, he shouted forcefully. "Hands in the air! *Now!*"

Dimitri slid to the side, blocking me totally with his body, so I couldn't see what happened. I heard scuffling and cursing and could only guess that Santos had taken down the shooter.

When it was safe, Dimitri staggered toward me. He grabbed my hand and jerked me around the moaning bodies on the alley pavement. "Hurry, Benny. This place could blow at any minute."

"Get her to the street," Santos shouted. "I've got Fire and EMS on the way."

The bat slipped from my shaking fingers and I gripped Dimitri's hand tightly. We hurried out of the alley and nearly ran into the two officers who rushed around the corner. Dimitri put his hand up and pushed me aside, ready to bear the brunt of whatever mistaken violence we might catch.

"They're victims! Let them through!"

With Santos' help, we got the hell out of there. Dimitri led me across the street to safety. He backed me up against a wall, trapping my smaller body between his and the brick masonry. He had a fierce look on his face. "What the hell were you thinking? Why didn't you run? You could have been killed!"

Breathless, I said the only thing that mattered. "I love you. You wouldn't have left me behind. I wasn't going to leave you."

"You stubborn, beautiful, brave woman." With a rough exhale, Dimitri touched his forehead to mine. "*Lyubimaya moya*. What the hell am I going to do with you?"

"Love me?"

A ragged sound escaped his throat. "I do, Benny. I love you."

Our lips met in a passionate, crazed kiss. The feel of his slick blood under my hand ripped me out of the romantic moment. He winced when I pressed my hand to his worst wound. "We have to get you to a hospital." I shot him a warning look. "A *real* hospital."

He snorted with amusement. "I won't argue with that."

Sirens grew louder and louder. Fire trucks, police cars and ambulances poured onto the street. Side by side with Dimitri, we watched the drama unfold. The backseats of the cop cars were quickly filled with the villainous thugs who had attacked and tried to kill us. The one I'd pushed down the stairs was carted out on a backboard. The sight made my gut twist.

"He'll be fine." Santos must have seen the worried look on my face as he approached us with an EMS crew and two police officers in tow. "You broke his collarbone but he's not paralyzed or anything." He flicked his fingers and pointed at Dimitri. "This one has a gunshot wound."

I stepped aside as the medics descended on Dimitri. He wore an aggravated expression as they poked and prodded his injuries. Santos questioned Dimitri first and then me.

"Do you know any of those men, Benny?"

"Just the fat one," I said and pointed to the stretcher where Carl rested. "He works for Jonah Krause. A few mornings ago, he showed up at the bakery to try to intimidate me."

Santos rubbed his jaw. "Krause, huh? Yeah, that's not the first time I've heard his name mentioned in circumstances like this. But never with a Latin street gang," he commented and frowned. "Some strange bedfellows."

"Not really," Dimitri interjected. "Jonah threatened Benny yesterday when she wouldn't accept his offer. He tried to blackmail her with threats of turning Johnny over to the rival gang and calling Immigration."

I replayed the conversation I'd had with the nasty real estate developer. "He did say I was playing with fire."

Santos' pen scratched away at his notebook. "I think it might be time to pay Mr. Krause a visit." He glanced at Dimitri who grunted in agreement. "In my official capacity with the Houston PD," he amended.

Dimitri didn't reply. Would he go behind Santos' back

to get revenge on Jonah Krause for orchestrating tonight's diabolical act? I decided then and there I was going to have a talk with Dimitri. With the police department involved, this whole mess could be dealt with legally. I didn't want him to cross that line for me.

"So you kicked that guy down the stairs and then what happened, Benny?"

"I saw the baseball bat. I grabbed it and started swinging."

"A baseball bat, huh?" Smiling, Santos shook his head. "Man, that brings back memories! Remember that time I dragged you down to the park for my home run derby team? Damn, we were so late getting home. I thought for sure your grandma was going to whip off her *chanclas* and give me a good smack."

The happy memory seemed so out of place in this nightmare I was living but I couldn't stop the smile spreading across my face. "Seems like forever ago, doesn't it?"

"Not that long," he said. "I was, what, a senior? You were a freshman?" He shrugged. "That's what? Ten years?"

"A lot can change in ten years," I said and stared at the inferno across the street.

"I'm really sorry, Benny." Anguish was clear on Santos' face. "I wish I'd gotten here sooner."

"What were you doing here in the first place?"

"I was worried Johnny might try to hide out at the bakery or with Dimitri. I'd heard that some private investigator was shaking down Hermanos members looking for him. When I drove by, I saw the flames and called it in. The gunshot caught my attention damn quick." He shook his head. "I'm glad I was able to reach you two in time."

"Thank you, Detective." Dimitri extended his hand, the skin caked with dried blood. Santos didn't hesitate to grasp and shake it. "You saved our lives. I'm in your debt."

"Just doing my job," Santos replied. He glanced at the crime scene tech who came forward with three white boxes. She opened them to reveal guns they'd taken from the alley. I was stunned by how quickly they'd grabbed and tagged all that evidence but apparently they worked quickly when the threat of fire and a deluge of water were imminent.

"We recovered three guns in the alley. Is one these yours, Dimitri?" Santos gestured to the weapons.

"That one," Dimitri said with a lift of his head. "And, yes, I have a concealed handgun permit. It's all legal."

Santos' lips twitched. "I didn't say it wasn't."

"You didn't have to," Dimitri replied and then hissed with discomfort. One of the medics palpated his belly. "Hey, take it easy, yeah?"

"Sorry," the medic said with an apologetic smile. "You're going to need scans and x-rays when we get to the ER."

Dimitri grunted but didn't refuse treatment. Probably because he knew I'd raise living hell if he tried to avoid a trip to the hospital. The cut on his arm needed stitches and that awful bruise on his belly scared me.

"What if he has internal bleeding? Shouldn't we hurry?"

The medics and Dimitri glanced at me. "It's fine," Dimitri said. "It hurts but I'm not dying. I've had worse."

"I don't find that comforting, Dimitri."

He held out his hand and I moved closer to the stretcher where he now sat. He didn't have to say anything. The look on his face told me everything I needed to know. As he gripped my hand in his, the medics wrapped his arm and slapped dressings on his other bloody wounds.

Behind him, the blazing bakery lit up the night sky. Tears burned my eyes as I watched my family's history go up in flames. The firefighters battled the blaze and got the upper hand but the damage was done.

I'd been preparing to say goodbye to this chapter in my life but not this way. To lose it all because of arson and revenge and blackmail? It made me sick.

"Oh, Dimitri, what about Yuri? Do we still have a deal? Does he get this awful, burned shell of a building? That's not right! It's not fair to him."

His gaze skipped from my face to the street. "You'll have to ask him."

I looked back and spotted Yuri and Nikolai striding up the sidewalk toward us. Both men wore stony expressions. The cold glint to their eyes would have struck fear in the heart of even the most hardened man. I sure as heck didn't want to be on the receiving end of their wrath.

"What in the world? How did they get here so fast?"

Santos snorted. "The king's eyes and ears, I'm sure."

I frowned. Did he mean Nikolai? It didn't surprise me that Nikolai had a network of informants on the streets but why would they be watching us? Nikolai struck me as the kind of man who believed deeply in protecting his friends. Did he have some sort of tail on Dimitri?

Santos stepped back to speak with his colleagues but I noticed the way his gaze strayed to Nikolai's face. The men shared icy glares but neither formally acknowledged the other. Apparently there was some history there.

"Benny!" Yuri shocked me by engulfing me in a bear hug that squeezed the air right out of my lungs. He set me back at arm's length to look me over. "Are you all right?"

"I'm fine, Yuri. Your building—"

He waved his hand. "I don't care about the building. It's just bricks and mortar and money. I can replace any of those easily, but you and Dimitri?" He shook his head. His gaze fell on Dimitri. Carefully, he clasped his friend's shoulder. They spoke briefly in Russian. Whatever Dimitri said put Yuri at ease.

"Sir?" The medic who had been assessing Dimitri gestured to the ambulance. "We need to get you to a hospital now."

Dimitri glanced at me and then at Yuri and Nikolai. Before he even had to ask, Nikolai assured him, "We'll take care of her."

I opened my mouth to protest because I wanted to go with Dimitri. He caught my worried gaze and shot me a pleading look. I finally understood why he wanted me with his friends. At the hospital, we'd be separated and I would likely end up alone in the emergency room waiting area. I could only imagine how anxious he would be about my safety in that situation.

Desperate for him to be patched up and healthy again, I brushed my lips to his mouth. "I'll be fine. We'll see you as soon as possible."

Dimitri gripped the back of my neck and drew me down for the kind of kiss that left me dizzy and trembling inside. "When I'm out of the hospital, we're picking up right there."

All I could do was nod. "Okay."

The medics moved closer to the stretcher and I backed out of the way. Yuri put a hand on my shoulder, steadying me as I watched them load Dimitri into the ambulance. He got the name of the hospital where they were taking him. The doors closed and I experienced the crushing sadness of watching the man I loved be taken away in an ambulance—and it was all my fault.

"No." Nikolai dared to touch my face, using his heavily tattooed fingers to tip my chin. "I know that look. You have no reason to feel guilt."

"Don't I?" I gestured to the ambulances, fire trucks and police cars lining both sides of the street. "Dimitri never would have been hurt if it wasn't for me." I wiped at the tears dripping onto my cheeks. "Look at what getting involved with me has cost him! I'm, like, the worst thing that's ever happened to him."

"No," Nikolai replied with utter seriousness. "That honor belongs to me."

His frank rebuttal stunned me into silence. He tapped my cheek and let his hand fall to his side. "But you, Benny? You're the best thing that's ever happened to him. All this?" He gestured to the backdrop of destruction and mayhem. "It's nothing to him, not when it means keeping you safe and in his life."

Santos cleared his throat. There was a glint of surprise in his dark eyes as he regarded Nikolai. When he extended his hand toward me, I caught sight of my purse. "Is this yours? They found it in the alley."

"Yes." I cringed as I took the soggy bag from his hand. The zipper was firmly in place and I prayed the contents had been spared the brunt of the water damage. A quick peek inside relieved my worries. On my way out the door, I'd grabbed Dimitri's keys and wallet from the floor, where they'd fallen out his jeans, and the phone Johnny had given me. "Santos?"

"Yeah?"

I presented him with the phone. "I'm not sure how much help this will be but Johnny wanted me to give it to you."

Santos stared at the phone. "Johnny gave that to you? When? Where?"

I felt Yuri shift next to me. Even though I hated to lie to Santos, I did. "I can't give you the details. He was insistent I give this to you. He said there's video of the shooting on it. I don't know how the chain of evidence works in a situation like this—"

"It doesn't," he said with a frown. With a flick of his fingers, he gestured for one of the crime scene techs to join us. "Can we get this bagged and tagged?"

I waited for the tech to photograph and tag the phone while Santos took a sworn statement from me on its provenance. Whether it would help his case, I couldn't say but I felt a little better knowing I'd fulfilled my promise to Johnny. I didn't like being on the wrong side of the law and desperately wanted to get back on the right side, where I'd always lived.

Once I was cleared to leave the scene, Yuri took Dimitri's keys from me and Nikolai indicated I should come with him. I didn't miss the unhappy expression on Santos' face. I felt sure the next time we saw one another that he would give me a stern lecture on getting mixed up with the wrong crowd.

Suddenly, I felt so conflicted. The wrong crowd? What was that exactly? Was it Nikolai and Kostya? Were they really as awful as their reputations? I thought back to high school and the way nasty stories were repeated and exaggerated. I'd seen so many young women crushed by those ugly rumors—and God only knew how many of them were untrue.

Was that the case with men like Nikolai and Kostya? Were they as dark and dirty as their reputations would have me believe? I considered Johnny. Oh, he'd done some stupid, stupid things. He'd done dangerous and reckless things. Was he a bad person? No. He was misguided and he'd pay for the mistakes of his youth for the rest of his life.

What about Nikolai? I sneaked a glance at him as we rode through the streets of downtown Houston in the back of one of the private cars in his personal fleet. The two SUVs guarding us hadn't escaped my notice.

Was Nikolai as terrible as his reputation would have me believe? Was he like Ivan? Had he come here to start over but been unsuccessful in making a clean break? Was he slowly reforming his bad ways?

I honestly didn't know. I wanted to believe that it didn't matter but I wasn't that naïve. It did matter but I just wasn't sure how much anymore.

My jumbled emotions unsettled me. Dimitri's absence affected me deeply. In the last few days, we'd grown so incredibly close. Admitting that we loved and needed one another had been the most natural thing in the world. Now, being separated from him felt like the most awful, terrible thing imaginable.

At the hospital, the car pulled up to an empty space along the curb. I followed Nikolai out of the car and onto the sidewalk. Surprise filtered through me at the sight of Ivan, Erin, Vivian and Lena waiting for us there.

Lena was on me in an instant, flinging her arms around me and hugging me tightly. "Are you okay? We wanted to go to the bakery but Ivan convinced us to come here."

"I'm fine. Dimitri was hurt but not too badly."

She released me and rubbed my back. "You want me to come in and sit with you? The waiting room is crazy busy. They're a little grouchy in there about having too many family members waiting on one patient."

Family members? With a thud, the revelation that I

wasn't actually alone hit me hard. Yes, I'd lost Johnny tonight. My brother would be on the fringes of my life for the foreseeable future but that didn't mean I didn't have family. It wasn't always about blood connections. Dimitri, my friends, his friends—we were all connected in varying degrees.

Smiling at Lena, I accepted her offer. "I'd like that. Thank you."

After exchanging hugs with Ivan, Erin and Vivi and assuring Nikolai I wouldn't go anywhere alone inside the hospital except to rejoin Dimitri, I entered the waiting room with Lena. As she'd described, it was a madhouse.

With some difficulty, I made my way to the registration desk and asked to have Dimitri notified I was here. The nurse didn't seem in any rush to get on it but I didn't hold it against her. I could only imagine what kind of wear and tear she experienced working night after night of shifts like these.

Lena and I found a free spot against a wall. Leaning back against it for support, we talked softly about what had happened. I could see the terror reflected in her dark eyes as I related the awful details of our ordeal. I refused to think about how badly it could have gone. Dimitri and I truly were lucky to be alive. One wrong move, one miscalculation, and we could have both been shot or stabbed or beaten to death.

"Benny Burkhart?" A man in dark green scrubs stood in the doorway of the ER's entrance. Lena gave me a little shove and I hurried to cross the room. I glanced back at her, but she waved me on before gesturing outside, silently informing me of her intent to wait there.

I followed the nurse into the busy emergency department. We bypassed the larger trauma rooms for a small hallway lined with curtained cubicles. He dragged back the curtain on one of them to reveal Dimitri.

His pale blue eyes shot open at the sound. Though he tensed at first, he spotted me and relaxed. I couldn't get to him fast enough. A little sob left my throat as I pressed my lips to his. He gently caressed my cheek. "Don't cry, sweetheart. I'm all right."

"No, you're not." Here in the harsh, bright light of the hospital, I could see all the damage that the dark street had hidden from me. The stab wounds and gashes he'd suffered had been stitched and covered. There were smaller nicks and cuts on his forearms and hands. The deep, reddish-purple bruising along his jaw and belly made me wince. The arm he'd been favoring during the fight now sat in a sling. The other arm, the one that had been hit with a bullet, was cleanly sutured and covered with a neat bandage. "God, Dimitri! Look at you."

"It's temporary. I'll heal." He tilted his head toward the bullet wound. "This was only a graze. A few stitches and I'm fine. This arm isn't even broken. I need a couple of days to rest and I'll be back on my feet."

My eyes widened. "A couple of days? You need a week in bed to recuperate."

He made that grunting sound that meant he didn't agree but didn't want to argue. "That's overkill, Benny."

"I wasn't asking, Dimitri." I threaded my fingers through his unkempt hair. "Let me take care of you for once."

"Well," he murmured and lifted up for a kiss. "When you put it like that..." I let him have the long, sensual kiss he wanted. He touched the bed. "Climb up here with me."

I glanced over my shoulder at the slightly open curtain. "I don't think that's allowed."

"For what I'm probably paying for this horse stall, I

don't really care what they allow or don't allow. Come here."

Not wanting him to cause a ruckus, I slid onto the bed, careful to avoid his injured areas. He didn't seem the least bit daunted by the thought of discomfort and dragged me even closer to his side, tucking my head against his chest and kissing the top of my head.

"Was the building a complete loss?"

"No. I heard one of the firemen tell Santos that most of the second floor was salvageable. I hope we'll be able to save most of your things."

Dimitri nuzzled my neck. "It's only stuff. We're alive. That's all that matters."

"It's not just stuff, Dimitri. Your photos, your memories, my memories..."

"Sweetheart, I'm so very sorry about the bakery. I never wanted you to lose it that way."

I swallowed the urge to cry, pushing the painful ball of emotions down my throat and refusing to let it overwhelm me here. Later, in private, I'd grieve for the terrible loss. I repeated what he'd said to me. "We're alive, Dimitri. That's what really matters."

"But everything hanging on the walls? The art, the newspaper clippings and photographs..."

"Some of it can never be replaced," I conceded, "but luckily most of the framed letters and newspaper clippings and photos were copies. We switched those out back when my grandmother was still here."

"We'll start looking for a new building this week."

"Dimitri," I gently scolded him. "You have to recover first. Anyway, I don't even know who the building belongs to right now. Is it still mine? Does the deal with Yuri still stand? Will my insurance cover the fire? I don't even know how this works."

"We'll figure it out," he assured me. "Don't stress about it right now."

"I don't have a choice. There are seventeen employees who expect to start work in a few hours. How the hell am I supposed to pay them while I find a new building, get it outfitted and do all the other legwork? At least with the deal Yuri offered me, I could keep one business going while I setup the other one. That meant my employees would have a steady income but now I—"

Dimitri put his finger to my lips. "Hush. Not tonight, Benny. We'll sort it all out in the morning. If you keep worrying like this, you're going to be the one who needs a hospital bed."

I decided to let him be bossy tonight. After what he'd done, he'd earned it. With a little smile, I said, "Well I could use a vacation."

"We'll take one soon." He kissed my forehead. "We'll go anywhere you want."

"I'd like to see my brother."

"Then we'll do that. I'm sure he'll be some place wonderfully warm around Christmas."

"I like the sound of that." Snuggling closer to my big, sexy Russian, I enjoyed his loving embrace. The bustling noise of the emergency room swirled around us but none of it mattered to me. Here, in his arms, everything was perfect.

"Benny?"

"Yes?"

"Move in with me."

There was no questioning lilt to his statement. I leaned back and gazed into those blue eyes I'd come to love so much. He stared back at me with such love—and the tiniest hint of fear, as if he expected me to reject him.

Any other time, I probably would have politely done

just that or asked for more time to consider it but tonight? Tonight had shown me that trying to plan and control everything down to the very last detail was futile. I'd almost lost him and refused to ever have regrets where Dimitri was concerned.

I answered him with a playful grin. "Well, considering you're basically homeless now, shouldn't *I* be asking *you* to move in with *me*?"

He chuckled and nodded slowly. "*Da.* Yes."

Carefully, I interlaced my fingers with his. "After I sell the house, we can move into a new home together."

His eyes became suspiciously shimmery. "Yes. *Together.*"

CHAPTER SEVENTEEN

Dimitri winced as he slipped out of the sling that cradled his left arm. It had been six days and his damn elbow joint still ached painfully any time he extended it fully. The jarring impact of that bat against his forearm had rattled his joints badly but it was nothing time wouldn't heal. Like the sutures, bruises and scabs marking his body, the pain would soon fade.

Glancing around Yuri's office, he remembered the last time he'd been there. Then, Yuri had made him a business offer that he'd been conflicted about accepting. Now he felt surer of himself.

Front Door Security had grown about as much as it ever could in a city this size. He had great relationships with the clubs he provided bouncers for but he'd gotten comfortable with his success. Maybe it was time to be ambitious again.

Out of the corner of his eye, he saw Nikolai shift

subtly in the shadowed corner of the room. Yuri had dimmed the lights and the setting September sun spilled just enough light into the spacious office to give it a nearly sinister appearance. He hoped the ambience took a more ominous tone before Jonah Krause arrived.

Dimitri had taken Eric Santos' warning to heart. Though he'd like nothing more than to beat the shit right out of the real estate developer, Dimitri knew he was being watched. He could easily hire men to do the dirty deed but it would blowback on Benny in a way he wouldn't allow.

While he walked that gray line between the world of law-abiding citizens and the darker underworld Nikolai inhabited, Dimitri wouldn't cross it, especially not now that he had so much to lose. Benny meant more to him than any satisfaction he would have attained through pounding his fist into Jonah Krause's face.

The sound of voices approaching the doorway drew his attention. Yuri's ability to charm never surprised Dimitri. He'd seen his friend talk his way out of some truly legendary scrapes. How he'd managed to persuade Jonah to visit his office after regular business hours Dimitri would never know. No doubt there had been dollar signs attached.

All smiles and smarminess, Jonah Krause stepped through the door. Yuri came in right behind him and shut the door. From another corner near the entrance, Ivan appeared with stealth. If Dimitri hadn't known he'd been hiding there, he never would have seen the hulking fighter.

As he turned to make a joke with Yuri, Jonah noticed Ivan sliding in front of the door, blocking the man's only chance of escape. Dimitri could almost smell the fear radiating from Jonah now.

"What's going on?"

"What? Ivan?" Yuri's shoulders bounced easily. "He's filling in for one of my bodyguards. Food poisoning," he lied.

Dimitri knew the moment the other man saw him. Jonah stiffened and his eyes widened, the whites so big and bright Dimitri wanted to laugh. The real estate developer hadn't caught sight of Nikolai yet. Dimitri hoped Yuri's cleaning crew would be coming by tonight because the man was probably going to piss himself.

"What is he doing here?" Nervous and fidgeting, Jonah stepped to the side so he could talk to Yuri but keep an eye on Dimitri and Ivan.

"He's a business partner. I thought he'd like to be here for this discussion."

"Then I think I'll pass." He took a step toward the door but Ivan stepped forward. Jonah beat a hasty retreat. His gaze darted around the room in search of another exit. He froze suddenly. His Adam's apple slid up and down as he got his first look at Nikolai.

With the white sleeves of his shirt rolled up to his elbows, Nikolai had bared the impressive and intimidating swath of tattoos marking him from his knuckles to the edges of shirt fabric. The top few buttons of his shirt were undone, showing even more of the heavy ink on his chest. A cigarette clamped between his lips, he flicked open his favorite lighter and made sure the real estate developer got a good look at the bright flame.

After lighting up, he took a long, slow drag and eyed Jonah with that icy, bone-chilling glare he'd perfected. He held the cigarette between his fingers and pointed at the empty chair in front of Yuri's desk. "You. Sit. Now."

Jonah tried to look calm as he made his way to the chair but Dimitri spotted the trembling fingers he curled into his fists at his sides. Once seated, he glanced around nervously. "Is this where the four of you tie me down and take turns beating me?"

"Jonah, Jonah, Jonah," Yuri said with a laugh, "you insult me. Unlike you, I don't condone violence to frighten people into submission." Yuri walked to his oversized leather chair and got comfortable. "I don't find any enjoyment in terrifying those weaker than me by, say, setting their business on fire."

Jonah gulped. Dimitri waited for him to spout the same lie he was using to defend himself against the police and in the press—that a greedy, rogue employee had been acting without his approval or knowledge. Instead, the man exhaled a shaky breath. "I never meant for that to happen!"

Rage boiled over in Dimitri's chest, the anger bubbling hot and threatening his control. "You sent five men to my home, to my girlfriend's place of business, with lighter fluid, guns, knives and a baseball bat! What did you think was going to happen?"

Jonah slid back in his chair. "Not that," he said and gestured frantically to Dimitri's bruised and battered body. "They were just supposed to vandalize the place. They were supposed to make it look like they were after her brother. How the hell was I to know they would take it that far?"

"They shot up a car and killed people. That's what they do. They're stupid, barbaric thugs. They take things too far." Dimitri moved closer but muscled down the urge to strike the man. "The only reason you're still breathing is because Benny wasn't hurt. If one hair on her head had been singed, you would be wearing cement shoes. Do you understand?"

The man's head bobbled as he hurried to show he

understood. "I'm sorry. I'm really sorry. I'm not going to sue her over the building her brother destroyed."

"That's not good enough for me."

Jonah swallowed and glanced between Dimitri and his friends. "What do you want?"

Yuri's part in this evening's setup arrived. He grabbed a navy blue folder from the corner of his desk and tossed it at the man. "Sign this."

With shaking hands, Jonah opened the folder and started to scan the pages held inside. The color drained out of his face. "You want me to give you my retail development?"

"Not give me," Yuri corrected. "I'll buy it from you."

"For a third of what I paid for it!"

"You did acquire most of those buildings and the lots through blackmail and extortion." Yuri clicked his teeth and wagged his finger. "You were a very naughty boy."

Jonah's eyes took on the same malicious glint they'd had the day he'd been so nasty with Benny. He threw the folder at Yuri. "Fuck you."

Yuri didn't even flinch. "Fuck me?"

Nikolai stepped up beside the desk and lifted his shoe. He stubbed out the burning tip of his cigarette on the sole and dropped it into the trash. Cracking his knuckles, he asked, "Is this where I get to play?"

Jonah was out of his chair in the blink of an eye. He jumped behind it and held up a hand. "If he touches me, I swear I'll fucking sue!"

Yuri laughed. "If he touches you, you're probably going to need a trauma surgeon or possibly an undertaker but definitely not a lawyer."

Dimitri didn't think it was possible but the man paled even more. Sputtering, he shouted, "This is extortion!"

"Is it?" Yuri shrugged. "I'm just taking a page out of

your playbook. Isn't this how business is conducted here?"

Jonah's face reddened. Whether it was from the humiliation at finding himself outmaneuvered or the anger of screwing himself over, Dimitri couldn't say. He lashed out with such ire. "You lured me here with the promise of a multi-million dollar deal."

Yuri gestured to the folder. "That's a multi-million dollar deal. It's simply not one that's going to line your pockets."

Jonah breathed heavily as he tried to make his decision. Finally, he growled with disgust and stalked to the desk. He picked up the folder, jerked the contract out of it and yanked a pen from the holder on Yuri's desk. Furiously, he scribbled his initials and full name in the appropriate spots. He tossed the signed contract at Yuri. "I won't fucking forget this."

"No, I'm sure you won't," Yuri calmly replied and stacked together the pages. "Of course, if my contacts in the district attorney's office are correct, you'll have plenty of time to replay this moment where you're going."

Jonah's expression twisted from fear to sheer panic. He recovered quickly. "We'll see about that."

Yuri nodded and tucked the contract into the folder. "Yes, we will."

"Are we done?"

Yuri glanced at Dimitri. "What do you say? Should we let him go?"

Dimitri's jaw tensed and he gritted his teeth. Hating that he couldn't put his hands on the man who had tried to kill them, he nodded stiffly. "Get out of my sight."

Jonah didn't have to be told twice. He hurried to the door but Ivan blocked his path. Dimitri enjoyed seeing a grown man so obviously rattled. He wanted the real estate developer to experience the same fear Benny had that awful night.

"Hey, Jonah?" Yuri called out with a friendly air. "If things go well for you at trial and you manage to escape jail time, I'd be happy to put in a good word for you at one of the big-box stores I'll be opening next fall."

Jonah's eyes narrowed and he grumbled under his breath. Ivan smirked and opened the door. Jonah didn't even try to put on a brave air as he left. He scurried out of there so fast Dimitri was shocked his pants didn't catch fire from friction.

"You're lucky he didn't piss himself," Ivan commented with a gleeful smile. "I thought for sure that he was going to lose it when he spotted Nikolai."

Chuckling, Yuri slipped the folder into his briefcase. "I enjoyed that immensely. I'm sorry you couldn't relieve some of that bloodlust, Dimitri, but this was for the best."

Dimitri waved his hand. "I want to hurt him but I want to keep Benny happy more. She'd be furious with me if I put my hands on him and risked our life together."

Nikolai rolled down his shirt sleeves, covering the tattoos he usually kept so carefully hidden. "How is she coping? I overheard Vivian talking to her on the phone about nightmares."

"That's normal, I think," Yuri replied. "It was a traumatic experience for a sweet girl like her. She's had personal traumas, no doubt, but the last week has been particularly violent for her."

Dimitri hated that he hadn't been able to shield her from the uglier side of life. That she'd had to see her brother and boyfriend shot in the same weekend? It was terrible.

"She's strong," he said finally. "She'll overcome it."

"Erin was the same way," Ivan reassured him. His cheeks took on the strangest shade of pink as he suggested, "It helps if you hold her while she sleeps. They feel safe and secure that way."

Dimitri appreciated the pointer but Nikolai chortled with mock disgust. "If we start talking about our feelings, I'll throw myself out that window."

Yuri laughed and changed the subject. "I heard that you two had a look at the building Nikolai's friend has for sale. What did she think of it?"

"We're making an offer tomorrow. It's the right size and the area is one where the business would thrive. I hope to close by the end of next week. She's already in talks with a contractor she knows and trusts. She wants to be open in the new location in eight to ten weeks."

Yuri shrugged. "I've seen much bigger builds completed quicker than that. She should be fine." He picked up his phone and dialed the line for his car. When he had that arranged, Yuri added, "Tell her not to worry about our contract. We'll work it out once the dust settles."

Dimitri knew this was a point of much concern for Benny. "She feels like you're overpaying her by agreeing to honor the original price. She has a point, Yuri. The building is gone."

"I was going to have it razed. It's the lot that's important to me." He slashed his hand through the air. "Just tell her to worry about getting her fire insurance to payout so she can start over in her new location. I'm happy with the deal we agreed to before the fire. When her end is settled, we'll draw up a new contract for the lot and move forward."

Dimitri wanted to thank Yuri for being reasonable but didn't. Yuri didn't need to be told what he already knew.

"Are you all still coming over tonight?" Ivan leaned back against the door. "You know how Erin likes having these dinner parties." He shot Yuri a knowing smile. "Lena will be there."

"Why should I care if she's there?" Yuri's gaze dropped to his desk as he made a big scene of gathering together his things. "I can't stay long. I'm flying to London tonight."

Dimitri, Ivan and Nikolai exchanged glances but they let it go. He suspected Yuri's feelings toward Lena were as complicated as his had once been toward Benny. He didn't envy his friend for being in that position.

He caught Nikolai's eye again. "And you?"

Nikolai nodded and reached for his suit jacket. "I have to stop by the house and change first."

Yuri frowned. "Why? I wasn't aware there was a dress code. Ivan, I thought you were throwing steaks on the grill."

"I am."

Nikolai reluctantly admitted, "It's that damn cigarette. If Vivi catches one whiff of it on my shirt, she'll ride my ass for the rest of the week."

"My God!" Yuri guffawed. "She's worse than a wife!"

Dimitri watched Nikolai's mask slip into place. In their tight-knit group, Yuri was the only one brave enough to make that kind of remark. Ivan shifted uncomfortably but Nikolai played it off with a nonchalant shrug.

"I'm happy to let her practice on me. Someday she'll make a nice man a very good wife."

Dimitri caught the way Nikolai distanced himself from the equation. Whether Nikolai's affection toward Vivian was brotherly or, as Yuri believed, more romantic, Dimitri couldn't say. It wasn't any of his business and he sure as hell wasn't going to pry.

Still it was a curious situation. There were times Dimitri could swear he'd caught the briefest flash of unrequited love in Nikolai's normally cold gaze. It was only Vivian who inspired that look.

Like Ivan, Dimitri had long since suspected Nikolai wasn't capable of loving a woman in that way. To love as he loved Benny, a man had to open himself up to such vulnerability—and that was one thing Nikolai would never do. To show weakness? He'd never allow it.

Sometimes he wished Nikolai would come clean with Vivian about what really happened that night nearly ten years ago. It would do all of them some good to have the truth out in the open for once. When Benny had asked him about the pair's history, he hadn't quite known what to say. He'd sensed she didn't believe him but she hadn't pushed for more details.

Someday she would ask again and what would he say? It wasn't his secret to tell but he didn't like lying to Benny about anything. Protecting Nikolai's secret might be the only time he'd make an exception to his truth-only rule with her. There was no good that would come from opening that Pandora's Box.

Ivan's cell phone chirped and he fished it out of his pocket. Dimitri watched his friend's expression morph to confusion. Looking up, he asked, "What the hell is a parfait cup?"

Yuri laughed. "Another one of Erin's errands?"

Ivan tried to look annoyed but none of them bought it. "It would help if she would send me pictures when she sends me on these wild goose chases."

Grinning, Dimitri picked up the sling he'd discarded and joined Ivan near the door. "I know what they are. There's one of those kitchen and bath stores on the way to your house."

Ivan looked relieved as he texted his girlfriend back. After pocketing his phone, he glanced at the sling Dimitri held. "You'd better put that back on before we reach the house. I heard Benny lay down the law as we were leaving."

Dimitri grunted with annoyance but slipped back into the sling. He *had* promised to wear it and take it easy. As worried as she'd been about him, he didn't want Benny fretting unnecessarily.

"We'll see you soon?" Ivan's eyebrows arched as he waited for Nikolai and Yuri to nod. With a flick of his fingers, Ivan gestured for him to follow. They crossed the empty lobby.

Yuri's two bodyguards nodded at them as Dimitri and Ivan made their way to the elevator bank. The sight of them spurred his thoughts on the new business venture. Tonight, at dinner, he'd find a way to get Yuri alone to talk to him about it in more detail.

Dimitri stretched his neck and pushed the scratchy strap of his sling away from his skin. Ivan noticed the movement and shot him a sympathetic smile. "Those things are such a pain in the ass."

"It's truly unnecessary. I'm not a child. Hell, even when we were children, we weren't coddled like this."

Ivan chuckled and stepped into the elevator car that had arrived. "She cares about you. Mothering you is her way of showing how much she loves you." With a wicked gleam in his eye, Ivan punched the ground floor button. "Indulge her need to play nurse now. Later, when you're healed, she'll be only too happy to indulge your needs..."

CHAPTER EIGHTEEN

I watched Dimitri for any signs of discomfort as we stood side-by-side in my bathroom and brushed our teeth. It had been a long day and I worried he'd overexerted himself. Dinner with Erin and Ivan had been lovely but the night had gotten a bit raucous as we sat on their back patio and listened to the men sharing the wild tales of their childhood. It had been after midnight when we finally left.

"What?" Dimitri asked, his lips twitching with amusement as he patted his mouth with a hand towel. He reached over and dabbed my chin. "You look like you want to scold me."

"We stayed out so late tonight."

"We had a nice time." He touched my cheek. "Seeing you laughing with the girls made me happy. *You* need to relax more."

"*You* need to rest, Dimitri. Six nights ago, you were

stabbed and shot."

"And I'm fine now." He tucked strands of hair behind my ear. "You're blowing it out of proportion. The wounds were nothing compared to what I suffered years ago in Grozny."

I blinked. "Isn't that in Chechnya?"

Dimitri's jaw tensed and he glanced away from me. "Yes."

It was the first time he'd ever spoken of his time in the military over there with any specifics. I sensed it was a slip that he wouldn't make again. "We're not going to talk about your military career, are we?"

Dimitri's haunted eyes made my heart ache. "No, Benny. That is from a time I never want to remember." He cupped my cheek and rubbed his thumb across my skin. "I don't want any of that horror to ever touch you."

I lifted on tiptoes to kiss him. "I won't ever ask again."

Relief relaxed his features. "Thank you."

Certain he wanted to change the subject, I asked, "What were you and Yuri whispering about before he left for London?"

"Ah, that," he said with a sheepish expression. "I was going to talk to you about that over breakfast but we can discuss it now."

"Okay. What is it?"

"I'm going to expand the business. I've made a good name for myself selecting and training professional bouncers for the clubs here and providing personal security on a small scale but I'm leaving a lot of money on the table. You know I chose and trained Yuri's bodyguards?"

"I didn't."

"Well I did. He always receives questions about the firm where he hired them. That's big money, Benny.

There are wealthy people who need trusted security. I think I could fill that role."

"So you'd select and train them and then what? Hire them out like contractors?"

"Basically," he agreed. "We're going to sit down next week and come up with some concrete plans." Looking a bit nervous, he asked, "What do you think?"

"I think it's a great opportunity. Yuri wouldn't steer you wrong. He has great business sense. And you're damned good at what you do. You should go for it."

He breathed a little easier. "I'm glad you approve."

"Did you think I wouldn't support you?" I tried not to be hurt by the idea that he didn't find me supportive.

"Benny," he said my name in a rush. "I didn't mean it like that. I only meant that you tend to be extremely careful and conservative about taking chances. I hate thinking of you being anxious about my business ventures."

"I trust you to make the right decisions. Lord knows you've always been better at the business side of things than me."

His face softened. "You're not a bad businesswoman, Benny. You inherited a tangled mess. It has taken time to sort it out but you're going to make a success of the new location. Yuri's offered to mentor you. Lena's agreed to continue working PR for the bakery. You can't go wrong with those two in your corner."

"No," I agreed wholeheartedly. Rubbing his arm, I said, "You need to go bed. It's late and I'm sure you're exhausted. Tomorrow, you're going to spend as much time as possible on the couch, relaxing and resting."

He playfully tugged on a handful of my hair. "You know I love the way you're mothering me, Benny, but I'm not that guy. I can't sit on the couch and watch mindless television when there's work to be done."

I stepped closer and slid my arms around his trim waist. The yellowing bruises and scabbed over scrapes and healing sutured areas marred the wide swath of his sexy chest. I placed a tender kiss to the spot right above his heart. "I don't want you to have any setbacks in your healing."

Dimitri sifted his fingers through my hair. "It's stitches and bruises. There won't be any setbacks. I promise." He tapped his finger against my nose. "But you're right. We need to go to bed. We have to be at the realtor's office early."

Grasping my hand, he led me out of the bathroom. I smacked the light switch on the way into my bedroom. It felt so incredibly strange to have Dimitri in the bedroom where I'd spent my entire childhood. I was suddenly very glad I'd taken the time to redo the hot pink and lime green décor last summer. His reaction to my frilly white duvet and shams hadn't gone unnoticed. It was obvious we were going to have to find some middle ground when it came to decorating our place.

"I thought after we put in the offer on the building we might take a peek at some of the available lots in Ivan's neighborhood."

My surprised gaze darted to his. I folded the top of the duvet down toward the bottom of the bed. "Um…that's a pretty pricey area, Dimitri."

He frowned. "I suppose."

I decided to state the obvious. "I have, like, no money. When we agreed to get a place together, I thought we were talking something smaller and more affordable. The fire insurance payout and the sale of the lot to Yuri are giving the bakery a clean slate but my personal finances are still a mess. Half of the proceeds from selling this place will go to Johnny. The rest will go toward repaying the loan you've given me for the new building and paying salaries to my employees."

He sat down on the edge of the bed and pulled me between his legs. Hands on my waist, he insisted, "It's not a loan, Benny. You don't have to repay it."

We'd gone round and round on this one over the last couple of days. Even though we were in love and a couple, I still felt so weird taking money from him. "Dimitri, I never want you to feel like I'm using you."

He scoffed. "You're not using me—and I don't feel that way. I'm giving this money to you. I'm helping you because I like helping you. There are no expectations on this money, Benny."

"But—"

He silenced me with a demanding kiss. "We're not arguing about this. We're partners now. The money for the new building is not a loan."

"If we're partners, you should be on the paperwork. We should make it legal."

Dimitri stared at me for a long moment. "All right. Let's make it legal." He brought my fingertips to his lips and kissed each one of them. "Marry me, Benny."

My tummy wobbled wildly and my heart skipped a few beats. I swallowed hard and tried not to faint from shock. "Wh-what?"

Dimitri's lopsided, boyish smile made my heart swell with love. "I know this isn't the ideal proposal. I don't have a ring and we're in a bedroom and not some romantic spot."

"I don't care about that."

"No, I didn't think you would." He cupped both sides of my neck and gazed into my eyes. "We were meant for one another. It's no coincidence that life brought me here, to Houston, to that apartment, to you. That was fate. You were meant for me, Benita. It was always supposed to be you." He claimed my mouth ever so tenderly. "Marry me?"

"Yes." I didn't hesitate. I didn't think. I listened to my heart. I trusted my instinct. He was right. We were meant for one another. Our friendship had spanned five years and only grown stronger. In the last ten days, we'd survived more than most couples would in a lifetime together. There was no doubt in my mind that Dimitri was the man for me.

"Yes?" Elated, he breathed out in excitement. His enthusiastic grin filled me with such happiness. He gathered me tightly in his brawny arms and nearly smothered me with passionate kisses. "I'm going to spend the rest of my life doing everything I can to make you happy, Benny."

Teary-eyed, I whispered, "You already have."

With that sexy smile of his, Dimitri ran his hands down my back. He cupped my bottom through the sheer fabric of my night shirt. "How about we slide into bed and we'll see how happy I can make you tonight?"

"We can't do that! You're still healing."

He narrowed his eyes. Grabbing my hand, he dragged it down to the hard bulge in the front of his pajama bottoms. "Does that feel like it's in need of healing?"

"No."

"It's been six nights, Benny. I've been patient and gone along with your demands for rest but not tonight. The woman I love just agreed to be my wife. I'm not falling asleep until you've screamed my name at least three times."

I gulped and curled my toes against the plush carpet. "Three times, huh?"

His lips skimmed my throat and made me shudder. "Well—maybe four—but only if you hop on this bed without another argument."

He didn't have to make that offer twice. I climbed onto the bed and peeled out of my night shirt. There were no undies in the way tonight. He'd quickly made that one a rule after returning from the hospital. He wanted me completely bare in bed.

Even though I was burning up with need, I eyed Dimitri with some concern. "Are you sure we should tempt fate? I know your stomach still hurts and your arms are bothering you."

"Sweetheart," he grinned devilishly, "what I have planned doesn't require much physical effort on my part."

"Oh?" My nipples drew taut as the dirtiest images filled my head. Yesterday, I'd caught Dimitri flipping through my bookshelves. He'd zeroed in on my stash of fetish erotica and super sexy romance. I could only imagine what scenes he'd read and stored away as inspiration for our trysts.

He tossed pillows off the bed and reclined slowly. I slid my hand behind his back to guide him down. He didn't flinch or wince with discomfort but I knew he felt it. That stoic expression of his face didn't fool me.

Flat on his back, Dimitri reached for me. I found myself in the position he normally occupied, propped up on one elbow and kissing him. Those rough palms of his glided over my naked skin. Shivering with desire, I whimpered as he petted and caressed me.

"I love it when you make those sounds," Dimitri murmured before capturing my mouth. "You make my dick so fucking hard."

His dirty talk left me throbbing and so incredibly wet—and he knew it. I saw the wicked glint in his eyes.

He slid a hand between our bodies and pushed my thighs apart. "Are you wet for me, Benny?"

I gasped as he probed my tender folds. His fingertips circled my clit before slipping lower and pressing into my slick sheath. Moaning with pleasure, I widened my thighs and let him slowly fuck me with his thick digits. He nipped at my neck and drove me crazy by whispering all the dirty things he was going to do to me once he was fully recovered.

Our tongues tangled in a duel for supremacy. As always, he won and dominated me even with his kisses. He cupped the back of my neck but broke away from the kiss. "I want you to kneel over my face."

My eyes widened at his frank request. "You...what?"

He flattened his shoulders to the mattress and gave my butt a sharp smack. "Come here. Put your knees on either side of my head."

I formed a mental picture of what he was instructing. "But then my...*you know*...would be right over you."

He laughed and gave my butt another good whack. "That's the point, Benny. I'm dying for a taste of your sweet pussy. Now get up here!"

Trembling with excitement and anxiety, I did exactly as he commanded. It occurred to me as I wiggled into place that this was probably the only comfortable way for him to do this. I had a feeling I was in for a wild ride.

"Oh!" I tipped my head back as the pointed tip of his tongue swiped me. Careful not to move for fear of hitting his sutured bicep or jostling his sore elbow, I held as still as possible while his searching tongue flicked and fluttered over the most intimate part of me.

He groaned hungrily, showing me just how much he loved going down on me, and gripped my waist in his big hands. I nearly died when his tongue dipped inside my pussy. He fucked me with it, the sensation unlike any other I'd ever felt. Panting and aching, I squeezed my thigh muscles and tried to maintain some semblance of control.

That skilled tongue of his moved to my clit. He lapped at my swollen bud and suckled it gently. The tugging pull drove me closer and closer to the edge. With a strangled cry, I climaxed against his wonderfully talented mouth.

But he wasn't done with me.

Holding tight to my hips, Dimitri went wild between my thighs. He used that sinful mouth of his to torment me until I shrieked his name and came so hard I felt certain I would black out from the sheer pleasure of it.

Still shaking, I tumbled off him onto the bed. Rolled onto my side, I tried to catch my breath and stared at him with such awe. "You're going to kill me one of these nights."

Chuckling, he snatched me by the waist. "We're not done yet. I only heard my name once."

"Oh God!" I didn't try to fight him when he urged me to straddle his waist but first I decided to return the favor. Once I had him out of his pajama bottoms, I lavished his big cock with oral attention.

"Benny!" He groaned my name while I painted his shaft with my tongue. Sucking the tip of him, I stroked his hard length and cupped his taut sac. He let loose a string of Russian when I swallowed most of him. Loving the taste and feel of him in my mouth, I took my time and enjoyed every moment of it.

"Fuck me," he practically begged. "Ride me, Benny. *Now*."

When he used that tone, there was no denying him. I crawled over his hips and grasped the base of his erection. Dragging the ruddy crown of him through my wet folds, I pushed him against my entrance. He thrust up into me, burying himself to the hilt. We both groaned with delight.

Gazes locked, we found a rhythm that left us panting and gasping. I did most of the work, swaying back and forth like a belly dancer on his lap. Dimitri relaxed on the bed and swept his hands up and down my body. When he toyed with my nipples, I inhaled a sharp breath. He pinched and rolled the dusky peaks, causing delicious little shocks to travel right to my pulsing clit.

Licking his thumb, he brought it down to the spot where our bodies were joined. He flicked the rough pad side to side over my clit. My lower belly clenched as need pooled hot and heavy between my thighs. His other hand squeezed my breast and tormented my poor nipple. I gripped his wrist as the first panicked flutter shuddered deep in my core. "Dimitri! I—*ah*! *Dimitri*!"

I could hear him laughing as I climaxed hard. Snapping my hips, I rode his cock as the pleasurable ripples exploded in my belly and arced through my chest.

"That was two," he said and thrust up into me. "Let's see how fast I can get you scream again."

"No! *Wait*! Oh!" I wasn't ready to try to come again but he had that wickedly sexy grin on his face. I hissed when he brushed his thumb across my super sensitive clit. His thumb moved just to the side of the pulsing bud. The slow up and down strokes left me panting and shaking as that coil of ecstasy screwed tighter and tighter in my core.

This time, when I shattered atop him, I threw back my head and shrieked his name. My pussy fluttered around his cock. I could feel him growing harder and thicker inside me. With a growl, he thrust up inside me and joined me in an intense, shared orgasm. His fingertips bit into the fleshy softness of my ass so sharply I was sure there would be tiny bruises there by morning but I didn't care.

Slumped against his chest, I buried my face in the crook of his neck and inhaled the familiar scent of his cologne and sweat. His body heat soothed and relaxed me. Tucked against his steely body and safe in his arms, there was no place else I wanted to be.

CHAPTER NINETEEN

FIVE WEEKS LATER

"Congratulations!" Erin engulfed me in her embrace and did a little happy dance with me. Laughing, I hugged her back. "You already congratulated me when we broke the news a few weeks ago."

"I know." Grinning, she released me. "But what's an engagement party without another round of congrats?"

She had a point. I glanced around the Samovar and couldn't believe how many people were packed inside the restaurant. Nikolai had taken it upon himself to host a huge engagement bash. With Lena, Erin and Vivian's help, he'd organized the entire thing. So far everyone seemed to be having a great time. Of course, all the amazing food and free booze probably helped.

"Ivan and I bought you two a couple's gift but I got you a little something extra." Erin handed me a wrapped rectangle.

"Erin, you didn't have to get me anything."

"Take it." Smiling, she pushed it into my hands.

I peeled back the pretty pink wrapping paper and started giggling when I realized what it was. "A Russian workbook!"

Giggling, she explained, "I know how annoying it is to be unable to understand a dang thing that comes out of your man's mouth." She glanced over at Ivan who was laughing and telling an animated story with Yuri to a small group of men. Love burned brightly in her eyes for that giant bare-knuckle fighter of hers. Looking back at me, she added, "Ivan was seriously touched when I started learning his language. It meant a lot to him."

"I'm sure Dimitri will appreciate the gesture." With a self-deprecating smile, I said, "I'll probably have to hire Vivian as my tutor."

"Definitely," Erin agreed. Looking around, she asked, "Where the heck is she?"

"Um..." I rose on tiptoes to scan the crowd. My gaze landed on Lena first. She chatted with a couple of women and a man I didn't know. When she reached into her purse and withdrew business cards, I realized she was networking. Did that girl ever take a break?

"Oh, there she is!" Erin pointed Vivian out near the front of the restaurant. Her brows knitted together. "Did you invite Detective Santos?"

Surprised by the mention of my old friend's name, I shook my head. "I don't know. Lena handled all the invites. He's a friend from way back so maybe he got put on my guest list."

"Hmm," Erin hummed softly. "No, I think he's here for Vivian. He's still wearing his gun and badge."

"Why would he be here for Vivian?" I scooted over

268

just enough to see the pair huddled together. Whatever they were talking about, it wasn't good. Vivian looked really upset and Santos wore an expression of displeasure.

"They're cousins. Maybe it's a family thing."

I reared back in shock. "Vivian and Eric Santos are cousins?"

She nodded. "I didn't know either until after we had that run-in with the Hermanos gang at Ivan's place. Santos was the detective on our case. Later, Vivian told me they were cousins. Her dad and his mom are brother and sister. Apparently, Santos' side of the family doesn't speak to her dad. They basically shunned him because he was a criminal."

I remembered the sordid tale Dimitri had told me. Vivian's family situation seemed even bleaker now. Movement off to Vivian's right caught my attention. Nikolai stepped away from a group of partygoers to watch the intense discussion.

Dressed in all black with that bright white shirt he preferred, the imposing Russian crossed his arms and seemed to be fighting the urge to get involved. His demeanor relaxed suddenly. I glanced at Vivian and Santos. They were hugging and seemed to have resolved their spat. Santos handed her a wrapped gift and quickly left the restaurant.

Without even trying to hide her nosiness, Erin waved at Vivian. She crossed the room, winding in and out of the crowd to clear a path to us. Along the way, Lena joined her, looping their arms together at the elbow. When they arrived in our secluded little corner, Erin pounced. "What the hell was that, Vivi?"

Stiff and obviously uneasy, she radiated anxiety. "It's my dad. He's getting early release from the federal pen."

"What?" Lena's harsh tone made me flinch. "How?

When?"

Vivian shook her head. "I don't know how he got early release. Neither did Eric. It will be sometime around the New Year when they let him go."

Erin reached out and patted Vivian's arm. "What are you going to do?"

She shrugged. "What can I do? I'll probably have Eric help me put a restraining order against him but I doubt he'll let a piece of paper stop him from trying to talk to me."

Lena glanced over her shoulder before reluctantly asking, "Maybe you could ask Nikolai to do something about it."

Vivian looked back at her protector. Voice soft, she said, "I don't think I'll have to ask. Something tells me he already knew."

When she turned back to us, we exchanged uncertain glances. I, for one, had no idea what to say about any of this. We were all friends but I wasn't aware off all the dynamics involved in this Charlie-Foxtrot of a situation.

Lena sought to lighten the somber mood. She snatched my left hand. "Girl, you better be careful working in that kitchen of yours. You lose this in a batch of *pan dulce* or a tray of cupcakes and you're going to have to put up a big reward to get it back!"

Gazing at the gorgeous emerald-cut solitaire Dimitri had chosen, I confessed, "He made me swear I wouldn't wear it in the kitchen. I told him no problem."

"It really is a beautiful ring," Vivian said and tugged my hand closer for a better look. "It's so perfectly *you*. He did really well."

"Yes, he did." I found Dimitri across the restaurant. He sipped a beer and laughed with Ivan and Yuri.

"So how is the bakery setup going?" Erin snatched a

270

champagne flute from one of the passing waiters. "Ivan said you guys are getting close."

"We are. It's coming along a lot faster than I'd expected but we've got some of the bakery crew coming in to help. A lot of the guys who work for me do tile work or lay flooring or install drywall on the weekends anyway. They know the contractor I hired and he's only too happy to have more hands on the job."

"Probably because Dimitri inserted one of those bonus payments on early completion clauses," Lena remarked. "It's a good way to keep a contractor from milking you dry." She stepped away to grab a glass of white wine from another waiter. "Don't forget we're meeting at my graphic guy's place tomorrow. We have to okay the designs for the launch."

"I won't." I'd started using her color-coded scheduling system to keep track of everything. I wouldn't ever miss an appointment again.

"I heard the radio commercial on the way to class this morning," Vivian said. "It was catchy. I liked it."

"That's all Lena." I smiled at her. "This girl knows how to hustle."

Just then, a waiter stopped by our group with a tray of canapés. The overpowering scent of salmon and dill and some kind of egg salad made me queasy. I moved to the side and pressed my hand to mouth and nose.

Erin shot me a worried look after waving at the waiter to go. "Are you okay?"

"Fine," I said and swallowed hard. My stomach calmed slightly. "I think I caught a slight case of food poisoning from that Thai place the other night. I've been sick to my stomach ever since."

Erin frowned. "Benny, we ate there a week ago. You've been nauseated for, like, seven days?"

"Are you sure it's food poisoning?" Lena's dark eyebrows had arched to her hairline.

"Pretty sure," I replied.

Vivian lean forward and whispered, "Are you late?"

"For what?"

She rolled her eyes before focusing her gaze on my belly. "*You know.*"

"No! I..." My brain short-circuited as I tried to remember the last time I'd had a period. It had been a week or so before Dimitri and I had gotten together so that meant my period was due...

My tummy pitched as I hastily recalculated. "I'm three weeks late."

Calmly, Erin asked, "You're sure? It could be the stress of everything you've been through in the last month and a half."

"Yes, I'm sure."

"Is it likely that you have a little Dimitri bun in your oven?" Lena asked the obvious question. "I mean, have you two been together without...?"

I blushed as I remembered that first morning when we'd made love and then again the night he'd asked me to marry him. "Yes. Twice."

"There's a drug store around the corner that's open all night. I could run over and grab a test," Vivian offered.

"No." I caught Dimitri's questioning gaze across the restaurant. Even at that distance, he could read me so easily. Glancing back at the girls, I said, "If I'm going to test, I'm going to do with him. You won't say anything until I'm sure?"

"No."

"Definitely not."

"Your secret is safe with me."

Assured they would keep mum until the time was

right, I excused myself. Lena squeezed my shoulder as I left and smiled encouragingly. Moving through the thick crowd, I was stopped every few feet and hugged and congratulated. Some of the well-wishers I knew and others I didn't. Here, though, we were all friends.

Butterflies swarmed in my belly as I drew near Dimitri. He still chatted with Yuri, Nikolai and Ivan but his gaze skipped to me as I made my approach. I didn't know how the hell I was going to tell him what I suspected. I fought the urge to press a hand to my still-flat tummy.

Deep down inside, I knew it to be true. All the little things I'd been ignoring and chalking up to stress over the last couple of weeks made sense. The nausea, the headaches, the sleepiness, my super sore breasts—they were all clear pregnancy signs but I'd been blind to them.

Dimitri held out his big hand as I came close. I placed my palm on his and enjoyed the heat of his fingers enveloping mine. Dragged to his side, I wrapped my arms around his waist. He kissed the top of my head and caressed my lower back. "What were the four of you whispering about so conspiratorially?"

"Oh that?" I shrugged and managed to play it off. "Just girl talk."

Dimitri's eyes narrowed with suspicion but he didn't pry. Instead, he said, "Yuri was just bragging on you. Apparently, you're doing very well in your lessons."

I shot the billionaire playboy a grateful smile. "He's teaching me all kinds of useful tricks for running a business on lean margins. I'm starting to look forward to checking my email every morning for my next lesson."

Yuri laughed. "I'm enjoying it actually. It's nice to pass on some of the things I've learned to someone who actually wants to learn them. Usually when I get requests for mentoring, they're from people who want to make a fast buck."

"Well that's not me," I said with a laugh. "If I was after fast money, I've gotten into the wrong business."

"Fast is rarely good. Sometimes the slow, easy build is the best way to happiness."

His teasing smile told me Yuri wasn't talking about business now. He meant relationships. My relationship with Dimitri fit that bill. Was he also talking about his relationship with Lena? I wasn't really sure where that was going. They weren't friends but they weren't enemies either. They were...acquaintances with the possibility of something more.

The soft notes of music faded and the DJ switched to some truly old school R&B. Etta James crooned over our heads. Beside me, Ivan swore softly in his mother tongue. I spotted Erin coming toward him, holding out her hand. I sensed he didn't actually like dancing but he wasn't about to tell her that. He let her drag him onto the floor. Grinning and laughing, he pulled her close and wrapped his arm around her. There was no mistaking the love they felt for one another.

"Dance with me?" Dimitri gave me a gentle tug toward the swaying couples. I happily went with him. My eyes closed briefly as I pressed my cheek to his chest. His scent and heat soothed my raw nerves. I tried to decide if now was the time to tell him or if I should wait until we were alone and had privacy.

"What were you really talking about with the girls?" Dimitri peered down at me with concern in his pale eyes. "You looked panicked. Was it something to do with that tense discussion Vivian had with Detective Santos?"

"No. Did you know they're cousins?"

His surprised expression answered that one. "No, I didn't."

"Well they are. He was coming to give her a heads-up that her dad is getting out of prison early."

"Shit." Dimitri's gaze jumped from my face to some place behind me. I didn't have to look over my shoulder to know he was searching for Nikolai. "That's going to be a problem."

"I gathered that."

He slid a finger under my chin and forced me to meet his curious gaze. "If it wasn't that, then what had you so panicked?"

I gulped, my mouth suddenly dry, and tried to figure out the best way to tell him. "Um...what do you think about kids?"

"Kids?" He seemed taken aback by the unexpected query. "I think they're fun. I assumed we'd have some."

"Like...when?"

He laughed nervously. "I don't know. Whenever you'd like, I suppose. Why? Is this your way of telling me you'd like to start trying after we're married?"

"Well..."

Dimitri stopped dancing. Shock filtered across his face as he pieced together the hints. "Are you—are we—?"

"I'm not sure," I hurriedly patted his chest. "I'm late. Like *really* late and I have other symptoms and we did...you know...twice."

Slowly, his mouth curved into the most ecstatic grin. Gone were all traces of shock. He seemed completely and totally thrilled by the possibility. Touching his forehead to mine, he whispered, "We'll buy a test on the way home. I hope it's positive."

"Really?" I held his gaze and gauged his sincerity. "You're not upset?"

"Upset? About making a beautiful little baby with the woman I love? Never!"

I'd never seen him so happy. The anxiety I'd been experiencing fled.

"Are you upset?"

"No," I answered quickly and honestly. "I'm a little scared. Two months ago, I wasn't even dating. Now I'm engaged and probably pregnant. It's a lot—and really fast."

"Life doesn't follow prescribed timetables, Benny. Sometimes it just...happens." He cupped my face and captured my mouth in a loving kiss. "I promise I'll be a good father."

After the miserable childhood he'd experienced, Dimitri would probably spoil our baby rotten but he'd be a wonderful father. My heart threatened to burst as I gazed into the shimmering eyes of the man I intended to marry. "I know you will. That's one thing I never doubted. You're the best man I've ever known, Dimitri. I can't imagine sharing all this with anyone else."

He gathered me close and started to sway with me again. "We'll have to move up the wedding date. Yuri offered to let us use one of the yachts for the ceremony and reception so Johnny can be there." He chuckled and teased, "Of course, Johnny's probably going to punch me in the face when he finds out I got his sister pregnant."

"Probably," I agreed with a short laugh. He'd been so supportive when I'd called to inform him of the engagement. Honestly, my brother hadn't seemed the least bit surprised. I'd been left wondering if he and Dimitri hadn't already discussed the possibility of him proposing at some point.

"You'll have to cut back at work," Dimitri insisted. "What do you think of hiring an office manager to handle the part of the business you dislike so much?"

"It's not a bad idea."

"And you'll have to stop going in for the early morning shift. You'll need your rest. We'll get you a nice, comfortable stool for working at the decorating table. You can't be standing on your feet for twelve hours a day anymore. And fans for the kitchen," he added hurriedly. "It can't be healthy for you to be so hot."

Amused by his overprotectiveness but also a teensy bit annoyed, I started to argue with him. Then I remembered how he'd borne my mothering and coddling when he'd been injured. With a submissive smile, I replied, "Yes, Dimitri."

"Just like that? No arguing?"

"Would it help?"

He laughed. "No."

"Exactly."

Nuzzling my cheek, he murmured, "I can't wait to get you home. We'll have to start a new nightly routine for you."

"Oh?" My tummy trembled with excitement as I wondered what he had in mind.

"A nice, relaxing bath, foot and back massages and then I'll make love to you," he decided. "How does that sound?"

"Fantastic." I rose up to meet his seeking kiss. Ridiculously in love with my big, sexy Russian, I slid my hands up his arms and held on tight. "I love you, Dimitri."

Grinning, he kissed the tip of my nose. "I love you, Benny."

Cradled to his chest, I felt safe and secure. If this was how we were going to spend the rest of our nights, I couldn't wait to start the next chapter of our lives together.

AUTHOR'S NOTE

I hope you enjoyed the second installment of the Her Russian Protector series! The series continues with full-length novels featuring Yuri, Nikolai and Sergei. Upcoming books in 2014 include sequels for Nikolai and Sergei as well as new tales for Kostya, Alexei and Danila.

ABOUT THE AUTHOR

When I'm not chasing after my wild preschooler, I like to write super sexy romances and scorching hot erotica. I live in Texas with a husband who could easily snag a job as an extra on History Channel's new Viking series and a sweet but rowdy four-year-old.

I also have another dirty-book writing alter ego, Lolita Lopez, who writes deliciously steamy tales for Ellora's Cave, Forever Yours/Grand Central, Mischief/Harper Collins UK, Siren Publishing and Cleis Press.

You can find me online at www.roxierivera.com.

ROXIE'S BACKLIST

Her Russian Protector Series
Ivan (Her Russian Protector #1)
Dimitri (Her Russian Protector #2)
Yuri (Her Russian Protector #3)
Nikolai (Her Russian Protector #4)
Sergei (Her Russian Protector #5
Nikolai Volume 2 (Coming 2014)
Sergei Volume 2 (Coming 2014)
Kostya (Coming 2014)
Alexei (Coming 2014)

The Fighting Connollys Series
In Kelly's Corner (Fighting Connollys #1)
In Jack's Arms (Fighting Connollys #2)—Coming January 2014!
In Finn's Heart (Fighting Connollys #3)—Coming March 2014!

Seduced By...
Seduced by the Loan Shark
Seduced by the Loan Shark 2—Coming Soon!
Seduced by the Congressman
Seduced by the Congressman 2

Erotica
Chance's Bad, Bad Girl
Halftime With Craig
Tease
Eddie's Cuffs 1
Eddie's Cuffs 2
Eddie's Cuffs 3
Disturbing the Peace
Quid Pro Quo
Search and Seizure

CPSIA information can be obtained at www.ICGtesting.com
Printed in the USA
LVOW06s1028200114

370159LV00004B/94/P